One in Ten

One in Ten

A test of loyalty

by *Michael Roses*

Perth, Western Australia

ISBN 9780645719017

Dedicated to all good people on planet Earth

Be Good!

Nathan Butler

Nathan Butler arose in the morning on a day that would change his life forever. Everything seemed normal as he prepared himself for his day at work as the owner of his welding business, where he employed more than twenty workers. Today would be just another day in downtown St. Louis – surely! He was an early starter so gave his wife a parting peck on her cheek as she lay asleep in their bed. He took a carton of iced coffee from their refrigerator and headed to his garage, opened the roller door, started his Buick and set off toward the industrial area, about ten miles away.

It was normally only a twenty minute drive from his home in Bridgeton to his factory in Cottleville and he will be the first to arrive, to open the premises. There were a few sets of traffic lights on the way and, on this occasion, Nathan was required to stop at a set of traffic lights at McClay Road. Nathan glanced downwards to change his radio station when, suddenly, his car was jolted forward. Nathan looked into his rear vision mirror to see a woman holding her phone in her left hand. His car had been very slightly nudged from behind. Nathan motioned with his right hand for the woman to follow him as the lights had turned from red to green. She had her right hand up over her mouth as if to display her shame at what she had just done, then gave him a 'thumbs up' to acknowledge.

As there was a truck bay just one hundred yards ahead Nathan drove into the bay and the woman stopped five yards behind him. Nathan exited his vehicle to inspect any damage. He observed there was a very minor indentation in his rear bumper but no apparent harm to the duco. The woman approached him – and Nathan stared at the woman, but not because of what she had just done.

"Oh dear, look I am just so sorry about that, you know my phone rang just as I was about to stop and I could see it was a person I really needed to talk to about a very important conference I am attending today and ... ah ... I had been trying to contact this person all day yesterday to no avail ..."

Nathan was still staring at the woman.

"Lady ... look ... ah ... it's not all that bad ... ah ... maybe I can just pour some boiling water onto this bumper and hopefully it will just pop out into place. It's a plastic bumper, you know!

"Oh no, look, I can't have that, now I admit this was my fault and I want to make sure your car is repaired to be as new again, okay? My name is Cassandra, now I want you to take this cash and pay for a repair job today then just call me to bring me the change, but please keep a couple of hundred dollars for putting yourself out, okay?"

Cassandra handed Nathan two thousand dollars in cash.

"That's quite a sum of money you've handed me there. Look, I don't think this will more than a couple of hundred dollars so take half of this back."

"No, no, no, I insist, it's okay you can bring me the change, I just want you to know I am genuine with this. Now here is my card, you can call me later today because I will not be free until after four o'clock, but I am staying at the Hyatt Regency in Chestnut Street and I fly out early tomorrow so let's just get this cleared up today, if you don't mind. I'm sure you could obtain a quote and pay for this same day, even if they have to book your car in for another time, okay?"

"Okay, have it your way ... ah ... my name is Nathan, so I will take my car to a panel repairer just around the corner from my factory just down the road there this morning and I will give you a call to let you know.

"Okay, thank you Nathan, I will expect to hear from you but you might need to text me first because I will be delivering a lecture at the conference this morning. Actually, if you don't mind just text me now so I have your number also."

Nathan took his phone from his pocket and sent Cassandra a text, thinking to himself that he will just love to have the very beautiful woman's number on his cell phone. Never know what might happen in the future, he thought to himself, wondering already if she was a single woman, as there was no ring on her left hand. Cassandra's phone buzzed from Nathan's text.

"Okay, thank you Nathan I will hear from you later but after midday please."

"Okay!"

Both turned toward their vehicle but Nathan just had to glance back as Cassandra turned away. He noticed her amazing slim figure and slim legs. He muttered to himself.

"Wow, what a beautiful woman and I'm going to see her again later. Can't wait."

Nathan was gravely distracted at work that morning and couldn't stop thinking his brief interaction with the woman, who reminded him of actress Jaclyn Smith. He obtained the quote for his car repairs and paid cash up front. The panel repairer did, in fact, return the bumper to its former state simply with boiling water and booked Nathan's car in for a superficial touch up of the duco. The total cost was just seven hundred dollars. He looked forward to returning the entire change to Cassandra without retaining the two hundred dollars she had offered. Nathan sent Cassandra a text at two o'clock in the afternoon. A minute later his cell phone rang – it was her.

"Hello, Cassandra!"

"Yes, hello Nathan how did you go? Did you get the quote?"

"Yes and I have paid for the repair job and it came to just seven hundred dollars, so I will bring the change to you as you suggested."

"Hey, that's great - and thank you for getting that sorted because I fly out very early in the morning back home to Dover in Delaware."

"So, where will I find you Cassandra?"

"If you come to the Hyatt Regency after five, I should be back there by then, so just look for me in the lobby, okay – I should be there just enjoying a wine - or two."

"Ah ... okay I will see you then, bye for now."

Nathan closed his workshop half an hour early, telling the workers they could leave at four o'clock as his accountant was coming in for a review of the books. He had been drooling all afternoon on his planned rendezvous with Cassandra after five o'clock and was already planning ahead. He called his wife.

"Nathan - what's up?"

"Oh ... nothing too serious, just thought I'd let you know the accountant is coming in at five o'clock so I might be staying back for a couple of hours ... ah ... maybe I'll pick up some take away on my way home. Unless we just order from Uber Eats once I am home."

"Actually can you pick up a Chinese from the Peking Duck, that would be great – really feel like something special tonight."

"Okay, I'll get the usual!"

"Don't forget the prawn crackers!"

"Okay – prawn crackers! See you maybe eight or nine, hopefully sooner though."

Nathan terminated the call then sent a text to Cassandra.

"Leaving my workshop now, be about twenty minutes."

When Nathan arrived at the Hyatt, Cassandra was indeed sitting in the lobby lounge sipping a white wine. She waved to him as he entered. There was only one other person sitting in the lobby bar, a male person viewing a laptop computer.

"Well hello again, I have your change here ..."

"Hey, take a seat and let me buy you a drink ... what's your poison?"

"I will buy you a drink for what you've been through this morning. Here is your change and no, I do not want to retain the two hundred dollars you offered, thank you though."

"Well if you insist! I will have a vodka with lemonade, thank you."

Nathan signalled the waiter who came to the table.

"Could we have a vodka and lemonade and a pint of Foster's beer please."

"A beer man, eh?"

"Yeah, a hard working beer man Cassandra – though in the cold of winter I do prefer a fortified wine, actually."

"Such as?"

"Surprisingly a ... ah ... sweet sherry that my local liquor store imports from Australia – a McWilliams Royal Reserve sweet sherry which my grandmother used to drink, so I am following her footsteps."

"Is she still with us?"

"She is, in fact just turned eighty-five last week."

"And you are?"

"Me – thirty nine – last week."

"Do you still see her?"

"Not as often as I should but she now resides in a care facility in San Diego. She always wanted to live life out by the ocean."

The waiter brought their drinks to the table.

"And is she your father's mother or your mother's mother?"

“Emily is my mother’s mother – I used to be close to her. In fact I would drop in to see her when riding my pushbike home from school back in the day. On cold days she would be drinking that wine.”

“Is your mother there in San Diego?”

“No – San Jose! My parents split twenty years ago and my mother has developed her career in the Silicon Valley.”

“And you – are you with a wife with kids? You seem like the family man.”

“Yeah – three kids, all high schoolers. Bit of a rascal element there – always on the bloody social networking. Can’t get them off it, in fact.”

“How does your wife feel about that?”

“She’s done with it – seems they are totally hooked up and have reached the point where they just don’t want to pay any heed to anything we say.”

“Yes, it’s quite a social disease now isn’t it? So are you still a happy little family despite that from your kids?”

“Happy? Hmm ... content, yes, but having to tolerate life being somewhat dour at the moment and ... ah ... been that way for a couple of years – corresponding with the advent of Snapchat or Instagram or whatever.”

“Hey, I’ll buy now. Waiter ... hello waiter ... yes could we replenish our drinks with the same please. Thank you! So, you are still happy with your wife, though?”

“Oh ... you know ... just the usual ... things could be better.”

“Oh, how so? Your wife’s name is ...?”

“Janice! How so? Ah ... I suppose most men would like more loving and affection in their life, wouldn’t they?”

“Don’t know! I don’t know most men. Have known more than a few though.”

Nathan burst into laughter.

"Go on ... prey tell! With your looks you would have men banging down your door, surely!"

"Hey, no way! I'm not telling you about my intimate past."

"Past? So ... what? Nobody in your life at the moment?"

Cassandra hesitated, then intentionally scrolled her eyes up and down a couple of times, then sideways before returning her gaze upon Nathan.

"I've been single for six months now – not really on the lookout though, I'm enjoying my own me-time – I find it's peaceful."

"Yeah, well, I could certainly use some peacetime at the moment – been all work for a long time now."

"Well I'm sure your Janice appreciates you, being a successful business man, providing security for your family, educating your kids and all that. Do they aspire to undertake a college education?"

"Huh ... if there's a degree in social networking, I suppose they might."

"So your family environment isn't exactly as you would like. So, what is the most undesirable aspect of your family life?"

Nathan saw his opportunity though having no idea as to how this very beautiful woman would react.

"Touched on that already – the lack of affection ... from my so-called loving wife."

"You mean ... lack of sex?"

"Yeah ... well, yeah ... without putting too fine a point on it, just occasionally rather than regularly. Very occasionally, in fact."

"Ah huh! So how often do you think most men would like to make love with their wife?"

"Oh ... ah ... probably two or three times per week I'd say. You know, you spend a long day at work and a good roll can do wonders for stress reduction."

"Which is probably why so many men seek a little outlet away from the home environment. I had a partner for one year who was a lawyer and he was a member of a very exclusive club in New York which was merely a façade for engaging prostitutes during the daytime, where their wives or partners couldn't see what they were up to."

"Ah yes ... I have heard of such clubs."

"So ... you never have?"

"Never have what?"

"Been in a discreet liaison with another woman whilst married to your wife?"

Nathan shook his finger in Cassandra's direction.

"That's a line from that film, isn't it, with Michael Douglas and ... ah ... what's her handle ... Glenn – Glenn Close."

"Very good - almost! He said, 'am I what?'"

"And as for your query ... no, I never have been with another woman since I married Janice."

"So are you going to remain as a faithful husband just bearing the life you have with Janice, or are you going to be like many men and seek solace somewhere?"

"And where would I seek this solace from, Cassandra?"

"Well you may need to just look around you. A lot of men find a woman they turn to for a new life and live happily ever after. Which, I suppose, is why our national divorce rate is so high now – above fifty percent in many, if not most, western societies. So ... you may not need to look very far."

Now, once again, Nathan was wondering why this very beautiful Cassandra was not wearing a ring - and whether a new life might be awaiting him, after life with Janice.

"That sounds to me like very good advice, thank you!"

"And the other line from the film was ... something about him being a naughty boy, out with another woman, just as you are Nathan and ... ah ... you're quite a good looking stud, if you don't mind me saying so."

"Now why would I mind you saying that Cassandra – thank you."

"Well ... um ... if you do have particular needs Nathan, I need to leave this hotel at four in the morning for my flight, so I need you to leave before nine, is that okay?"

"Ah ... yeah, that's fine with me but ... am I to take that as an invitation to accompany you to your room here?"

"Let's just call it remedial therapy by two people who are in need of some love and affection, for their mutual benefits sake."

Nathan left at ten minutes past nine o'clock to head home. As soon as he left, Cassandra made the call.

"Cassandra?"

"Hello Janice - your Nathan has just left so he should be home within thirty minutes."

"Oh ... ah ... so am I to ... ah ... assume that he did stay with you for the last four hours?"

"Yes he did! Now Janice, I know there is a shock factor in this because you will be thinking about your man having been with another woman, but just reflect on your conviction in the greater cause okay. Your Nathan took the bait and he has failed the loyalty test ... as you wanted him to. So you now have the chance to move on and if you need the graphics for Baker and Hall attorneys, just let me know. My assisting investigator was sitting nearby in the lobby and has recorded everything."

"Okay ... thank you Cassandra, goodbye."

"Goodbye Janice! I do, honestly, wish you the best in the future."

Joel Robbins

Joel Robbins was driving to work on a typical Tuesday morning in Chandler, Arizona and was just a couple of blocks from his office when he stopped at traffic lights. As he stopped he glanced into his rear vision mirror.

"Hey!"

There was a mild thud as his car was jolted forward slightly.

"Oh shit! Stupid woman!"

Joel exited his vehicle and walked back to glance at the rear of his Honda Accord. The woman in the car behind his reversed about one yard, so he took the few steps back to woman's car as she put her driver's side window down. She was immediately apologetic.

"Oh look, I am so sorry I don't know how that happened, I am so sorry."

"You don't know how that happened? You had your cell phone to you ear as you hit my car – that's how it happened."

Despite being very annoyed, Joel was rather reticent as he spoke as he couldn't believe just how extremely beautiful the woman who had just hit his car was. He noticed there was now traffic approaching.

"Ah ... we need to move so let's just go over there and pull into the car park in front of that office building, okay?"

"Okay, look I am so sorry!"

Joel returned to his vehicle and proceeded to the car parking area, noticing that she was, indeed, following him. They stopped in the carpark and he exited his vehicle to inspect the damage. She exited her vehicle and was again so very apologetic, as he looked at the damage to his rear bumper. She was now standing alongside him and endeavored to placate him.

"Look you don't need to worry about anything, I will pay for this today, okay. Here is my business card with all my details, now I want you to obtain a quote for this repair job and have this fixed, okay? I am Cassandra, I am from out of town and I am staying at the Sheraton in Wild Horse Pass, so you can give my details to the panel repairer and I will cover everything, okay? Now if I call your cell phone number right now I can save that on my phone and you can verify that this number on my card is my number, okay? My name is Cassandra Young. And your name is?"

"Joel ... Joel Robbins."

"Well I am pleased to meet you Joel, now don't worry, everything will be taken care of."

Cassandra extended her hand to shake Joel's hand. "Well, I am pleased to meet you too, but not in this way obviously. I can call my insurer this morning to lodge a claim but it looks like quite superficial damage so I don't know if they would cover this regardless."

"Okay ... ah ... I'll tell you what I can do. If you take this cash and get the quote for the repair and pay for it today, up front, just bring me the change, okay, to the Sheraton this evening okay - because I fly out of Chandler in the morning. Oh ... and keep two hundred dollars for yourself for the inconvenience Joel, okay?"

Cassandra handed Joel a bundle of notes.

"That's actually three thousand dollars you have there, so that should cover this repair job – just bring me the change less the two hundred."

Joel accepted the cash.

"Okay, I will take my car in to Ace Body Repairers in the industrial sector at lunch time and pay for the repair job up front - as you have suggested."

Joel was typically quite an assertive person and would normally have been quite terse at being put out, but was finding it difficult to be assertive as he was also struck by the absolute beauty of this woman – thinking to himself that she was one of the most beautiful woman he has ever met. She reminded him of actress Jaclyn Smith – a stunning brunette woman with the most beautiful blue eyes.

"Okay I will take my car to the body repairer and will bring you the change this evening. I'll let you know how that goes and when I am on my way."

Joel and Cassandra went to their respective vehicles and proceeded to join the traffic. As he drove off, Joel was somewhat dumbstruck at meeting Cassandra and how beautiful Cassandra was. He then had to wonder whether this beautiful woman was married or attached – or even if she was single. He pondered whether he might be able to make good with her when he did see her in the evening. His mind was racing already. When her reached his office he called his wife.

"Hello, Joel!"

"Deb ... ah ... I just need to let you know I have had a small bingle on the way to work and might be home late tonight."

"Oh! What's happened?"

"Ah ... a woman nudged the rear bumper of my car but don't worry, she has offered to pay for the damages. It's nothing too serious but just going to put me out a bit for the day. I've got to complete the programming for the Chase Manhattan Bank by close of business today so could be a late finish tonight."

"Okay text me when you ae on your way home, okay?"

Joel arrived in his office and called the auto body repairer.

"Ace Body Repairs Cliff speaking, how can I help you."

"Oh Cliff, it's Joel Robbins calling, look my ... ah ... my car was rear ended this morning, nothing too serious, but I need to initiate a search for a rear bumper for my car, the Honda Accord okay. You might be able to do a repair job but, if not, be best to have a replacement on standby ... ah ... preferably the same color - Passion Rose – okay? I mean, I can bring it in about midday to show you but just in case you decide to do a replacement I would like you to jump onto the repairers' webnet."

"Okay, Joel, will do ... ah ... bring it in as you say but I will try to find a replacement too in case we need it. Whichever way, that would cost, maybe, fifteen hundred dollars all up. You okay with that?"

"Yeah that's fine Cliff! The woman has agreed to cover that, so I'll see you at lunchtime."

Joel took the car in to the repairer at one o'clock and Cliff had a replacement bumper ready – 'Passion Rose' in color.

"Lucky you! This bumper was on a car that was hit from the front so it's in perfect condition and is obviously better than your bumper was."

"Yeah ... looks great Cliff ... ah ... can you do the exchange now?"

"I'll get Jacob onto it straight way – probably take about three quarters of an hour. He's done this model a few times before. Hope you don't mind taking a seat in the lounge."

"Fantastic ... I can be back in the office within the hour."

Joel took possession of his car and paid the repairer, then called Cassandra Young.

When Cassandra's phone rang she noticed it was Joel calling.

"Joel, hello, this is Cassandra, how did you fare?"

"Hello Cassandra, you won't believe it, the repairer was able to source a replacement bumper the exact same color as mine, so they did a swap while I was there ... and ... the total cost just fifteen hundred dollars. So I will bring you the balance this evening as you suggested."

"Hey, that's great, so just bring me the thirteen hundred balance, okay and I will ... ah ... be back at the hotel from a seminar by about five o'clock, okay?"

"Five, that suits me fine, so I will see you then."

"Okay, bye for now!"

Joel disconnected the call and was quite chuffed that he would be able to lay his eyes once again on the very beautiful Cassandra at the end of his work day. He called his wife Debbie again.

"Hi Joel, what's up?"

"Hi Deb, it's worked out all good, Ace panel repairers managed to get a same-color replacement and they have fitted it to the car, but I have lost so much time with this hassle today I am going to have to stay back to complete that bank programme."

"Gotta do what you gotta do babe so just keep me in the loop if you are going to be ... like ... really late."

"Yep will do, will see how it's going by about eight o'clock or so."

"Okay, bye!"

"Bye!"

Cassandra Young's phone rang again.

"Hello Deb, how are you?"

"Yeah good actually, Joel just called me and the car has been repaired, so all is set. He should be able to call by your hotel after five tonight."

“Yes he called me too, to let me know so I told him to swing by after five. Are you ... ah ... still fine with this?”

“Oh don’t worry, I’ve been hoping to offload that bastard for years – ever since he had his affair way back then, not even two years after we married. Do you believe it?”

“Ah ... yep, I’m afraid so, been there, been through that. So ... no compunction on your part about what might take place tonight if he is willing?”

“If? Cassandra ... let me say it plain as day - fuck the bastard for me okay? He’ll be right onto you soon as – hundred percent. Have to warn you though, he’s a real goer so be prepared.”

“Okay, well you seem to be in no doubt about putting him to the test.”

“Cassandra, I am looking forward just so much to starting the next chapter of my life and to find a good man, one who will remain loyal to his wife. My grandmother took me to church for her diamond wedding anniversary last month and I met a man there who was widowed and got to having a bit of a chat. He told me that he had always been loyal to his wife and always would have been – had she not passed away over three years ago – so he is the type of man I want to be with.”

“Hmm ... church eh? And will your photographer be at the ready? My associate was available but you have saved money the way you are doing this.”

“Yes! He will take photographs of Joel entering the hotel and sitting with you in the lounge and exiting the lounge with you, then leaving the hotel later. But the pics will only come out if there is legal action over our assets. Until then he will be told that he was seen by someone who knows us, that’s all.”

“Okay, well as I have indicated, Baker and Hall will present his attorneys with my photograph and statement if it comes to that. Now, I will call you as soon as Joel leaves me, okay?”

"Thank you Cassandra and, good luck!"

"Okay, bye Deb!"

Joel left his office at the end of his work day and drove to the Sheraton Hotel to rendezvous with Cassandra. He parked his car and called her.

"Hello Cassandra, it's Joel – I am here now, just parking up outside."

"Okay thanks Joel, I am in my room but will be down soon as, so will meet you at reception."

Joel entered the foyer and proceeded into the lounge area where he could buy a drink. He noticed Cassandra come out of the lift, caught her attention and waved to her. Cassandra entered the lounge and Joel greeted her.

"Hello Casaandra, good to see you again ... ah ... you may not believe it but my car has been repaired already and I have your change right here."

"Wow, how did you get that done so quickly?"

"As my good luck would have it, there was an identical replacement part available right off the shelf, so my mate at the repair shop fitted it while I was there."

"Fantastic, so how much did that cost you Joel."

"Just fifteen hundred dollars actually so I have the fifteen hundred change right here, thank you."

Joel handed Cassandra the fifteen hundred change.

"Don't forget the two hundred I told you to keep for the trouble I have put you through, Joel."

"Ah ... well, as your luck would turn out, the replacement bumper was better than mine which, actually, had very slight pre-existing damage, so no, you can have the fifteen hundred actually."

"Are you sure about that? I was prepared to compensate you for the inconvenience I have put you through."

"Ah ... no worries, I have had a bit of a win already."

Joel was not only thinking of acquiring a better rear bumper for his car but also of being able to stare at this beautiful woman.

"Hey Joel, can I buy you a drink while you are here?"

Joel looked around at the bar and the lounge area and accepted Cassandra's kind offer.

"Yeah, can't say no to a drink, thank you!"

Cassandra led Joel to a table in a corner of the bar and they took their seats. A man with a laptop was seated nearby.

"Ah, time to relax after that tiresome day."

"Oh! So what are you involved in here in Chandler this week?"

"I deliver training seminars to corporations to allow them to, hopefully, educe greater productivity from their employees. I majored in industrial psychology at Harvard back in the day."

"Hmm ... sounds complex, but I'm sure you will be good at whatever you do."

"Oh ... how so?"

The table attendant came to the table to take their orders.

"Would you like to place an order now?"

Cassandra ordered first.

"I would like a Bloody Mary cocktail please."

"One Bloody Mary for miss and ..."

"Same here please ... a Bloody Mary, thank you."

Joel looked at Cassandra.

"Always been my favorite!"

Joel had never had a Bloody Mary in his entire life, but was already beginning to be a tad fawning toward her, hoping to spend a little more time with the beautiful Cassandra.

"So, where were we, oh yes, you said something about me being good at whatever I do, Joel."

"Well, yes, you convey an impression of being articulate and very confident in the way you communicate, so, yes I'm sure you are probably a valued member of staff, or whatever."

"Oh, no, I am a freelance consultant, so, self-employed – you know, it's my own business, what I operate. They pay me a decent fee because they have problems with staff morale and they feel that reflects on their productivity. It only takes a few adverse responses from staff dealing with customers who have a grievance and that can result in loss of revenue."

"Hmm ... well I'm glad that's you and not me – too ... ah ... how shall I say, too people-messy for me to dabble into. So where is your home town?"

"I'm from the city of Dover in Delaware! Been there for the last twenty years, bought my apartment there just a few years back."

"And what line of work are you into Joel?"

"Computer programming ... getting into AI at the moment. It's the latest big thing."

"And have you lived here in Chandler all your life, or have you moved around a little?"

"Been here since the day dot, you know, born here at the maternity hospital."

"And do you enjoy living here? It seems like a good city to live in – clean, vibrant, lots of night life from the little I could see these last three days."

"Yeah, I suppose Chandler is quite a great place to live."

"So you probably live quite a happy life here, Joel?"

"Oh, life could always be better."

"And ... what would you say would achieve that for you."

"Oh, just the usual – the love of a good woman would go a long way towards achieving happiness."

"You don't have a woman in your life?"

"Nope ... been single far too long now – ended a relationship last month actually and ... ah ... still looking. How about you? Who is the lucky man in your life?"

"Lucky man?"

"Well you are obviously a very attractive woman, Cassandra – you must realize that. A lot of men would be extremely keen to form a relationship with you."

"Well, thank you ... I have had that mentioned to me before, yes, by a couple of previous partners. Nothing too long term though – three months to six months here and there."

"What ... so nobody in your life at the moment? Not married or attached?"

"I've been alone for more than a year now. Oh I've had my share of suitors ... men I have met in doing my job who ask me to socialize once my three-day seminars have completed. You know, the corporate dinner, drinks, let's kick on a little, like to go to a night club, etcetera."

"Don't you get lonely at times for a little ... ah ... company, love and affection, some intimacy perhaps?"

"Oh, I think most women would reach a point where they would need a little ... ah ... love and affection, Joel."

"So ... ah ... if you don't mind me asking, when are you likely to reach that point, Cassandra?"

Cassandra shrugged her shoulders.

"Could be any time, Joel."

"So if a man was to, say, hit up on you while you are here in Arizona, how do you think you would react."

"I completed my presentation here in Chandler at four o'clock today and was invited out by the board members for drinks after work, as they say. Fortunately I was able to tell them that I had to meet somebody and was able to scoot off. I suppose there was one good looking guy there I felt a slight attraction to but, I didn't want to let you down, Joel."

"Must have been quite a good looking guy, eh – for a woman like yourself to be attracted to?"

"No better good looking than yourself, Joel."

"Well, thank you! So would you like to kick on a bit, downtown ... ah ... I know a great Nepalese restaurant if you would like to go for dinner."

"Thanks Joel but, I have a really early flight in the morning so ... no that's not really an option for me tonight. I need to hit the hay by ten at the latest so I'll just have to stay in, here at the hotel, I'm afraid."

Joel looked disappointed and a tad despondent.

"So ... would you ... um ... like to come upstairs for a couple of hours, Joel?"

"Yeah! Was hoping you would ask ... shall we go ... now?"

Cassandra took Joel to her room where they stayed for three hours before she asked him to leave.

"Hey, I need to hit the hay now, so, I'll have to ask you to leave now, okay. But I must state, you've certainly been very good for me."

"Phew ... be a bit of an understatement for me to say the same. Have to state, Cassandra, you are the best lover I have ever been with. I ... ah ... don't suppose there is any chance of hooking up again? I could make trips to Dover whenever you might be free of work commitments. You know, see how it goes."

Joel started to dress himself. Cassandra also started to dress with a night gown.

"Well you do have my number, Joel, so yeah, we will see how that goes okay."

Joel gave Cassandra a hug and one last kiss then she saw him to the door. The time was now a few minutes after nine o'clock.

Once the door had closed, Cassandra picked up her phone and called Debbie, assuming she would probably need to pacify Joel's wife.

"Hello Cassandra, how did it go?"

"Your Joel has just left and, yes, I can vouch for him being a real goer, Deb."

"Huh ... so he went for it, eh?"

"Didn't take much convincing. I hope there are no regrets with what you have done."

"Cassandra, I can assure you, within the next month I will start to cause a few issues and be able to move out of this house. I don't think you are not the only woman he has been with in recent years so it doesn't bother me that you took my Joel in tonight. Thank you!"

"Now please remember the deal – he is not to know that you set him up, okay. I rely on my clients remaining confidential about that to generate my business, okay! And can you have your observer email me the pics."

"Yes, mom's the word at this end and, yes, the pics will come from me as he will send them to me."

"Now you have the details of the attorney who will handle your case – Baker and Hall okay. Now with the pics as evidence it should be totally straightforward for them to come to an uncomplicated settlement if your Joel is in denial to his own attorney. Baker and Hall will have a photograph of me and a statement from me, supposedly from identifying me in the discovery process, via the hotel. That's all from me so, goodbye Debbie. I do hope everything works out well for you with the new man you have met through the church. He should be a good man – one of the best."

“Goodbye Cassandra.”

“Yes goodbye Debbie, I am very pleased to have helped you dear.”

Ross and Robert

Joel arrived home just after ten o'clock and walked into the living room where his wife, Debbie, was watching a movie.

"How did you go? Did you get the job done?

"Almost! We have a few issues with the client's corporate governance policy so we might have to make a visit to the client in Dover within a week or so to sort things out. How was your day, Deb?"

"Oh ... mine? I had a very peaceful day actually, just had some rest outside contemplating the green trees in the garden and the beautiful blue sky - after I finished the housework. Feeling so peaceful I wonder if I should be good to you tonight, dear."

"Ah ... I'm feeling a bit washed up ... ah ... that contract is our biggest and it was pretty stressful at the office today. Maybe tomorrow, eh?"

Deb shrugged her shoulders.

"I can wait!"

The following day Joel went to work as usual and after work met with his best mate, Ross. They had arranged to have after work drinks at their local bar. Ross was seated when Joel arrived. Joel ordered a beer and strolled to the table where Ross was seated.

"So ... how's it going buddy?"

"Don't mind telling you Ross ... I have to say I have had one of the best sexual experiences in my entire life last night."
"Oh yeah ... what's her name, I wonder?"

“Yes, well, you are pretty much onto it already. Was involved in a slight bingle yesterday on my way to work and ... ah ... I don’t mind telling you because you are my best mate, but this drop-dead gorgeous woman rear-ended my car, then offered me three thousand dollars to get it fixed and I had to take her the change ... to the Sheraton where she was staying.”

“Hotel?”

“Yeah, she’s from Dover in Delaware ... jut here for a couple of days for some kind of work conference. Stayed at the Sheraton for a few nights.”

“So you took her the change and ...”

“I made good mate – I fucked her!”

“What? You lucky bastard. How was it?”

“Went through her four times in just three hours mate. Don’t mind telling you ... the best fucking sex I’ve ever had with a woman. I mean ... you wouldn’t believe how beautiful this woman was ... and ... I’ve got her phone number.”

“You weasel, Joel! Hope your Deb doesn’t find out.”

“Nah ... can’t happen! Told her I was working back on that bank programme I have been working on.”

“That still going?”

“Oh yeah, but it’s not due for another week or more. But Deb believed me.”

“Never too hard to fool a woman, eh, mate. So have you called this ... ah ... what’s her name?”

“Cassandra! Cassandra Young. No I am going too soon enough though – told her I could make the odd trip to Dover to maintain the friendship. Just need to tell Deb I have some out of town jobs to do. She’ll buy it!”

“Same story you fed her with that ... ah ... Julieanne eh? What’s become of her, Joel?”

"Ah ... said she wanted to try to save her marriage. You know how some women get!"

Ross nodded in concurrence.

"Why don't you ring that Cassandra now ... see where she's at? Should be home from work by now."

"That's not a bad idea actually."

Joel reached into his pocket for his phone and called Cassandra. There was an automated message instead of a ringtone.

"The number you have dialled is not connected. Please check the number and dial again. The number you have dialled is not ..."

Joel disconnected the call and dialled again.

"The number you have dialled is not connected ..."

Joel disconnected the call again.

"Hmm ... strange, that! She gave me her business card with that number just yesterday and we sent each other a text message last night. Hmm ... must be some kind of a glitch in the line somewhere."

"Oh well, not the first time you've played around, you cad. The strange thing really is that, you know, your wife Deb is such a wonderful person Joel. A lot of men would envy you for that!"

"Yeah ... I know she is Ross but ... can't break the old habits ... you know ... before I met Deb I had more than three hundred lovers in my day. Got a bit of an affinity for women, mate."

"Yeah you've told me before ... about two hundred more than I have had, mate. Thank God for Tinder, eh?"

"Or – thank the devil?"

Both men broke into vociferous laughter for a few seconds then ordered another round of drinks.

"I'll try that number again before we leave."

He did – with the same result. Joel Robbins didn't realize that the so-called Cassandra Young purchases bulk SIM cards from Walmart, then dispenses of them once they have been used. She wears the ongoing cost for twelve months, which she builds into her fee.

"I'll try her number again later, before I arrive at home."

The men left the bar at half past six o'clock and Joel pulled over off the road just a couple of blocks from home to dial Cassandra again – but with the same result. He walked into his house, placed his brief case down and walked into the kitchen, where Deb was standing in a corner with her arms folded.

"Hello dear!"

Deb gave Joel the death stare and remained silent for several seconds, blinking a few times. Joel sensed there was something amiss. He frowned then put the question.

"You okay?"

"Am I okay ... ah ... well, no, not really. I had a call from a second cousin whom you met very briefly at Uncle Tony's funeral last year. He was having a drink at the Sheraton night before last and believes he saw you with a woman – a very beautiful woman and you left with her and got into a lift together. You told me you were working that night."

"A second cousin! Which second cousin?"

"Never mind that, you only met for a second or two. Was it you he saw with that woman?"

Joel became somewhat frantic and shook his head.

"Must be a case of mistaken identity I'd say. Quite a few guys out there who look rather like me, you know, last year I was sporting a beard when we went to your uncle's funeral. Would have been someone else that he saw – just someone with similar looks."

Joel's denial gave Deb the feeling of conviction she was seeking to leave her philandering husband for good, which she would effect within just a couple of weeks. The following Sunday while Joel was playing golf in the morning, Deb went to the Catholic Church where she waited in the foyer near the entrance for the same man, Robert, whom she had met at her grandparents' anniversary function. She had decided to set the wheels in motion for her new life. Deb perused some publications but kept a watchful eye through a window as people entered the church. She saw Robert approaching the entrance and as he stepped through the doorway she replaced a booklet and stepped toward the main entrance.

"Oh hello Robert, nice to see you again."

"Hey, Debbie, yes nice to see you again too. Are you a regular here now?"

"Oh I will be for sure ... ah ... I have been going to a parish nearby but I prefer the service here actually. Seems like such a friendly community here."

"Yes, well I can vouch for that, they have been so welcoming here for me since my wife passed away."

"Oh yes, you told me she passed on about three years ago Robert. No doubt you are still grieving but time is the great healer, as they say. You might be ready to meet somebody else soon."

Debbie gave Robert a slight nudge with her right elbow. Robert laughed quite spontaneously and gestured with a pleasant frown with his eyebrows.

"Time to go inside Robert, I hope you don't mind if I sit with you."

"Please do!"

Debbie was so nervous during the service and looked with great anticipation at the moment she could turn to Robert to wish him the sign of peace, meaning they would hold hands so momentarily and mutter those words 'peace be with you'. The moment arrived and Debbie turned to Robert with a beaming smile and Robert reciprocated. After the celebration of the Mass they went out to the foyer and Debbie took her chance.

"So Robert, what did you think about the gospel today ... the ... parable of the Prodigal Son?"

"That's so special isn't it, because it gives hope to everybody that no matter how badly we live our lives, if and when we make a genuine turnaround in our lives to be a good person, the Lord almighty is there ready to forgive us and to welcome us home to heaven. It amazes me that when he saw the boy returning, the father ran to the boy."

"Yes, that truly is amazing isn't it - and just as intriguing as my favorite parable – the vineyard workers."

"Hmm ... so why would that be your favorite parable Debbie?"

"Well because the Lord welcomed the latecomers with the same reward as those who had worked all day – just one denarius or, eternal life. So when the early starters queried him because they expected more, he stated that it was his money to be generous with as he chose and they really couldn't ask for more than eternal life now, could they?"

"Yeah, fair point, so where are you off to now Debbie ... ah ... would you like to take in a coffee at the café by the lake?"

"Oh ... love to Robert, thank you so much for asking me, yes, my car is right there so I will follow you to the café and ... see you there."

"Great and ... ah ... might even have a bite to eat so, see you there. Don't worry – it's on me!"

Robert was really struck by Debbie's beautiful sparkling eyes and her rosy lips. He wondered whether he had, in fact, recently met his future partner. He could only hope. They arrived at the café and took up their seating overlooking the water.

"So what would you like Deb - it's on me today?"

"Oh thank you Robert - and I will reciprocate next week if you meet me here again after church."

"Yeah ... ah ... okay sounds good. Might even sit together for the Mass again eh?"

"So I will have a café latte and a toasted avocado and salmon sandwich if that is okay?"

"Absolutely, hey that was my choice here just last time I was here - fancy that."

"Wow good to be on the same page, so is that what you are going to have?"

"No I can tell you that in church I was literally drooling over the thought of having a bacon and egg toasted sandwich this morning so that will be my order. Haven't had one for about three months actually."

"Oh, tell me more! Is this where you come regularly after Mass on a Sunday?"

"Yes, almost every week, depends on what the girls are doing for sport. Sometimes they start and finish before church but other times I have to collect them straight afterwards."

"So do you have two girls or ..."

"Three actually ... all aged between seven and eleven. And you?"

"Two boys, eight and ten!"

"So together we have children seven, eight, nine, ten and eleven!"

Debbie broke into a raucous laughter.

"Hey, yeah that's true eh - we'll all have to meet up sometime. Perhaps organize a picnic or a ball game sometime."

"Sounds great ... ah ... sometime in the next few weeks, will that be good for you?"

Deb had to think quickly. She knew she had just a short time to make the move, from her house, to secure premises and to take her boys with her.

"Oh I promised to take the boys away for a few weeks but as soon as we return from Cody's Camp, for sure Rob. Look forward to that immensely."

Deb and Rob enjoyed their late morning breakfast together and stayed in the café for an hour before parting in the carpark.

"Thank you for that Robert and will see you next week, now, give us a hug."

Robert smiled and was blown away as they embraced for a few seconds. They agreed to meet again next Sunday at church.

Janice Butler

Cassandra's phone rang.

"Hello Cassandra this is Janice, Nathan's wife."

"Hello Janice, how are you coping?"

"Fine, look I really want to thank you and am just calling to let you know that I have secured a condo for myself and the kids so I will be leaving Nathan within a week or two, just as soon as I can have a heart to heart with him. I don't know how much he disclosed to you but there really hasn't been a marriage between us for a couple of years now and ... ah ... some friends of mine have introduced me to a couple of really great guys, so if you want me to keep in touch I will okay. Oh – and I have made the appointment with Baker and Hall, the lawyers, thank you."

"Well Janice, I don't actually need to know too much about what happens in your future, you know, once the job is done but feel free to let me know if Baker and Hall do the right thing by you. Hopefully Nathan won't put up much of a fight for your other house that you want. I suppose you will consider putting that out as a rental Janice."

"That's the plan, yes, I honestly don't think I could live there again having lived there with Nathan for several years - and there are tenants there at the moment."

"Now, you might want to refer somebody else to me if you do know of anybody who needs to separate – just give them this number, okay, it's not a number I give to the men."

Janice was a little miffed at Cassandra's response, her not wanting to know how things went, but accepted it was just her job what she did, so they parted ways amicably.

"Okay Cassandra, thanks again."

"Oh just finally, Janice, it ah ... might sound a little like arrogance but believe me it's not, I just want to say that your Nathan was a very ordinary lover. It was all about him, you know, so I think you could probably find a future partner who can provide you with a much fuller sex life, so I do wish you the best."

"Okay, thank you Cassandra, goodbye."

Raymond Brookes

Raymond Brookes was one his way to his office in San Diego on a Tuesday morning, where he worked as an accountant, when his cell phone rang. He noticed it was his wife, Natalie, calling.

"Hello dear!"

"Hello darling, are you near the office yet?"

"Almost – just a few minutes away ... ah ... just approaching the traffic lights at the ... ah ... Stevens Avenue intersection. Is everything okay?"

"Oh yes, I just wanted to ask if you could call in to the supermarket on your way home this evening as I want to make a casserole for dinner and I will need some beef stock and some chicken stock, if you could do that for me please."

"Okay, beef stock and chicken stock, will do, casserole - sounds great!"

Raymond stopped at the traffic lights and looked into his rear vision mirror.

"Oh no!"

There was a mild thud as his car was jolted forward slightly.

"What is it dear?"

"Oh shit, some woman has just rear-ended my car – I saw she was on her phone, it was actually in her hand while she was driving. I had better go, I need to sort this out."

"Oh my goodness, you don't need that happening today - it was going to be a big day for you signing off the sale".

"I'm just going to get out of the car and ask this woman to meet me around the corner – we can't stay here at the lights."

“Okay, bye for now.”

Raymond exited his vehicle and walked back to the woman’s car as she put her driver’s side window down.

“Oh look, I am so sorry I don’t know how that happened, I am so sorry.”

“Well I know how it happened – I looked in my rear vision mirror and noticed you had your cell phone to you ear as you hit my car.”

Vehicles behind started to toot their horns.

“Now look, we need to move so I want you to drive around this corner and we need to pull into the coffee stand bay just over there, okay?”

“Okay, I am so sorry!”

Raymond returned to his vehicle and proceeded around the corner noticing that she was, indeed, following him. They stopped in the bay where the Muzz Buzz coffee outlet was. He exited his vehicle to inspect the damage and she exited her vehicle. He looked at the minor damage to his rear bumper and shook his head. She was now standing alongside him and observed that she had caused some minor damage to his rear bumper.

“Look you don’t need to worry about anything, I will pay for this today, okay. Here is my card with all my details, now I want you to obtain a quote for this repair job and have this fixed, okay? I am Cassandra, I am from out of town and I am staying at the Hilton in Jimmy Durante Boulevarde, so you can give my details to the panel repairer and I will cover everything, okay?”

“From out of town eh? Hmm ... well I hope you don’t mind if I call your cell phone number right now just to save that on my phone.”

“Yes, please do, that way I will have your number also. And your name is?”

"Raymond ... Raymond Brookes."

"Well I am pleased to meet you Raymond Brookes, now don't worry, everything will be taken care of."

Cassandra extended her hand to shake Raymond's hand. "Yeah, well, I can't say I am pleased to meet you in such circumstances, but thank you for assuring me ... but ... how do I know you won't do a runner on me? This won't be sufficient damage to make an insurance claim justifiable."

"Okay ... ah ... fair call, tell you what I will do. If you take this cash and get the quote for the repair today and pay for it, just bring me the change, okay, to the Hilton this evening okay, because I fly out of San Diego in the morning. Oh ... and keep two hundred dollars for yourself for the inconvenience Raymond, okay?"

Cassandra handed Raymond a bundle of notes.

"That's three thousand dollars you have there, so I think that should cover this repair job – just bring me the change less the two hundred."

Raymond opened his hand and accepted the cash. He was somewhat dumbstruck by her generous offer, not that a mere two hundred dollars was significant to him, as he had recently become a very wealthy man from property transactions, but her offer did placate his immediate concerns. He was also struck by the shocking beauty of the woman – thinking to himself that she was one of the most beautiful woman he has ever met in his entire life.

"Okay I will take my car to an auto body repairer I know of and will bring you any change there might be, this evening, thank you. I'll give you a call when I am on my way."

Raymond and Cassandra went to their respective vehicles and proceeded to join the traffic. As he drove off, Raymond was completely flabbergasted at his recent experience in meeting

Cassandra and kept thinking to himself what an extraordinarily beautiful woman Cassandra is – probably the most beautiful woman he had ever met in person. His next thought was completely understandable – is this beautiful woman attached or is she, possibly, single. No doubt there will be some very fortunate man in her life, he thought.

Raymond arrived at his office and before proceeding called his wife, Natalie, to assure her there was no great drama.

"Raymond, what's happened?"

"It's okay dear, nothing serious, just a slight dent in the rear bumper and a bit of a paint scratch, but the woman handed me three thousand dollars cash, would you believe it, to have the repairs done. But I need to pay today on the quote and to take her the change."

"Oh that's very kind of her, but you don't need that type of inconvenience on a day like today."

"Ah ... no worries, the repairer is not far away so that will only take fifteen minutes and she told me to keep two hundred for putting me out."

"Oh ... fantastic, we can go out for dinner tonight."

"Will see, okay!"

Nathan spent the day with his lawyers and those of the property development party that wanted to purchase the one hundred acres he had bought as a twenty year old man, when he got wind that the area in question would, one day, be earmarked for residential development. He was really pleased and relieved when the deal was sealed by three in the afternoon and, with some excitement, called his wife.

"Nat ... sealed the deal ... seventeen million! The money will be in the bank tomorrow afternoon. Now don't you go off and spend it, alright."

“Wow ... fantastic, congratulations darling and as if that is something that I would do to you, eh? I mean, really! So dinner tomorrow night will be on the cards don’t you think?”

“That will be highly appropriate, yes, looking forward to that so, choose a top restaurant, okay?”

“Oh ... I will, don’t worry, no holding back tomorrow night dear.”

“Okay I’ll finish up at my office, take that woman her change and see you about six o’clock.”

“Okay darling, I’ll make a booking with Mister A’s for seven o’clock tomorrow.”

“Excellent, see you when I get home.”

Natalie ended the call and immediately called Cassandra.

“Hello Natalie.”

“Hello Cassandra ... ah ... Raymond has completed the deal so I will be financial soon enough and be able to go my own way. So make sure you do a good job on him tonight because I need to catch him out. I don’t mind telling you it has taken me years to save your fee in an account he knows nothing about so I want to split from Raymond soon as I can. I’m a bit skint, you know.”

“Okay, now we have discussed this at length and you do understand that I will seduce your Raymond as long as he is willing, okay?”

“Oh, yes, please do – you have my permission, Cassandra.”

Raymond left his office at five o’clock and headed for Cassandra’s hotel to hand her back her change. He entered the hotel lobby and Cassandra waved him to come to her table.

“Hello Raymond, so pleased you could make it. Have you had a good day despite the trauma I caused this morning?”

“Oh that was nothing really – had it all sorted within a couple of hours.”

“Hey, let me buy you a drink.”

"Well I have your change here and I really appreciate you resolving that as soon as you have. The repairer managed to procure a replacement bumper and fitted it while I was there – all done, good as gold. In fact, a little better than the bumper that was on my car, in fact, so there's no need for the two hundred dollars you offered me."

"Oh, that's very good of you Raymond, now, what is your poison?"

"If you insist – a whiskey and dry please."

Cassandra hailed the waiter and ordered the drinks.

"So, apart from the inconvenience, I suppose in a way you might have had a small win."

"Yeah, the car does look better than it did this morning – my wife Natalie had scratched the bumper removing shopping bags from the boot, but nothing major."

"Huh – wives! What would you expect, so clumsy when it comes to motor cars, Raymond. And how is your Natalie apart from destroying motor cars?"

"She's ... been a good wife, been married for ten years, no kids though."

"Oh, why would that be Raymond?"

"We tried and she became pregnant but unfortunately experienced a miscarriage the first time she became pregnant, then was diagnosed as having a dysfunctional uterus ... so we've contemplated adoption but, just been too busy in the business to proceed with that to date. Maybe next year!"

"Well I hope that goes well for you with the adoption ... such as shame that you can't have your own children though. I don't have kids but ... can't really say I've been trying very hard."

"Oh ... do you think you will in the next few years ... ah ... how does your partner feel about that – assuming you have a partner?"

"Well, no I don't, I have been single for almost a year now and withdrew into my shell a little after my last experience, he was just so possessive, you know, wanted to know everything I had done every day, where I had been, who I had seen or been talking to ..."

"I know the type, one of my best friends was like that with his wife and myself and a few other friends warned him about that and ... ah ... eventually she flew the coup ... took off and left him."

"Yes. Well, I did the same and had to move to another city so he couldn't stalk me. Took a long time to shake him off."

"Well he was probably quite devastated – you would be quite a catch for any man, as you probably know."

"Well, thank you, Raymond, for the compliment but ... I'm not in a hurry, enjoying my me time, you know. Don't doubt I'll find happiness one day though."

"No doubt about that!"

"And you, Raymond, are you happy with your Natalie?"

"I have been ... or at least I thought I was ... until recently. One of my ex-girlfriends called me just two weeks ago and hinted that my Natalie may be having an affair with a senior executive where she works. You see, I play competition golf and am required to go away for weekends every so often playing the amateur tournaments, so Natalie goes to Las Vegas with her management team. My ex-girlfriend, Roxanne, has told me she heard from a friend that my Natalie may be playing up but that is just inuendo at this time. They have a mutual friend who still works with Nat. I ... ah ... haven't accepted that she does play around, but Roxy is going to make an attempt to procure evidence of that through her friend."

Natalie had said nothing about this to Cassandra, which did not surprise her, as many of her clients were in the process of separating to secure assets from their marriage and to go their own way.

"So ... if your Natalie is being unfaithful to you, Raymond, how do you think you will respond to that?"

"Well, I hope it's not true but, if that does come to light, I suppose the first step would be to seek counselling from a ... ah ... marriage guidance service or the local priest – I really don't know yet. Marriage is very important to me, Cassandra. Natalie and I were married in the local Catholic Church, you know."

"Hmm ... sounds like you might be in for quite a shock, Raymond. Let's hope that's not true then, eh! But supposing for a moment that it is true, what your ex-girlfriend has divulged to you, how will you feel about that, within yourself?"

"I'll be surprised quite honestly. I mean, I know Nat goes away virtually every weekend that I do but, I never suspected she had given up on our marriage. If that's the case then she's putting up quite a convincing charade in our home ... although, we don't share the same intimacy that we did a few years back. I've assumed for a few years now that ... ah ... that's the way it goes in many marriages."

"Perhaps you need a little therapy of your own, Raymond? Two can play the same game, you know. I know it's not my business but have you ever desired another woman since you've been married to Natalie? It's something you don't have to talk about, of course, if you don't wish to."

"That's okay, because, I have never been unfaithful to my Natalie and ... oh look there have been many women I have met who caused me to think that ... ah ... if I was a single man I would certainly pursue a woman like her, of course. Every man experiences that. Beautiful women don't lose their beauty when a man marries his wife."

"Well from what you said to me earlier, that compliment you paid to me, you might be thinking that of me, too, perhaps."

"Ha, ha, ha ... well I do have to admit, Cassandra, as a woman you are quite a stunner, yes, if I was a single man I would definitely be a suitor to you, no doubt."

"Perhaps you need to consider leveling the playing field a little, Raymond."

"How so?"

"Well your ex-girlfriend has told you that your wife may be playing around and that may be true, you don't know yet. So, in case that does come to light, why don't you consider having some fun of your own?"

"Ah ... with who? I don't actually know of any women recently who would be interested in a covert liaison with me."

"Well ... as I said, I've been alone for about one year now ... women do have needs too, you know. I'm no different! I'm here from out of town, staying here in this hotel and have a few hours to spare before I hit the hay so ... do you want to play?"

Raymond looked shocked as he sat there thinking, pondering.

"Just feeling a little empathy for you, actually, Raymond. I have quite a few friends who have evened the playing field because their husbands are unfaithful. Happens all the time! It's no big deal and some friends have told me that having a bit of a fling of their own actually deepens their own commitment to their partners."

"Are you ... ah ... asking me to spend a few hours with you in your room, making yourself available to me, Cassandra?"

"Sounds like that to me, Raymond."

Raymond stood, stepped sideways and placed his chair back into position underneath the table.

“Well thank you so much for the empathy Cassandra but ... I think I had better go home now, before I succumb to the temptation. It has yet to be confirmed that my wife is having an affair so until then I will give her the benefit of doubt. I’m sorry I can’t be there to meet your needs so ... ah ... goodbye for now. Oh and, thank you for having my car repaired, I really appreciate that.”

Raymond started towards the door and Cassandra took her phone from her bag to make the call to Natalie.

“Hello Cassandra.”

“Yes, hello Natalie.”

“Ah ... it’s not six o’clock yet - did he not stay with you?”

“I’m afraid to say, Natalie, that your Raymond turned me down ... and I did make a blatant play for him ... for sex. I invited him to come to my room for a few hours ... told him he would need to leave by nine o’clock, but he wouldn’t be in it. Pretty much got up and left - soon as, really.”

“Oh shit! Okay well I suppose I will just have to go about this in another way but, thanks for trying. I thought he might have stayed with you.”

“Perhaps your husband is a good man, Natalie. If so, he’d be one in ten so, perhaps reconsider your intentions.”

“Yeah, well, that’s my call okay, but thanks again. Goodbye Cassandra.”

“Goodbye Natalie. I wish you the best.”

Rachael and Damian

The next day Cassaandra's cell phone rang.

"Cassandra Young speaking, how may I help you?"

"Oh hello Cassandra, my name is Rachael and I was given your details by a friend who has informed me that you successfully put her despicable husband to a loyalty test and ... ah ... a test that he failed, actually. I am hoping you can do the same for me."

"Okay ... ah ... do you mind if I ask you who recommended me?"

"No, not at all, it was an old friend named Sheralyn and you sorted out her ex-husband named Jed who was, to put it quite bluntly, fucking around with anyone he could actually."

"Oh yes, I do remember Jed and Sheralyn from last year, yes, he was not very difficult to sway. Now has she given you any details of how I go about my business and the nature of my fees?"

"Well yes, Sheralyn did inform me that you require ten thousand dollars for what you do."

"And are you okay with that?"

"Absolutely! I would pay twice as much to get rid of my husband, Damian. I am an English teacher so I subscribe to professional ethics, but my Damian is a boilermaker. I don't detest his occupation, per se, but he and all of his mates voted for Donald Trump at the last election – so there's a bit of a gutter mentality quite prevalent there."

"That's good Rachael, because I will have a paid observer there with me to take photographs and you will need to inform your husband that a person who knows you intimately, observed him at the hotel with me, okay? You are never to disclose that you engaged my services because I cannot have my work publicly disclosed and you will need to consult family lawyers Baker and Hall who are experienced in marriage separation and with what I do, okay? Do you agree with my requirements Rachael?"

"Yes, I agree with that!"

"And has Sheralyn informed you that to seal the fate of your husband, I will provide him with sex if that is what he chooses?"

"Yes, she did and I have no problem with that because I found out that he has been calling in to his best friend's house when his mate is out of town doing railway repairs, so I believe he has been fucking his best friend's wife. I was going to her house myself one day but as I approached I could see Damian's car was parked outside and he stayed there for two hours, when he was supposed to be at work. I believe he may have been fucking around for years, including with some of his ex-girlfriends who like to contact him occasionally. He gets calls every couple of months from somebody then disappears for a day or two, supposedly for conducting his business."

"Hmm ... yes an all-too-common reason for leaving home for a few days, for sure. So which city are you in Rachael?"

"Sacramento! Can you come to this city?"

"I am willing to go anywhere Rachael so, yes, I can be there virtually any time that I am free of other appointments. Have you gone beyond the point of counselling for your marriage?"

"We went through all of that years ago Cassandra and it has made no difference to him whatsoever."

"Okay so I need you to provide me with certain details about where you live and where your husband works and how he gets to work and so on, because I need to meet your Damian with a slight traffic bingle and then to ask him to meet me at the hotel where I will be staying, okay"

"Yes!"

"And Rachael I need to let you know that I require payment of the ten thousand dollars in advance, once I arrive in Sacramento. Are you okay with that?"

"Yes! I have thought this through so very thoroughly so believe me there is no future for us and I need evidence for my attorney to move on. I can't see how him having sex with you is any different to what he's been doing for years – having sex with a lot of women. Can you be here next week?"

"I can be there on Monday morning, Rachael, if you wish."

"Excellent! Please call me when you arrive."

"Yes I will and I will be staying at the Hyatt Regency at 1209 L Street so you need to meet me there because I will need some details about Damian, okay. Then if things go to plan I will arrange to meet your Damian on Tuesday morning by causing the traffic incident. I will provide him with cash and ask him to return the change to me at The Hyatt. So I will need the details of the route that he takes to drive to his place of work and what car he will be driving and you can show me a photograph."

"Very good, thank you Cassandra, I look forward to meeting you."

"Now I can fly in on an early flight so I will text you once I have booked into The Hyatt. You can come to see me there at a time that suits you."

"Oh thank you, yes, that will be ideal, I will see you there. Goodbye for now!"

"Goodbye Rachael."

Cassandra flew into Sacramento on the Monday morning as pledged and met Rachael in the Hyatt Regency lobby.

"Hello Rachael."

“Hello Cassandra.”

The two women shook hands and Rachael was momentarily stunned by the appearance of Cassandra as she was of immense beauty. Cassandra outlined the conditions of her service pertaining to confidentiality and that her attorneys Baker and Hall would have to be the lawyers that Rachael utilized. The lawyers had her photograph on file and a generic statement that simply needed to be signed by Cassandra.

“Now are you sure you want to proceed with this?”

“Oh, absolutely Cassandra, I haven’t disclosed this yet but my marriage has been quite precarious for some time now. There has also been some confrontation toward me by Damian. He can become quite belligerent if I provoke him and insinuate that he has been up to no good when he has been out all night – supposedly with the boys. He is such a mendacious bastard and he has the temerity to lie about everything. He is just so totally devoid of any integrity so it is futile trying to save my marriage. I can no longer condone what he is doing and I am positive that he will transgress if offered a liaison with you. I desperately need to avert any escalation of the confrontation this causes, so it’s imperative that I bring this marriage to an end now because I am not willing to persevere any longer.”

“Oh, I am sorry to know that Rachael, so I do believe you are going about this the right way and I wish you the best.”

Rachael knew that if her Damian had, indeed, been unfaithful before today, he would fall into the trap set by Cassandra. Damian did not let her down - and Cassandra trapped Damian in the usual way. Rachael was extremely relieved to know that her suspicions of her husband, Damian, were correct and that she had the evidence she would need to effect an acceptable divorce and to start a new life.

Raymond and Roxanne

Raymond Brookes was at his work desk when his cell phone rang, with a number he did not recognize.

"Raymond Brookes, hello!"

"Hello Raymond it's Roxanne calling, how are you?"

"Roxanne, hello, I am really good actually. How is everything with you?"

"I am fine too Raymond, but I do need to talk to you for a little while in confidence, so, do you mind if I see you for half an hour sometime soon?"

"Ah ... yeah, no issue with that, but would this be in relation to what you intimated to me previously, about my wife, Natalie?"

Raymond had been in a relationship with Roxanne for almost two years before she introduced him to her best friend at that time – Natalie.

"Yes it is, but I really should talk to you in person, Raymond. It's not the type of subject to talk about aver the telephone, so can you find half an hour free after work tonight? We could meet somewhere at your choice, but say, the Crocodile Bar, downtown? "

"Well I could spare a half hour from four thirty, but after that Natalie would expect me to be making my way home."

"Yes, well it is Natalie that I need to talk to you about, Raymond, so I will see you there at four thirty, okay?"

"Yeah, okay, I will see you there and then, Roxanne."

When Raymond arrived at the Crocodile Bar, Roxanne was already there waiting to see him. They gave each other a small hug.

"Roxanne, hello, how are you going darling?"

"I'm fine Ray, but please take a seat and let me buy you a drink."

Roxanne signalled the bar attendant for two drinks. She had already informed him of what their drinks would be.

"Okay, so ... ah ... what's this about my wife, Natalie, then?

"Raymond, I need to let you know that I am extremely happy with Gareth and, as you know, we have three children now. So this is not about you and me, okay. It's just about your wife and certain things you probably do not know about her, but that I intimated the last time we spoke."

"So do you believe you have some more detail about Natalie? We've been married for almost eleven years now."

"Raymond, as you know, Natalie and I used to work together until I left the company just two years ago. There was no dearth of conjecture floating around within the administration section back then - rumours about the relationship between your Natalie and the proprietor, Graham Bridges."

"What type of rumours?"

"Rumours that when you go away for weekends with the golf club, as you seem to quite regularly, Natalie would accompany Graham to weekends away in Las Vegas, staying in top class hotels and spending the nights in the casino."

"Uh huh!"

"And that included staying in the same room for their weekend away, Raymond. Now, I have just recently been to a type of re-union meeting with some of the girls from admin - not including your Natalie – and one of them, Glenda, a relative newcomer, corroborated on Graham Bridges and your Natalie being an item, Raymond."

"An item? As in ... lovers?"

"Yes! Your Natalie has deceived you, Raymond, so your future with her is fraught with peril. I don't know how a woman can be so flippant about her marriage to a wonderful man such as yourself."

"Well, I do hope that's not true, Roxy, but ... I'm just going to have to take that on board and ... ah ... see if I can ascertain the truth, somehow. Got to admit though, she hasn't been the best of lovers these last two years."

"That's something I can possibly help you with Raymond and, I want you to know, I would only do such a thing because I know what a wonderful man you are and that you deserve better. You do not deserve a disloyal wife, Raymond. You must know that yourself. I would have been so very happy with you, myself, had I not introduced you to Natalie."

Raymond seemed to sit there in shock for a minute.

"So how could you assist me to find out the truth, Roxanne?"

"One of my long-term friends, Jessica, who is still there at the corporation in the admin section, sometimes goes to Vegas when Graham and Natalie go there and is willing to get some graphic evidence for you. She is a lovely woman you have never met, but I see her occasionally and the topic of discussion came up. I told her what a wonderful man you are so she agreed to help. Her name is Jessica Robertson."

"How would she do that?"

"Now I believe this is quite a feasible plan. When they go to Vegas, the corporation books a number of rooms in very close proximity to each other. Being the sole owner of the enterprise, Graham Bridges can take his entire management team as he wishes - and he does – about seven or eight of them.

Apparently he tells them it's their reward for gaining new contracts and he wants to keep their motivation levels up. So they all go there together, about ten of them. But according to Jessica, it's just a front so he can be with your wife for the weekend. Now, Jessica can probably get a few snaps or video that will allow you to deduce enough to put you in the loop."

Raymond put his face into his hands. He wasn't expecting something like this but he was recalling those recent utterances from his wife pertaining to the sale of the land, as she had taken an unexpected interest in recent months in the progress of the sale.

"Shit! I never thought!"

"So when is your next golf weekend with the club, when Natalie will probably go to Vegas while you are away?"

"Oh, we have booked that for the weekend after next, actually, in San Francisco."

"Okay, so if this is true, you really do need to know about this because you are quite financial and if she leaves you, you will need to be prepared to surrender about half of everything you own. You've been married long enough for her to legally claim that you know."

"Oh shit!"

"I recall you had that parcel of land down south when we were together so ..."

"Sold it two weeks ago for a packet, Roxy."

"Really, oh shit!"

"Yeah ... seventeen million!"

"Holy shit, Raymond, she could walk away and be upside forever and never have to work again. That Graham is pretty well off, bit of a billionaire you might say. He's into all this artificial intelligence software and it's going gargantuan Ray. He has made billions from the AI bubble, Raymond. He invested ten million in Nvidia five years ago and sold recently for three hundred and fifty million, so the weekends he provides to his staff are just a front to spend weekends with your wife, Raymond."

"Not much I can do about that now – there was no pre-nuptial in place, though I wouldn't go down that road of vindictiveness regardless. If she wants to leave me I will split everything with her."

"I know you will Raymond – you are such a good charitable man."

"Okay so ... ah ... probably does explain some things about our marriage, that she has been a little aloof in recent years. I had put it down to menopause or something similar."

"No ... she's only thirty eight Raymond and she has had a lover all that time ... leaving you out in the cold. How totally fucking callous of her, if you don't mind the expression. Now she can leave you with millions. I suppose the upside for you, if there is one, you will still be very well off yourself, even if she does take you for half of everything you own."

"Yeah ... I can thank my God for that."

"You still believe?"

"Yes, of course – always will, Roxy."

"Well ... maintain your faith and your hope, okay. Things can improve for you Raymond, somehow! I will arrange for Jessica to see what she can do in Vegas next weekend while you are away."

"Rox, this ... ah ... goes a long way to explaining why a woman who caused a traffic incident with me at traffic lights a couple of weeks ago tried to seduce me into her room at the hotel where she was staying. She gave me cash for the repair job and I took her the change. So now I am suspecting that Nat tried to set me up with that woman. So thank you Roxy, I really appreciate you assisting me this way. I'll have to act as though I don't know anything so as to not let her in on this."

"Yes, well, good luck with that Raymond, just be natural okay."

They bade each other farewell and Raymond left in a very pensive mood.

Phillip Mason

Three weeks later Raymond Brookes was driving one morning in his home town of San Diego and had cause to take a different route to his office that morning, having delivered some documents to his lawyer's office at eight o'clock. On his way back toward his office he noticed two vehicles parked up on the side of the road with a man and a woman standing alongside chatting to each other. To his total surprise, Raymond realized that the woman was the very same Cassandra whom he had met just a month prior. Raymond found a place to pull off the road to observe what was happening. Cassandra Young handed the man a couple of items and they shook hands and departed.

Raymond followed the man to where he ended his journey and parked alongside the man's car. He approached the man in question.

"Excuse me ... I just noticed that you were having a chat with a woman not far from here and ... ah ... can't help wondering if she is the same woman I met a few weeks ago, not far from here."

"What's it to you?"

"Look, my name is Raymond ... Raymond Brookes and just four weeks ago she ran into the back of my car and caused some damage. Then she handed me cash to have the car fixed and asked me to take her the change to her hotel. Can't help wondering if that's what she has done again here this morning."

"She might have, but why would you want to know?"

"Ah ... because ... just let me put it this way, she tried to seduce me into her hotel room, okay. Tried very hard to, in fact and since then my wife has been making noises to split from me, even though I did not accompany that woman to her room. An old friend tipped me off that my wife was possibly scheming something so I just have to wonder whether my liaison with this Cassandra was a part of that, somehow. So ... be very careful with her, if you are married and want to keep your marriage intact."

"Cassandra? The name on this card is Beverly ... Beverly Granger. Perhaps you have the wrong woman."

"Okay, yes perhaps that is the case, I'm sorry. I feel so foolish, have a good day."

Raymond was already planning ahead. He had noticed that Cassandra was driving a similar vehicle to the one she was driving previously, but had not seen the registration number. At four o'clock that afternoon, Raymond was parked up in the car park at the same hotel, even though he knew that Cassandra might stay elsewhere. There was, however, a very similar vehicle parked there in the same place so he assumed that might be Cassandra's hire vehicle. The man concerned did not disappoint him, arriving on que at five o'clock. He entered the hotel and stayed there until about nine o'clock. Raymond was in a quandary about what to do but decided to bite the bullet, hence parked his car alongside the man's car. He approached the man who saw Raymond and stopped in his tracks before reaching his car. The discussion ensued.

"What's going on man, are you stalking me or something?"

"No! I just needed to know if that woman seduced you as she tried to seduce me. That's the only reason I am here because, despite the different name she has given to you, she is definitely the woman who introduced herself to me as

Cassandra Young. Did she give you her phone number, so you could meet her here?"

"Yes!"

"Does it end in four, four, triple two?"

The man did not respond but simply stared at Raymond. Raymond took that as a positive, so gave a better explanation.

"Look, according to an old girlfriend, my wife is planning to leave me, just after I sold a property for a substantial sum. That friend informed me that my wife is having an affair with her manager where she works, so I sense there could be a lot more to this woman meeting men like you and me the way that she does. Okay?"

"You think this might be a setup?"

"Not sure but it could be – seems really strange that she has deliberately caused that traffic bingle with you as she did with me. That might even be the same vehicle she hit my car with – it was a Toyota SUV with the bull bar on the front. Wait a minute ... it was a hire vehicle but I'll check the registration number. Was it a private number ... Budget 007?"

"No! Budget 009 – same hire company though! So you went with this woman here too, eh?"

"No! That goes against my upbringing – Catholic parents, Catholic education, attended Sunday Mass, ex alter-boy. All that stuff!"

"So a little sanctimonious are we, holier than thou perhaps?"

"Bit of a crass comment, that one! We all have choices to make in life. I've made mine okay, that was my prerogative and what you do is your volition. So for your sake I hope you have not been set up. I'll leave that with you so have a good life ... ah ..."

"Phillip! Phillip Mason."

"Phillip ... I hope all goes well for you. Goodbye!"

Raymond bade the man farewell, feeling slightly concerned for him. Cassandra had used the same number she had used with Raymond because, she believed, Raymond was unlikely to contact her again. Raymond went home to his wife Natalie who asked where he had been.

"You're home late!"

"I was a witness to a traffic crash dear, so I had to stay there to make a statement. Sorry about that."

"Hmm ... anything serious? Thought you might have been out with some floozy."

"Do you really think I would do something like that?"

"Well a lot of men do, of course. I suppose I am like a lot of women in some ways and, at times, have had to wonder. I know we've never talked about this before but, have you ever been unfaithful to me Raymond - you have been rather aloof lately?"

"No! I have not, never have, never will either. Unless for some reason we agreed to go separate ways – and as you would be aware, this property deal has been dragged out for more than a year now, so ... ah ... might just have to put that down to stress, okay! I will always be with you only. I've got my ticket to heaven and I will preserve that. Won't give that up for all the money in the world – nor for anything else. Might even be male menopause if I have seemed aloof, as you say."

As this was the very first occasion that Natalie had raised the subject, Raymond left it at that but intending to raise the matter again within a week, as he would.

Natalie had reheated a plate of casserole that she had made up two days before and after dinner Raymond went to his office to use the internet. He searched for a private investigator and found what he was looking for, with assignment requests online followed by a twenty four hour contact. Raymond requested an investigator to meet him at the airport the next morning at five o'clock. He did!

"Hello, I am Raymond Brookes and you must be Scott from Eagle Eye Investigations."

"Yes, how are you? Now, from the details you provided you want us to tag a woman who is likely to fly out from here this morning?"

"Yes, nothing totally certain about that but when I met her previously she informed me that she would be on the first flight out of town, so she could be here soon. Now as I indicated, I need you to follow her and to ascertain where she is from – where she lives, okay. You assured me your team can achieve that."

"Yes, when we arrive at the destination we will have a few vehicles involved in the trail and each vehicle has a drone and is in constant communication with all others, so as one drops off the trail, another picks it up."

"Great – I really need to find out what this woman is up to, she seems to be setting up married men for a fail. She's an absolute stunner, as you will see, so a lot of guys will take the bait. She tried that on me but I turned her down – caught out another guy though. Oh and this ... ah ... beard is a fake – can't have her recognising me."

"Now you've given us the downpayment of six thousand and we may need to bill you some excess depending on how complex this trail becomes. She could live a hundred miles from her destination airport, you know."

"Yeah – that's fine, I appreciate what you are doing."

Cassandra entered the terminal building.

"There she is – that's her okay, so you need to book yourself onto the same flight."

“Will do – there’s always seats available this early in the morning regardless of where she is flying to. We’ll keep you up to date on how it’s going.”

“Champion! Now don’t get roped in, yourself, somehow.”

“No way of that – I’m the consummate professional.”

Scott lined up in the line on the same flight and immediately booked himself on the same flight to Cincinnati using his cell phone. He could have simply informed his cohorts at the other end of the flight of her appearance as he had already taken a graphic of her. However, although being the chief executive officer of the company in his region, he had decided to be involved in this himself – personally. He had taken a good long look at the woman concerned – the very beautiful Cassandra Young.

Raymond had set the wheels in motion to ascertain the identity of the woman who had tried to seduce him - and had successfully seduced the other man.

Natalie's Share

It was five o'clock on a Friday evening and Raymond Brookes was driving home from work.

"Nat, I'm on my way so I'll stop at the Peking Duck for take-away. I've phoned through the order already."

"Great idea Ray, I haven't bothered with dinner yet. Feeling a bit jaded about a few things."

Raymond arrived home and after dinner Natalie decided to broach the subject of the proceeds of the property sale.

"So how was work today dear?"

"Mainly same as, but I did make some calls to property developers just contemplating on expanding the business interstate. I have heard there is a paucity of bottom-end accounting services in San Jose, which is understandable I suppose, given all the wealth they generate there. The accountants could be charging a fortune and who would care. I might have to purchase my own parcel of land on the outskirts though and put a building on it – the rents for established properties are sky high."

"So what do you plan to do with the windfall from the property sale?"

"Well that's where I would draw the funds from, of course, if I had to purchase my own parcel of land and build an office complex. Though I could expand the business into other cities first, for starters. Orange County, Riverside or even Santa Barbara would be good options – not too far from home. Would need to recruit a good management team for each though."

“On the other hand you do realise that with the sale of the property you could simply retire and live happily ever after. You would be able to play golf every day. Or we could buy a yacht and sail around the world.”

“No, that’s not me, you know that! If we are going to expand our business it would be best to go as far upmarket as possible. Like I said, those mega-rich companies in the Silicon Valley are not your typical penny-pinchers darling – they’ll pay a substantially higher hourly rate for top quality accounting. Might need to invest the entire seventeen million in one hit. That type of investment could double itself in just a few years, then every few years thereafter. Could go national!”

“I have some good business ideas, things I have always wanted to pursue and have never really had the chance to.”

“Such as?”

“Well I have completed the degree in info-technology so I could establish my web design venture.”

“Hmm ... a bit risky that type of thing – the technology is always replacing itself with the next round of innovation. Rather like electronics technicians designing devices that do themselves out of work.”

“Don’t you think it might also come down to a joint decision? I mean, I suppose I am legally entitled to half of that money, aren’t I ... so we should be deciding together what to do with it.”

That was the first occasion that Natalie had expressed any notion of splitting the proceeds of the property sale - and Raymond had been expecting that to happen, based on what Roxanne had told him.

“Well, legally I suppose you are but ... we are a team aren’t we Nat?”

“Yes, of course we are darling! It’s just that, I have some other ideas too like ... ah ... a graphic design business.”

"Hmm ... there's a pretty high failure rate in new business startups Nat. It gets reported in the accounting journals on a regular basis just how tenuous they are. People go bankrupt every day of the week by trying to start something up. It's a bit of a jungle out there, people stealing ideas from their former employers, for example, then trying to start up as an immediate competitor or conducting the same line of business in a different area. They are prone to high failure rates."

"Well, I do have quite some guile so I could explore a few tentative options, but I might need some capital to even get that started, you know, maybe to engage a consultant or two. Perhaps we could set up a new bank account for me in a business name and transfer some funds Ray?"

Raymond sensed from this that his wife Natalie was now starting to make specific plans to separate from him and was already thinking that, if Roxanne was right with her allegations about his wife, he would actually want to let her go – for her to move on. He also had in the back of his mind that the beautiful Cassandra Young was not wearing a ring and was quite possibly a single woman, as she had stated. Also that she had told him that she had not been with a man for a long time and that she had expressed to him that, as a single woman, she had needs. He felt pleased with himself that he had initiated the investigators to ascertain her identity.

Eagle Eyes

"Raymond Brookes, good morning."

"Raymond it's Scott from Eagle Eye, how are you?"

"Yeah fine, Scott – how did you go?"

"Yeah good result man, we have tracked your esoteric woman to a housing estate in downtown Cincinnati and I can send you the photographs we took of the house."

"Wow, excellent result ... hey thank you ... ah ... you can send them via text or email as you wish. So ... ah ... any preliminary details you might want to disclose already?"

"Yeah - you could say that!"

"How so?"

"We were able to park up a vehicle nearby to catch some snaps and ... ah ... the woman concerned came out of her house in the morning and waved goodbye to a male person who remained at the house and that was at eight o'clock in the morning. In fact his car had been parked outside that house all night. No telling who he is but we have his vehicle rego number and hers too, so are working on that to ascertain their identity. He could be a friend or a boarder or a relative, who knows?"

"Hmm ... that's rather interesting Scott. I wonder if she is in a relationship with a man while she is offering herself to other men as a one night stand and if he knows of her activities. All seems just a bit strange!"

"Well we should have more detail in a day or two, we do have some contacts within the FBI and, obviously, they have access to vehicle registration details, so I will get back to you within a day or so on that. However, what you really need to know is that we tagged her from her house to see where she went to and she went straight to the airport again, Raymond."

"Holy shit, she only just got home last night from San Diego."

"Yes and she flew to Phoenix today, so we followed her to the hotel she booked into. If she's up to the same we should see her acquire a vehicle today and follow her target in the morning and then meet him back at the hotel in the evening."

"Huh ... well if she does she's onto it that's for sure. Must be making a small fortune from what she's doing. How much do you think Cassandra would charge her clients for this?"

"We had a similar case once before a few years back and the ... ah ... hooker was charging women ten thousand to assist in offloading their male partners."

"That seems a lot!"

"No, it isn't – when there are millions of dollars at stake or, in some cases, even many billions of dollars, having irrefutable evidence for one's attorney can save many times more than this cost when things get into court."

'Yes, I suppose you are right on that, eh?"

"Yes now our account has gone out to then thousand now and by the time we complete this assignment it will probably be fifteen thousand. You okay with that?"

"Yes that's fine! This could be worth a lot more than that to me, but am not going to elaborate on that now."

"Okay, I will let you know if we observe her creating a traffic incident in the morning. Meanwhile I will email you these graphics of the house and the address details. Must admit though, she certainly is a very beautiful woman. How the fuck did you say no?"

Both men chuckled at Scott's query but Raymond did not respond to answer his question, as he had done to the other man, Phillip, who had stayed with Cassandra. Raymond disconnected the call and opened his email. Cassandra's house appeared on his screen, a rather stately, well-kempt two storey structure with two balconies on the top floor. He wondered whether there might be two separate bedrooms on the top floor – one for Cassandra and the other for the man. He was hopeful!

Raymond then noticed that the house next door seemed to have a 'For Sale' sign standing near the pavement in front of the house. He zoomed in to see the details and found it was, indeed, for sale. He was also able to identify the name and number of the agent listed as selling the house.

So, reflecting on recent events, that his wife was now starting to make noises about taking half of the proceeds of sale of his property, that she may have been having an affair with her manager where she works and that he might have been set up by his wife for a fail with this beautiful woman as he believed Phillip had been, Raymond pondered what his immediate future might be. He wondered whether he could possibly find happiness with this Cassandra. He certainly felt some powerful chemistry in her presence and, for all he knew, the man who seemingly resides in the same house could very well be Cassandra's brother.

Raymond made the call.

"Good morning Happy Homes, James Randall speaking, how may I help you?"

"James, good morning my name is Raymond Brookes and I am enquiring about the house you are selling in Emerald Parkway in Hamilton County. Can you send me all the details you have please."

"Why certainly Raymond, I will do that straight away, it's in need of a bit of a makeover as it hasn't had any work done on it since way back in the nineteen fifties, so ... just keep that in mind when you view the interior, okay."

"Understood and I'm really not too concerned about the state of the interior as we are quite into renovating, so will do our own thing about that. Can you tell me the asking price please James."

"Yes, that is listed as offers above eight hundred thousand."

"Okay, fine, can you also send me an offer and acceptance form to sign and I will discuss it with my wife tonight."

"Will do Raymond but I do need to let you know that I took a couple through the house yesterday and they are really keen but have offered seven ninety hoping to save a few thousand dollars so the door is open if you want to make the offer up to eight hundred thousand. Of course I can't guarantee that the seller will accept that but they probably will."

"Okay James, tell you what I'll do, flick me the docs now and I will go straight to eighty twenty, okay - I don't want to be stuffed around trying to outbid somebody else so hopefully the sellers will accept. I'm keen to move to that area to set up my new business center as soon as possible."

"Eight twenty, eh? I like your style Raymond Brookes and I think they will too, so I will do that now and as soon as you have returned the docs, I will call the seller to arrange an appointment. So, bye for now."

"Bye James and thank you."

James made the call to the seller and sounded as enthusiastic as he possibly could over Raymond's offer. The seller was surprised and accepted the offer, signed the document that had been emailed to her and returned it to James, who contacted Raymond within the hour.

"Raymond Brookes good morning."

"Raymond it's James from Happy Homes, congratulations Raymond your offer has been accepted already."

"Hey, fantastic, thank you for acting so promptly on that James."

"My pleasure, Raymond! Now I will forward the documents to the settlement agents and the property title should be transferred within a week, which leads me to ask, how soon do you intend to move into the house?"

"Ah ... just need to sort a couple of issues so will talk to my wife about that - but it could be very soon after the settlement date, perhaps just a matter of a day or two."

"Okay, I will get busy and thank you Raymond for dealing with Happy Homes."

"Thank you James, goodbye."

Raymond called Roxanne.

"Hello Ray, how is everything?"

"Going well Rox, I have just sealed a deal on a house next door to that Cassandra I met and who tried to seduce me."

"Why would you do that Ray?"

"Long story but if you are right about Natalie then I will just find out what I can about that woman and ... ah ... take it from there. I must admit Rox, that on that night if I had been a single man I would have been quite profoundly attracted to that woman. There was just something about her, you know, how sometimes two people meet and there seems to be instant chemistry."

"As it was with us, Ray! Then with Natalie, Ray!"

"Yes, well it certainly was and Natalie coaxed me away from you, as you know. You are both very attractive women it's just that Natalie was so vivacious, as you know."

"Yes, well I suppose I am just a little dour, in the comparative sense. I suppose I regard the serious sides of life as being of utmost importance, rather than being exuberant or ebullient. You do know that I would never have been unfaithful to you, don't you Ray?"

"Yes, I do know that to be true Rox. You are an angel of a character and always have been. So please keep me in the loop about anything Jessica finds out."

Raymond went home that evening to his wife, Natalie.

"Hello Nat, how was your day?"

"Yeah, fine – how was yours?"

"Yeah work was good, got a few big payments in for corporate tax returns. Also got a call from Ralph who asked if I would like to go to San Jose this weekend for a four ball tourney. Told him I would talk to you about that because I am already committed to that tournament in San Francisco next weekend. He wants a low handicapper to partner him."

"Oh he's a good golfer isn't he?"

"He plays off three, I'm on two, so we are a good team."

"Oh good for you, yes, of course you can go and play with him and go to San Francisco also. Did you tell him you are available?"

"Not yet, but I will text him soon. What did you get up to?"

"I enrolled in an online graphic design diploma with the state technical college and I ... um ... paid for the course for twelve months. So I hope you don't mind but I used my own bank account for that so I would like to top up my account if you don't mind."

"Yeah, that's fair so, how much do you want me to transfer?"

Natalie was not going to request half of the proceeds at this point of time but was keen to secure funds to pay her lawyer once she decided to split.

"I don't know, what do you think? I would like to feel secure and not have to come back to you all the time for more funds so ... how much do you feel comfortable parting with?"

Raymond was thinking ahead and thought that if Roxanne could gain evidence of Natalie's alleged affair, he would like to separate from Natalie and take a chance on Cassandra being available.

"Well, as you said you are legally entitled to half of our joint assets, so why don't I just transfer a few million to you so you can pursue your dreams as you wish. I wouldn't want to be an impeding factor in you self-actualizing into some type of new creative enterprise. So I'll do that tomorrow as I will need to call the bank to increase my transfer limit."

"That's very good of you dear, thank you."

"Now I will just text Ralph and make some arrangements."

"And have a great weekend in San Jose."

"Yeah thanks – it should be a good one. I like playing with Ralph, he's good fun, a bit of a joker."

Raymond went to his office and sent a text to Roxanne.

"Hello Rox, I have told Nat that I am going to play golf in San Jose this weekend so will appreciate it greatly if you can liaise with your friend to procure some evidence against Nat, as she will probably take the opportunity to go to Las Vegas as you have suggested. Same the following weekend please as I am going to San Francisco. Also let me know how much your friend Jessica needs to cover any costs she might incur over and above whatever the corporation covers. I am willing to pay her a couple of thousand to make sure she is on the ball with this."

"Thanks for that, Ray. Will do!"

The next day Raymond contacted his bank and transferred the entire eight and a half million to Natalie's bank account. He then called Natalie.

“Hello Ray!”

“Nat hello, I’ve just transferred the money into your account, okay. I think you’ll be happy with what I’ve done. No sense stuffing you around doing things in dribs and drabs, so whatever it is that you decide to do as a business venture, you shouldn’t have anything holding you back, but, just keep me in the loop on what you decide, okay.”

“Oh Ray, thank you so much for that, wow, I feel as if I could fly now, I’ll check my account and see you tonight dear.”

“Okay, bye for now!”

Natalie checked her bank account and was astonished that Ray had transferred so much money. Her mind was racing now, contemplating what she could do.

Graham and Frank

The next morning Natalie called her boss Graham Bridges from her office.

"Morning Graham, I have some good news for you."

Graham invited Natalie to come to his office within thirty minutes, soon as he could brief his management team.

"Graham, you won't believe it, Ray is going to golf this weekend and next. A friend asked him to accompany him to San Jose this weekend and he has that tournament in San Francisco next weekend. I also set the wheels in motion to have a substantial sum transferred into my bank account from the property sale and yesterday Ray transferred eight and a half million dollars. The money is in my account now, Graham."

"Hey, great stuff! I'll go ahead and make the booking in Vegas for this weekend, today. I have next weekend booked already too."

"Wow, can't believe it! Won't be long now we can be together permanently. It's a good thing you divorced your Mary last year."

"Yeah, she's come out of it pretty well. Apparently she is with a lawyer now, a partner in the firm that represented her."

"Well very soon we can sail off into the sunset on a yacht, Graham."

"Can't wait! Hopefully it won't get too messy with your Raymond."

"He'll be okay! He's a good man but has allowed the passion to fade away. Always working, you know!"

"Yep! Bad habit that of too many men. Got to look after your woman."

In the early morning just a day later, Scott from Eagle Eye called Raymond.

"Raymond it's Scott, how are you?"

"Scott, hello, just fine thanks ... ah ... any news yet?"

"Yes we had an agent book into the hotel where your Cassandra stayed and, guess what, she caused a traffic incident with a man in the morning and he arrived at the hotel at five thirty in the evening. Our agent waited for her to be seated then sat at a table opposite with his tablet with his microphonic boom directed at their discussion. Went the same way as the discussion she had with you."

"You mean she tried to seduce him into her room?"

"Yes!"

"And did your agent observe that he was with her for a few hours?"

"No! They sat at the table for about forty minutes then he arose from his chair and left her. On the surface of it, seems he might have given her the thumbs down as you did."

"Hmm ... hope for the male species yet, eh?"

"Ha, ha, ha ... could be Raymond, who knows, but our agent is going to have a brief chat to the guy today. He might want to know that his wife tried to set him up. Got to ask why that would happen to a guy who turned down an offer from such a beautiful woman though."

"Yeah ... got me intrigued too. Sure would like to know what becomes of that."

"We'll see what we can do. Goodbye for now."

"Yeah, bye Scott."

That morning the Eagle Eye agent, Sam Collins, was able to approach the man concerned upon his arrival where he works.

"Excuse me, yes excuse me ... ah ... look my name is Sam Collins from Eagle Eye Investigations and this is my card ... ah ... we hope you don't mind us asking you something about what happened to you yesterday, please."

"Yesterday?"

"Yes, the traffic incident in the morning and the woman who paid you to have your car repaired."

"Oh that, well, there's no insurance claim involved in that, she paid for my repairs with cold hard cash."

"Yes we understand that but look, we have reason to believe that the woman involved deliberately causes such incidents then pays cash for the repairs in an attempt to lure men into her hotel room. Now it's not strictly our business but can you volunteer whether she tried that on you? Sorry I don't know your name."

"Frank – Frank Jeffries!"

"Well hello, Frank, I am pleased to meet you and hope you don't find this unnerving, but we believe women are paying that woman you met yesterday to put their partners to a loyalty test, hoping they fail that and open the door for a divorce. So did that woman who has previously gone by the name of either Cassandra or Beverly try to coerce you into having an affair last night?"

"Well, took her about half an hour to get into it but, yes, she did offer me a few hours with her in her room. I said no."

"Yes, I was sitting at the opposite table and got the drift but needed to confirm that with you. Do you think your partner might have put her up to something like that?"

"Well, she is not of the same character as me ... ah ... I'm a Pentecostal Christian and there's no way I would commit adultery. She thinks my religious beliefs are a load of bunkum but, that's the way I was raised – believing in the Lord Jesus

Christ. She's become increasingly cynical and when I am at church she is at the casino, gambling."

"Hmm ... that may be the case but it is also possible that she is with another man while you are at church, Frank. That's the way these cases usually pan out, so the women want evidence on their partner to facilitate divorce proceedings. Sorry to let you know that if it does apply to your wife."

"Never mind, I'll take that information on board and have my wife checked out, myself. If that is happening I sure would like to know about that."

"Okay, Frank, thank you for talking to me. I know this may all seem quite odd but we are checking her out for another man also who found himself in the same predicament."

"Well I hope for his sake he did not go with her."

"That's correct Frank. Raymond did not for the same reason as you. He is a devout Catholic man but now has doubts about his wife's activities. Thanks again!"

"My pleasure, good day to you Sam."

Sam alerted his supervising agent, Scott.

"Scott it's Sam – good news, the guy's name is Frank Jeffries and, yes, she did try to seduce him into her room but he refused her. Same reason as our Raymond did - he's a Christian."

"Huh! No doubt about those churchies eh?"

"Ha, ha, ha ... yeah, better get back there myself someday."

"You were raised into which church Sam?"

"Baptist! Went to Sunday school until I was twenty odd, then found more fulfilment in girls, actually."

"Well didn't we all! Got to admire these guys who stick with it though eh?"

"Yep – that's for sure! I'll head back to the office now and get on with the next case."

"Which one is that?"

“The alleged fake injury claim by that guy who claims he has damaged his knee on the job.”

“Oh yes, he’s a fake for sure so keep at him. Had a report from a neighbor recently that he goes off every Sunday to Lake Michigan to go fishing in a boat. A very close neighbor reckons there’s nothing wrong with guy.”

“Will do, we’ll catch up and I’ll send the graphics for you to forward to Raymond.”

“Thanks Sam, bye for now and ... ah ... good work Sam.”

“Thanks Scott!”

Las Vegas

Raymond arrived home early from work that Friday afternoon and packed his suitcase and his golf gear into his car.

"I'm off darling, Ralph is expecting me to collect him in twenty minutes time."

"Okay dear, have a great time and I'll see you Sunday night."

"Okay, bye!"

Raymond drove away from the house and called Roxanne.

"Hello Ray!"

"Roxanne, hello ... ah ... this might sound a little weird but I have just left the house and am going to park my car up at the office and am going to fly to Las Vegas within two hours. When I arrive I will hire a car and I have bought myself a makeup outfit to disguise myself. I'll get a hairpiece and a fake beard and some padding for my waistline, because I am going to book in to a room in Vegas myself and I would like to meet your friend Jessica there to liaise with her."

"Hmm ... that sounds rather dramatic if you don't mind me saying so, but do you mind if I ask you why?"

"Look, I don't know if it will come to anything but if there is the off chance that Jessica and myself can, together, obtain some incriminating evidence of Natalie's liaison with Graham, I will feel so much better – especially if there is any way I can see with my own eyes."

"Uh huh! Well that is understandable so what's your plan, where will you stay and meet Jess?"

"Not sure, but ideally in the same hotel if that is possible, I mean, if I go about this in a covert manner there should be scope for me to observe Natalie and Graham on the gaming floor or in a bar or whatever. I'm fairly confident that they won't recognize me and your friend Jess and I can stay in touch by phone about what their movements are. So I would like some details from Jess about which hotel they will stay in, even what floor they will be on etcetera. Can you give her my number?"

"Okay I will call Jess right now and ask her to contact you. They will all be flying out sometime around nine o'clock tonight for Vegas and I believe they stay in the same rooms each time at the Golden Nugget – and you might be pleased to know that the room they book for Jess is on the same floor, room 1326 on level thirteen and is virtually straight across the hallway from Graham's room which is 1329. That's how Jess has come to observe them together a couple of times."

"Great - I'll see if I can book a room on the same level now and I hope to hear from Jess soon."

"I'll call her for you now Ray."

Two minutes later Raymond's phone rang. It was Jessica.

"Hello this is Raymond!"

"Hello Raymond this is Jessica - your friend Roxanne just called me."

"Hey, Jess, thank you so much for helping me out on this and for the information you've passed on to Roxy regarding my Natalie. You know, until recently I really had no idea that my Nat was up to anything like this and ... ah ... it seems she endeavored to set me up with a prostitute just weeks ago."

"Yes, Roxanne told me about that and I have to say, I think that is so really devious of her to do that when she is the one who is unfaithful. That is just so reprehensible."

"Well thank you for that Jess, now I believe you will be staying in the same hotel again, room 1326 which is just across the hallway from Graham's room."

"Yes, Graham called a meeting yesterday afternoon to inform us that he was paying for another trip to Vegas for his ten management staff so we are flying out at nine tonight. We'll be in our rooms by ten thirty, oh and thank you for your kind offer to cover some of my expenses, that's very kind of you. When we are here I am supposed to mix in quite a bit, you know, a few drinks and have a bit of a flutter on the roulette, but to be honest, I really deplore the gambling side of it all."

"Well I'm pleased to hear that Jess, got to say I have quite a profound aversion to gambling, myself."

"So where will you be staying Ray?"

"I am just about to call the Golden Nugget to see if I can procure a room on the same floor - thirteen."

"Well, now, don't read anything into this but, once you have booked your own room why don't you just observe from my room. We would be like ships in the night most of the time and when I need to sleep you could go out to your own room. You'll have a bird's eye view from my room whenever they are heading upstairs and I can let you know when that will be, so, what do you think?"

"Jess, thank you so much, look, if you can do that for me I will pay you an extra one thousand dollars just for the sake of having the proximity to Graham's room. Thank you so much, so when I arrive in Vegas I will make my way to my room and will just wait to hear from you."

"Oh don't worry, they will be on the gaming floor within ten minutes of arrival – get some of that out of their system first before they return to his room. Always the same and Roxanne told me you will be disguised."

"Yes, I took the trouble of purchasing a hairpiece and false beard yesterday."

"Okay look forward to catching up. Bye for now."

"Goodbye Jessica!"

Ray called the Golden Nugget and managed to book room 1302, from where he would not have direct view of Graham's room but would be able to use Jessica's room to spy on Graham and Natalie. He then booked his flight and arrived at the airport and caught his flight at seven o'clock.

Graham's management team would take the usual flight at nine o'clock and be chauffeured from the airport to the hotel. Apart from Graham, Natalie and Jessica, there would be four other men and three other women – the usual team.

Fiona

Cassandra Young's cell phone rang again.

"Hello Cassandra speaking, how can I help you?"

"Oh, hello Cassandra, my name is Fiona and I have been given your details by a friend name Rachael who received your assistance to sort out her husband, Damian."

"Hello Fiona, yes I remember Rachael and Damian very well, I dealt with him just a couple of months ago. How are they doing?"

"Oh, Rachael split and she's now with her new fella, Shane, in Baltimore so, she's doing very well. Fortunately, when they went to the mediation conference Damian decided to concede half of assets to go to Rachael because his attorney informed him that he really had no case because of the photographs that your observer took of him with you. So it ended quite amicably really, which was good for Rachael because they had two houses worth about the same amount. But she sold her house and bought a new house and lives near Shane. I think she'll wait and see how it works with him before she makes a commitment, you know, he just might be a bad apple too, you never know."

"Well I'm pleased to hear that she is happy for now Fiona, so how can I help you?"

"I want to put my husband to the loyalty test, as you referred to it with Rachael, because I think my husband is having an affair with a friend of my husband named Angela. They always seem to be together whenever I am engaged in doing something that takes me out of town, which happens a lot because I am a journalist."

"Oh, I see yes, well that would require you being out and about wouldn't it. Now I need to let you know that for the purpose of testing your husband I require you to deposit ten thousand dollars into my bank account so I will text you the account details. You need to provide me with the location where I will be able to cause a minor traffic incident and pledge that you will never disclose to your husband how you went about this, okay? I will travel to your city with an accomplice who will be there to take photographs so you have some evidence which you may need for the courts. If it comes to that you need to engage Baker and Hall solicitors who will provide you with representation in the family court for a reduced fee because I do refer a lot of people to them, okay!"

"Yes, that's fine, I can agree to that."

"So which city are you in Fiona?"

"St. Louis!"

"No problem and how soon would you like this done?"

"As soon as you are available Cassandra, please."

"Okay, I am in Cincinnati but I can be in St. Louis at the end of next week to ... er ... arrive on Thursday and set up your husband on Friday. Does that sound okay with you?"

"Yes, that's fine! Now we live in Chesterfield and my husband works at Logan University so if you take Wild Horse Creek Road to Chesterfield Parkway West, then go into Schoettler Road, you should get a chance to cause a bingle there, somewhere."

"Okay now once I have your address, I will check out the roads and traffic lights. Now what is your husband's name?"

"Charlotte!"

"Charlotte? Er ..."

"Yes, my husband is Charlotte."

“Okay, so am I correct in assuming that your husband is, biologically, a female person, Fiona?”

“Well, yes, Charlotte was born as a female and we went through high school then college together as female but, once we graduated we both realized that we are both gay. So we’ve been together for six years now and we both turned twenty seven last month and we went to a college reunion and I met up with another old friend named Jasmine who sounded me out for some bonding.”

“Oh, I see and, do you think you might want to form a close friendship with Jasmine?”

“Well if my Charlotte is fucking around with Angela, yes, I will leave him and start a new friendship with Jasmine.”

“Hmm ... well I do need to let you know Fiona that in my work I have never been with another woman and that I am one hundred percent heterosexual, so I am not really sure that I can help you on this.”

“Oh please, please Cassandra ... if you do I am prepared to pay you fifteen thousand dollars and, I know what you are saying but all I want you to do is to find out if Charlotte is willing to be disloyal to me, with you - and you don’t really have to do anything with her. Just determine if she is willing to. Can you do that for me because I do so much want to be with Jasmine if Charlotte is fucking Angela.”

“I’ll have to give that some thought ... er ... not really sure at this point how I could go about that, you see, these men that I expose actually come to my hotel room and I fuck them you know. That’s the deal I make with their wives because they want that irrefutable evidence for Baker and Hall. In one case the guy was deny, deny, deny so we had to expose him by Baker and Hall supposedly contacting me via the court discovery process. His attorney was informed that they got information from the hotel pertaining to my contact details and that I confirmed in an affidavit that I fucked him. So then his goose was cooked and he had to hand over half of his estate to his wife. That was a really considerable amount of money that he lost in that, millions actually, but he got his comeuppance."

"Okay, well, I'm not expecting you to have sex with my Charlotte but is there anything you can do to put her to the test ... I mean, perhaps take your meeting her to the point where she propositions you and then you turn her down. Could you do that?"

"Well I need to, firstly, ask myself how I would educe a proposition whilst sitting at the bar having a drink or two, then entice her into my room ... er ... I suppose there are some possibilities. You see, with the men I am able to delve into their innermost psyche and draw out their frustration at not getting enough sex from their wives, which is what most men would be feeling."

"Oh ... ah ... is that verifiable ... I mean ... has there been any research on that question that you know of?"

"Yes, there are probably far too many post-graduate theses completed on that very topic. So college researchers question hundreds or thousands of men who, generally, state they would like to have sex about three or four times per week and their partners only come good about once or twice per week. That's common knowledge now. So I put some rather subtle questions to them about their life quality and they typically share how frustrated they are with their sex life. It doesn't take much from that point to entice them to my room."

"Oh, I see but I would be happy enough if she propositions you in the lobby bar if you can achieve that, but she would have to reiterate her proposition so that there's no possibility of a misinterpretation."

"Look, tell you what I will do. I will tell your Charlotte that I have written a novel and that I would like her to have a copy so as a parting gesture I will invite her upstairs to my room so I can hand her the novel, okay. Then, rather than asking her to leave straight away, I will give her a little latitude as she will probably want to discuss the novel."

"So, what novel will you be offering to her?"

"It's a novel that I wrote titled 'UFO's, Aliens and Religion' under my pseudonym of 'Michelle Roses' for the purpose of maintaining anonymity."

"Oh, that is so interesting, it's one of my own areas of interest, you know, the aliens who are here and all that."

"Yes, well they probably are. There really is just too much evidence out there now that confirms that."

"Hey I am just going to have to buy that novel Cassandra ..."

"I will give a copy to your husband, Fiona."

"Oh yes, okay ... so please go ahead and see what happens and if she does not proposition you I will reconsider my feelings for Jasmine, okay."

"Okay, well I will see you on Thursday morning Fiona. I will book into the Hyatt Hotel and we need to meet up that day. I need details of your husband's car and a photograph or graphic so I know what she looks like."

"Okay Cassandra, I look forward to meeting you."

"Goodbye Fiona."

The following Thursday Cassandra flew into St. Louis and booked into the Hyatt Hotel. Fiona met her there at ten o'clock in the morning and provided Cassandra with graphics of Charlotte and the details of her car. Fiona was quite stunned at Cassandra's beauty and thought about it herself, while she was there, but then thought better of it.

“Thank you Fiona, now after Charlotte has left I will call you with the details, okay.”

“Okay Cassandra, thank you.”

The next morning Cassandra waited for Charlotte to leave her house and joined the traffic north of Wild Horse Creek Road. As her luck would have it, she only had to wait until Schoettler Road to cause the incident. There wasn’t a lot of traffic so Charlotte got out of her car at the lights and stormed back towards Cassandra’s car.

“Hey, bloody hell what do you think you are ... doing?”

Charlotte’s first glance at Cassandra caused her to temper her immediate anger. Cassandra responded.

“Oh I’m so sorry but, look, if you pull up over there I will give you all my details and some cash to cover the repairs, okay?”

“Okay, but I don’t have much time. I have to be at work in ten minutes.”

The women parked up and inspected Charlotte’s car and Cassandra did the usual and handed Charlotte two thousand dollars in cash for the repairs.

“Now what I suggest you do is obtain a quote and pay for this today and just bring me the change, less two hundred dollars for the inconvenience okay. I’m staying at the Hyatt and I will be there from about five this evening but, I fly out in the morning so please make it this evening, okay.”

“Don’t worry I will get the quote during my lunch hour and meet you there about five this evening. Thank you.”

At five o’clock Cassandra was waiting in the lobby bar and Charlotte walked in.

“Hello Charlotte, thank you for honoring our agreement – how did it go with the quote for repairs?”

“Too easy actually – they took my payment for just eleven hundred dollars so here is your seven hundred change.”

"Thank you Charlotte, I am sorry to have put you out but I hope I have managed to make amends. Now can I buy you a drink?"

"Yeah, thanks Cassandra, I'll have a pint of beer actually."

Cassandra signalled the table attendant who wasn't paying attention so went to the bar herself, while Charlotte looked her up and down. She thought that, by looks, Cassandra reminded her of Sarah Palin.

"One pint of Cascade beer for you Charlotte. I'm on the Jack Daniels myself!"

"Could do worse ... so you fly out tomorrow so what are you doing in St. Louis?"

"I deliver training packages to corporations in human relations hoping they can educe a better performance from their employees. I majored in industrial psychology so it's right up my alley. Had a good day – apart from the shaky start sorry about that, not used to the hire car you know."

"Yeah, that's understandable - don't worry about it. I appreciate the fact that you took care of that situation so expeditiously the way you did. My immediate thought was of lodging an insurance claim and all that shit that comes with it. You must have quite an interesting life doing that work, flying around the country."

"Yeah, I get around. Been here in St. Louis before so I knew which hotel I would like to stay in. It seems like such a well-planned city this one. Some are a nightmare to negotiate. Do you like living here?"

"It has its ups and downs like most places I suppose. Bit too cold for me in winter though. I grew up in Florida so am more accustomed to the sun and the heat. I came here to study at Logan University in music production, theatre management and ballet. The ballet was great until I broke a leg – had to give it away unfortunately. Now that I am twenty seven years of age it's virtually too late to pursue that further, so I work as a data entry operator for admissions."

"Oh, that's a shame that you had to give away the ballet but, you would have made quite a few friends there doing that."

"Yeah, I still see a couple of girls from college on a regular basis ... ah ... Angela, Dianne and Fiona whom I went through college with. We hang out occasionally, you know, hit the night club scene, drink at bars where we might meet somebody."

"Ah huh! Looking for mister Right eh?"

"Or miss Right! How about you? Are you married with kids and living the life of bliss?"

"Me? No I am still single even at my age – turned thirty three last month so better get a wriggle on I suppose, but, not really in too much of a hurry – had my share of boyfriends over the years. Hey would you like another drink – my buy?"

"Yes, thank you!"

Cassandra signalled the table attendant who brought the drinks over.

"So where do you live Cassandra?"

"Cincinnati! Born there, probably die there too. Not a bad place, I ... ah ... like to get out into bushland on weekends where I can be creative writing my books."

"You write books? Tell me – fact or fiction?"

"Novels actually! My latest novel is titled 'UFO's, Aliens and Religion' – went on sale last year."

"Hey that sounds interesting – I would like to read that one."

"Well I have one in my room upstairs I could give to you before you go but, we'll finish our drinks first, eh!"

"That'd be great, thanks. So you write in bushland?"

"Oh yeah, I know of some quiet spots just off Sleepy Hollow Rd. I do find it very peaceful there and highly conducive to creative thinking. I just take a notebook and jot down my thoughts then I go home and put those lines onto a spreadsheet which I use as a schematic plan before I write the text on word processor. So every line I write can be expanded into a paragraph or two or ten."

"Interesting!"

Casandra finished her drink while Charlotte still had half a pint in her glass but made the move.

"So I will be rising at four in the morning because I fly out at five so I need to hit the hay early ... so I'll be turning in soon, but if you come upstairs I will hand you the novel."

Charlotte sculled the remainder of her drink in anticipation.

"Great ... let's go!"

The women went upstairs and entered Cassandra's room.

"Here you are – my aliens novel."

"Wow ... great cover, I like it. Hovering above the United Nations building in New York and I see they are Raptors and Apache circling there."

"You seem to know your aircraft Charlotte!"

"Yeah ... thought of joining the U.S. Air Force actually. Would have missed my friends too much though. So apart from writing books what else do you get up to - social life wise? A woman like you would surely have guys buzzing around. Have been trying to think of someone you remind me of, actually. Might be ... ah ... Jaclyn Smith, the brunette actress from Charlie's Angels."

"Oh that's very nice of you to say, Charlotte – I've always thought of Jaclyn as being a really attractive woman."

"So ... do you have lots of guys chasing after you ... or are you not into dating or something else?"

"Oh I've had a few relationships for sure, never been married though. Was with one guy for two years but ... he just became so totally possessive, you know, wanted to know everything I had done each day, who I had seen and all that. He would put me through the ringer every day after dinner. So I got rid of him – don't need that shit going on in my life."

"So apart from him, being thirty three now you must have had a few others? Like, short term or even casual affairs, one night stands? Now be honest, with your stunning looks, you'd have every guy gawking at you Cassandra – women too I suppose, eh?"

"Yes, I suppose I've had my share of guys, although I must admit, I have been rather circumspect about who I decide to go with, knowing that any relationship is going to become sexual, you know, if you have a friendship with a guy for more than a few weeks it's bound to go that way isn't it?"

"Yeah, I suppose so but do I discern that you have a lot of guys chasing you but you turn them away?"

"Yeah, I'll date a lot of guys for a week or two then let them loose because, to go beyond that they start to assume the friendship is going to become sexual. Then it just becomes too difficult to end it, you know."

"Yeah I would expect so. Had the same problem myself years ago though I didn't have your stunning looks. You know – guys always trying to hit up on me at bars and nightclubs. Got so pissed off with it all I decided to get close to a woman, actually."

"A woman, Charlotte? Go on tell me more."

"Well, we all need love and affection sometime so I ... ah ... met up with an old friend from college and we shared the same feelings and I stayed at her apartment one night and before we knew it, really, we found we were touching each other and it just felt so natural, we slept together that night."

Cassandra recalled that Fiona had mentioned that she and Charlotte had been together for several years so decided to pry a little further.

"Oh and you are now twenty seven years of age so when did that happen Charlotte?"

"Ah ... Fiona and I, just after we finished college actually, so we've been together for several years now."

"So you are both gay?"

"Yes - and there's another friend named Angela who wants to be with me but, I value my relationship with my wife Fiona too much to go with anyone else. So I've put Angela in her place – it's just friendship – even though I suspect Fiona wants to go with another friend of hers named Jasmine so ... I'll just have to trust her."

Cassandra had an awakening when she heard Charlotte say this, realizing that Fiona might have been trying to rationalize her own desires to leave Charlotte to be with Jasmine. She was also duly impressed with Charlotte's expression of loyalty toward Fiona. She decided to test Charlotte's loyalty a little further.

"Hmm ... interesting ... very interesting in fact, if you don't mind me saying so!"

"How's that?"

"Oh, I've always been one hundred percent heterosexual and have been approached by women a few times but have never been with any of them. I suppose have always just wanted to remain hetero and couldn't quite get my mind around the actual act, you know, the act of sexual activity with a woman. I suppose it's mainly oral sex, is it?"

"Ah ... that's how it starts for sure but, then it can progress to the use of vibrators and strap on vibrating dildo's and things like that. But it's also the kissing and hugging that gay women indulge in as much as sex. That's been my experience, anyway. But don't worry Cassandra, as beautiful a woman as you are, I wouldn't try to hit up on you because my love and loyalty is toward my wife, Fiona. She's my soulmate - I know that!"

"Well I am very pleased to hear that from you Charlotte so, now that you have my novel, I'll have to ask you to allow me to retire because I didn't get a lot of sleep last night and really need a long one tonight."

"No worries, thank you so much for the novel, I'll read it within just s few days and, good luck with that Cassandra."

"Thank you Charlotte it's been nice to meet you."

Cassandra let Charlotte out of the door and called Fiona.

"Hello Cassandra?"

"Yes, Fiona, I am pleased to tell you that Charlotte has just left and she's been here since five this evening so, just an hour and a half ..."

"Did she proposition you?"

"No, Fiona she did not and, it seems to me that you have one very loyal partner there in Charlotte so good for you."

"Oh no ... I mean ... sorry, I thought she might proposition you and ... ah ... didn't realize she would be loyal to me ... ah ..."

"You might be pleased to know that she mentioned her friend Angela and that she has made it clear to Angela that she is your husband and will not do anything to hurt you. It seems she simply socializes with Angela when you are not with her, so you should be happy you are with Charlotte, Fiona. She thinks of you as her soulmate."

"Okay, okay - I am a little surprised but I'll ... ah ... make an arrangement for Angela to meet Jasmine, actually. You never know, there's might be a marriage made in heaven too. Just like me and Charlotte."

“I hope so Fiona and I wish you the very best with that. Goodbye for now.”

“Goodbye Cassandra - and thank you for all your help.”

Debbie and Robert

In Chandler, Arizona, Debbie Robbins was preparing to leave her husband Joel and, unbeknown to him, her supposed second cousin had taken a picture of Joel sitting with the woman in the hotel just days earlier. The photograph was actually one of many taken by the investigator she had engaged to secure the evidence she would need to separate from her philandering husband and to lay claim to half of their estate without the risk of substantial legal fees.

Joel arrived home from work. Deb stood in the kitchen with arms folded again and Joel suspected she was not in a favorable mood.

"Ah ... hello! What's up?"

There was no immediate response from Deb.

"What's up? I'll tell you what's up. I called my second cousin who sent me a picture of you with that woman last month. That is definitely you with that woman, but you denied that Joel – you lied to me about that didn't you?"

Deb handed Joel the phone and Joel looked at the picture.

"So you were there with her and you went to her room and came out several hours later – and told me you were working back. And it's not the first time, is it? You had it off with that, that Stephanie when you went to Chicago last year for the conference. She kept calling you for weeks - remember? So, Joel Robbins, I made an appointment to see a family attorney and he has booked us in to the family court for a separation conference next week. I have also placed a deposit on an apartment I am going to rent for myself and the kids so we are going to move out – and I mean, soon as."

"Deb, I'm sorry I let my guard down ..."

"Let your guard down? No you didn't let your guard down Joel Robbins, you put your dick in, that's what you did. So you and I are no longer husband and wife. Got it! Now you can sleep in the spare room tonight, I don't want to be anywhere near you Joel."

Deb went to her room, stayed there for the entire night and did not see Joel off to work next morning. That day, she packed her essential belongings and took her two children to the apartment she had rented. Debbie then had a removalist van come to the house to remove certain belongings she needed, including a small refrigerator and the washing machine. The next week, Debbie and Joel attended the court conference where the decision was made that all assets owned by her and Joel were to be shared equally.

Deb Robbins went to the Catholic Church service the next Sunday to meet her new friend, Robert. He seemed so excited to see her again so she suggested they go to the same café they had gone to previously for breakfast and a cappuccino.

"So how did the trip away go with the boys, Deb?"

"Oh ... ah ... we had a few minor issues so I just took them to some amusement attractions for a few days, you know, improvised a little. The trip might have been a little too much for all of us actually. They were happy with what we did – they're good boys! I'll take them for a trip within a few weeks, I reckon. But I really wasn't in a position to be able to meet with you and your girls last weekend, I'm sorry."

"Hey no problem! We can all get together some other time in the next couple of months – there's no hurry."

"Actually I really want my boys to meet your girls Robert so, perhaps the weekend after this weekend. Would that be okay with you?"

"Great! Let's book that in for sure – perhaps they can all play ball together?"

"Yeah ... that'd be great ... ah ... baseball?"

"No my girls are all into soccer actually and, as a sport, it's just so easy to involve several kids so that would be good."

"Sounds great – might give it a go myself!"

"Yeah, well I might just have to defend your shots on goal Deb if you don't mind ... you know ... let a few pass now and then, impress the kids."

""Oh don't you worry Robert – I'll get my shots on goal past you. You just wait and see."

Robert and Debbie shared some precious moments together and much laughter. Robert was so very pleased to spend the morning with Debbie he invited her back to his house to meet his children. Debbie obliged and stayed at Robert's house until midday, then returned to her apartment to prepare lunch for her two boys.

"Well ... better be off, got to collect my boys from their father and get them home for lunch."

"Okay, can't wait to meet them Deb."

Within the next few weeks they met every Sunday after Mass and it wasn't long before they started a steady relationship. Debbie felt so relieved that she had managed to contrive a well-founded basis for ending her marriage to Joel. She was so grateful for Cassandra's service as she knew her husband Joel would not be honest about his disloyalty and would be extremely selfish in his fight for assets.

The Golden Nugget

Raymond Brookes arrived at the Golden Nugget and booked into his room - 1302. He had arrived more than two hours prior to his wife Natalie's work party and, anticipating that he might have to be awake in the casino gaming rooms for a few hours, decided to have a sleep for more than an hour. Raymond set his alarm for twenty one thirty hours and lay on the very comfortable bed.

Jessica called Raymond at ten o'clock to say they had landed and would be at the hotel within half an hour. Raymond replied saying he would await her advice that they had gone to the gaming area. He waited patiently. At eleven o'clock, Jessica had observed Natalie and Graham leaving their room for the gaming area, had gone downstairs to ensure they were seated, then called Raymond.

"Hello Raymond, how are you?"

"Hello Jess ... ah ... to be honest, I am actually feeling quite apprehensive about going downstairs to observe Natalie and Graham, but I do think my disguise will prevent Natalie from identifying me."

"Well we've never met so I suggest you come here to my room and allow me to see how you normally look and then with your gear on, okay. I have just come up from downstairs so I can confirm that Natalie and Graham are down there. So I am in room 1326 on the same floor."

"Okay I'll be there soon. Thank you Jess."

Raymond walked down the corridor and around the corner to Jess's room and knocked on her door, which was open already.

"Hello Raymond, I'm Jess, please come in. Hmm ... not a bad matching outfit that. I think you'll be pretty safe from being identified, but just show me how you usually look."

Raymond removed his glasses, his hairpiece and his false moustache and beard.

"Yep – you'll be safe down there in that massive crowd! Now when we go down there I want you to follow me and I will point out to you where Natalie is and who Graham is okay. Natalie is at a poker machine and Graham at a black jack table. Now there is a roulette wheel where we could stand for a while and observe if you want to but, I must warn you, they could be seated where they are for several hours. I don't expect them to go back upstairs until about three in the morning. So here's a plan – I would prefer to get a couple of hours sleep so we could return to our rooms and get some kip and I will set my alarm for, say, one o'clock and call you back to my room. Then I will go downstairs and when I see they are about to come back upstairs I will return before them, okay. That way you can observe for yourself that they will go to his room."

"Sounds like a plan!"

Jess's plan went like clockwork. She allowed Raymond back into her room at one o'clock then returned to the gaming floor. Natalie and Graham prepared to leave the gaming area just after two in the morning. Jess got to the lift before them and alerted Raymond who kept Jess's door ajar by the tiniest margin, but was able to see his wife embraced by Graham entering his room.

After observing Natalie and Graham returning to Graham's room, Raymond closed the door and slumped into a couch in

Jess's room. Jessica could perceive Raymond's trauma was palpable. He was a man whose wife was just several yards away with another man in the room across the aisle. Within him he felt the urge to rush the door and to storm in.

"No doubt you are feeling quite some trauma at the moment Raymond. This is a situation that not many people would experience in their lifetime. I feel your pain and that is totally understandable but this has been going on for several months now and, if you don't mind me saying so, in this hour of anguish you really need to keep a focus on your future. For whatever reasons she may have, your wife Natalie has made her decision that she wants to be with this man, Graham. So I can only suggest that, for you, there are probably better times ahead."

"Yeah, thank you Jess, you're right – I am feeling really badly hurt right now but in a way I am also pleased to know the truth. She's been deceiving me for a long time now. My wife! Huh! Feel like a bloody fool at the moment, couldn't see the signs – lack of love and affection, you know!"

"Yes, well, all I can say is, keep a positive outlook on what your own future might hold – there should be better times ahead for you, Raymond. You're a good looking man and a successful businessman and you have financial security and you are active in sport with the golf you play so you, yourself, will be quite a catch for any woman, Raymond."

"Yeah, thank you Jess, I understand what you are saying but, shit, it just hurts so much to know that right at the moment in that room across the corridor my so-called wife is with another man."

"Well if it helps you can stay here for a while and chat, you know, tell me whatever it is you want to share about your marriage to Natalie and the times you've had together. It's only just gone three o'clock so there's no need to go anywhere. They will be in there until ten at the earliest, so if you want to chat you can sleep in the bed in the small room – and I will sleep here in this main bed. It might help to have some company, rather than returning alone to your own room in isolation. You won't have to leave here until midday tomorrow. When do you plan to fly back home?"

"Oh ... ah ... I booked my return flight for four this afternoon – didn't see any point in staying another night."

"Okay, well, I'll make sure you are awake for two o'clock this afternoon, but until then just try to relax and take your mind off the fact that your wife is in that room over there with that other man. She's gone, Raymond, okay! So talk to me about what your own future might hold for you. Then just doze off when you will – you're most welcome to stay here for now, probably best thing for you at the moment."

"Thank you Jess for being so understanding about this. You're right, of course, I can't stand the thought of returning to my room to be alone. Thank you for talking to me. My friend Roxanne was right, Jess, wasn't she. God bless her, you know, I actually did contemplate whether I should propose to Roxy before she introduced me to Natalie. God, I know now that I should have married her. She is a top person, Roxy – a really good woman of exemplary character. She will be totally loyal."

"She is Raymond, yes, but she would have no regrets about the way that went with you, because she met her husband, Gareth, shortly after you went with Natalie and she has a really happy life. She just couldn't stand the fact that your Natalie was being unfaithful to you. She did ... um ... put me in the picture about what a good man she believes you to be."

"So, here we are talking about me and I literally know nothing about you Jess, apart from the fact that you work with Natalie at Graham's company."

"Me ... um ... I am a psychologist, did my degree through UCLA Berkeley, married a psychiatrist who turned out to be quite the psycho, himself, actually ..."

Raymond broke into raucous laughter.

"Sorry Jess but ..."

"Oh that's okay, it's what I expect from people when I tell them that, yes ... um ... he was pretty straight when I married him but I think he became a victim of his own profession, actually. It seems some of his clients had too profound an influence on his own mental capacity."

"How so Jess?"

"Well I was never privy to his confidential interactions with his clients but some of the situations he did tell me about were extraordinary ... like ... people still believing that the world is flat and that we didn't go to the moon or the U.S. Government destroyed the twin towers or the President is an alien or ..."

Raymond broke into raucous laughter again.

"... or that the Vatican has been infiltrated by the devil and they keep him in a room below the tomb of Saint Peter ..."

Raymond broke into raucous laughter yet again.

"Jess, Jess, stop please, you're killing me now."

"Well that's no bullshit, you know, it's the kind of thing that vulnerable people choose to believe when they lack a suitable screening process against the shit that others will tell them. It's very sad, really, that, for example, a lot of his clients were, say, former Jehovah's Witnesses or from the Branch Davidian or Heaven's Gate groups who had spent many years or even decades alienated from their family members. It's just so destructive what they have inflicted upon them, but after so many years apart, they really have great difficulty re-integrating with the people in this world who are the most important to them – their own family. So spending years listening to such people must surely have some kind of effect on the listener."

"So that affected your husband ... ah ..."

"Martin!"

"Martin ... and he became, what, a little unusual himself?"

"Well he was totally non-spiritual as many of them are because they seemingly choose to believe that fundamental tenet of sociology, that if almighty God did not exist, society would create him. All for the purpose of getting into people's minds for the purpose of social control, of course. So my Martin was quite staunchly atheist ... and let's face it, if you don't believe in God you have far fewer reasons to be good. So he was quite adept at evading his true income tax liability and he eventually had an affair with a fellow psychiatrist named Louise."

"Well I'm so sorry to hear that Jess ... it must have been quite traumatic for yourself, too, then."

"Oh, the initial shock was there but it only took a couple of days for me to get over it. Was quite relieved actually, not having to listen to his weird comments."

"How long were you married for?"

"Twelve years – about three too many! Life was good for the first nine years. Same happens to so many people now, doesn't it?"

"Yeah ... seems that for people around the forty years of age mark, where we are, life's circumstances can cause one to question certain fundamental truths. You'd have a good handle on that yourself being a psychologist, Jess."

"That's one reason I avoid the clinical stuff Raymond – don't really want to get too far into people's heads, actually."

"So how long have you been single for?"

"Three years!"

"Well you are certainly a very attractive woman so there will, surely, be prospects for you in your future."

"Oh ... look ... I lectured for two years at Berkeley and have had several fellow academics and fellow alumni pursue me since I separated but, just haven't met one with that initial chemistry yet. Sure that will happen one day it's just a matter of time."

"I'm pleased you mentioned that Jess, because ... ah ... that woman I told you about, the hooker, she is a very beautiful woman so I suppose a lot of men would feel the same, but I'm sure I felt that with her, actually."

"Yes, well, it's definitely there – it's in the eyes, the lips, the facial structure, the smile, the voice – it's there alright."

"Yes, well, as you know you are a really beautiful woman, yourself, Jess, but if you don't mind me saying so, apart from feeling rather nauseous right now, I don't feel that peculiar chemistry with you Jess."

"No! Nor do I with you either Raymond Brookes and that is understandable. I think in our case it's in the nose, actually. My mother always said that people who are a good match for each other have the same shaped noses. Your nose is straight and mine just a little concave so we are not a good match on the chemistry side of life. Now, are you thinking of trying to see that Cassandra woman again, Raymond?"

"She did give me her telephone number but I've had no reason to call her before now. Though I did have her followed by an investigator after I witnessed her setting up another guy."

"That's a bit dramatic!"

"Well I only did so after Roxy told me what she suspected about Natalie. Might give that Cassandra a call tomorrow – see where she's at."

Jess and Raymond sat together for several hours talking about their past and discussing various aspects of life – attitudes, values, the Golden Rule, life's crises and life's bliss also. It was soon seven in the morning when Jess decided to bid farewell to Raymond for the night.

"Okay, well, best you get some sleep now Raymond Brookes. I have set my alarm for midday too. I'll turn off the lights with the remote once we are in bed. Goodnight Raymond, you're a good man. Sleep well!"

Cincinnati

Raymond returned to his home that same day and arrived late afternoon. He stood in his house and looked around at the rooms where his life with Natalie had been lived, feeling that his marriage was soon to be over and contemplating his future. Natalie arrived home on Sunday afternoon and was there when Raymond seemingly arrived home from the airport after his golfing weekend. Natalie acted as though everything was normal, believing she had once again had a good weekend away with Graham and that her husband was oblivious to what she had been up to on this occasion – or for several months.

"Raymond how was the golf?"

"Rather too much damn rain actually – got far too wet to be enjoyable."

"Oh well, you are home now so just relax."

The following week the pair went through the motions of almost-normal life. Raymond had trouble maintaining eye contact with his wife knowing what she had been doing for some time behind his back. On Friday night of that week, Raymond let Nat in the loop on his intentions.

"Now I need to let you know that I have been contemplating establishing an outlet in Cincinnati and there is a house there I want to go look at in case I need a base to work from, so I have decided to scrap this weekend's golf game and to fly there tomorrow to check things out. I need to look at commercial properties that are up for leasing. Will you be okay with that?"

"Yes, of course darling, it's your business you need to expand as you said so, good luck with that. I'll be okay here!"

Raymond had already bought the house next door to Cassandra without informing Natalie of his purchase. He knew that she would be close to informing him that she needed to be alone to pursue her own self-actualization, whatever that meant – perhaps more time at the poker machine! The next morning, Raymond packed his suitcase and left for the airport. He had contacted the sales agent, James Randall, to inform him he needed the keys to his new house. James agreed to hand over the keys to let Raymond into the house on the Saturday morning, so Raymond flew into Cincinnati, hired a car and drove to the house in Hamilton County where he met James, who was there at the house when Raymond arrived.

"Raymond, great to meet you, how is everything?"

"Fine James, good to meet you too and, thanks so much for arranging the sales so expeditiously."

"My pleasure, it's not very often something goes through as quickly and as smoothly as your purchase did. You must have a specific purpose for moving here from San Diego."

James was looking around at the house from the front garden and as he looked to his right, he noticed a man standing on the front porch of the house next door – Cassandra's associate who had bade her farewell on the investigator's video.

"Yes, I will be setting up an office outlet for my accounting business here in Cincinnati. So I will make a trip to Walmart this morning to buy my furniture, bedding, kitchenware and whatever else I need and arrange for delivery this afternoon. Hopefully the house will be sufficiently set up for me to stay here for the night but, if not, I can motel it for a couple of days. I'm not in a hurry!"

"Okay so in we go and as you can see already, it really is a spacious house. This is your main living room and through to the family room then to the dining room and on to the kitchen area. All bedrooms are on the other side of the house apart from your main bedroom which is upstairs, together with an entertainment room and the home theatre room."

"Yep! Certainly is spacious, James! I like the look of the outside garden too – quite exquisite!"

"Ah yes, the vendor was a keen gardener but in her later years it was just becoming a little too much for her. She was very close to the people next door there though, ah ... Bradley and Phillipa, who assisted her a lot in her final years here. They're a lovely couple – I'm sure you will like them."

"I hope so!"

"So, Raymond Brookes, I give you the keys to your new future and wish you the best in this glorious house."

"Thank you James, thank you for all your assistance."

Raymond saw James to the door and spent an hour to look at the rest of his new house, but wondering why James had referred to Cassandra as 'Phillipa'. It was about half past ten when there was a knock on the front door. Raymond opened the door and it was the man from the house next door.

"Oh hello, I saw you arrive with the estate agent so I assumed you might be the new owner. My name is Bradley McPherson and I live next door. I think you saw me earlier."

"Bradley, yes hello, I am Raymond Brookes and, yes, I have just purchased this grand old lady. Please come in, but there's no furniture here so I cannot offer you a seat or even a coffee."

"No problem, oh I did push the button to ring the doorbell but it might need a new battery, so that's why I knocked."

"Okay, I'll see to that thank you and you probably knew the vendor reasonably well?"

"Oh yes, Jennifer, she was in her late eighties and finding it all a bit too much, you know, health issues and not being able to keep up with the gardening and so on. So she actually moved out to a care facility a couple of months ago and the house has been vacant since then. A few people have been through but it does require some renovating as you can see. Do you plan to move in and live here or is it an investment for you Ray?"

"Not exactly sure about that yet – depends on what happens, a few things can go either way, whether I sell my accounting agency in San Diego, whether I establish a practise here, whether my wife accepts moving to Cincinnati ..."

"Always the way eh, wife makes the biggest decision!"

"Yeah she's pretty settled where she is with her group of friends and her outside activities but there's more to life than ... ah ... bingo, croquet and crochet. I'm into golf, myself!"

"Hey, excellent, I will be able to nominate you to join at Western Hills Country Club if you want me to but you might want to check a few courses around Cincinnati first, eh? Could take you out for a game at Western Hills though, when you have settled a little."

"Yes, I'd appreciate that Bradley, thank you. I am a member at the San Diego Country Club so I would expect no issues in joining wherever. I do like to play on a championship golf course because I do play off a two handicap. Some of the municipal courses are just too short for me."

"Yeah, two handicap eh, that's good - I play off six myself, we might enter some foursomes comp's together."

"Be a good idea but, we'll see. Don't know if I'll be staying long term or renovating then moving on. I did consider moving to Columbus so a big decision to make on that. Might come down to whatever response I get from some major corporations on the tax front. I recently completed my master's degree pertaining to international corporate structuring. A lot of legislation is about to change on the corporate tax front. But that will take some time so in the meantime I plan to move in here and do some repair work like repainting all of this room and others and maybe even instal a home theatre. No kids to worry about so don't really need five bedrooms. What about you – do you have kids, Brad?"

"Yeah two girls! My wife Phillipa isn't planning on any more than the two though. She travels a lot, presenting seminars to corporations and ... um ... she's away at the moment, back tomorrow. She'll do one or two trips every fortnight and it's a good income for her."

"Phillipa eh?"

"Yeah, she completed a master's degree through Harvard in industrial psychology so she can pull in a few thousand dollars with every trip she makes."

"Sounds rather boring to me – industrial psychology? Too many stats for sure!"

"She'd probably say the same about accounting Ray! So you don't have anything here at the moment so, what are you planning to do ... ah ... have a removalist bring your stuff over or what?"

"No, not yet! I'll head on down to Walmart shortly and just start to buy up, you know, a bedroom suite, dining setting, kitchen stuff, kettle, frypan, air fryer. Will stop by at Maccas on the way for a coffee though."

"Hey, come next door I'll make you a cappuccino Ray. Sorry, I should have asked."

"Ah, thanks Brad, that'll be great but I won't stay long, I need to make sure Walmart can deliver today or I'll be moteling it tonight."

Brad took Ray to his house and provided Ray with a coffee and showed Ray some pictures of his wife and daughters that were on a shelf in the living room.

"That's Phillipa and the girls – they are eight and six years, not really much chance of a son though."

Ray had a good look at two photographs which absolutely confirmed to him that Phillipa was the same woman he met who introduced herself as Cassandra Young. The Eagle Eye investigators had that right.

"Nice place you've got here Brad!"

"Yeah, been here for five years, no plans on moving for at least two years though – my line of work keeps me busy."

"Sorry, I haven't asked!"

"I'm an engineer, major civil construction so, roads, bridges, housing estates. I have twenty seven staff working for me now and we are presently developing a new estate at Amelia which is about twenty miles south-east from the central business district. It's a big one though – big enough for six thousand homes so that will keep me busy for years. We have considered selling up from here to move down that way ourselves but probably not until we can build on top of the hill so, that could be two or three years away. Don't like to live in a low area and find myself surrounded by houses."

"Twenty seven employees Brad - that's fairly substantial. Does Phillipa do any work for you pro-bono?"

"Ha, ha, ha ... no way Ray – my wife charges me double for anything she does for me and I think she overstates the time she takes. She must think of me as her cash cow I'm sure. She did come in a couple of times to refine some duty statements and job descriptions but there was something going on between her and one of my staff so, she didn't want to do any more work for me. Never did query that very much though - thought it must be just a woman thing, you know."

"Yeah, women can be like that, eh – I call it the cat factor! Might have been a bit of a beauty contest going on Brad."

"Well, could be, both my wife Phillipa and my employee Roberta are very beautiful women - make no mistake. You'll have a chance to meet Phillipa tomorrow night. Hey make yourself available for dinner Ray - I'll order Chinese take-out through Uber Eats and let Phillipa know we will have our new neighbor as a guest."

"Yeah, that'll be good, thanks Brad. Now I better head off to Walmart and start buying up before it's too late for deliveries today."

"Yeah you do that and if there's anything else you need today just come on over – and don't forget the battery or recharger for the doorbell."

"Will check it out, thanks Brad. Oh and here is my business card with my cell phone number."

Brad entered Raymond's number into his own phone then called his wife, Phillipa.

"Hello dear, how's everything?"

"Hi darling, just calling to let you know we have a new neighbor and I've met him and invited him over for dinner tomorrow night, but don't worry, I will order Chinese to be delivered and it will be ready as soon as you arrive home. His name is Raymond and I brought him over for coffee because his house is bare, as you know, so just putting you in the picture darl, okay."

"That's interesting Brad! I hope he'll be a good neighbor and thank you that you will take care of dinner because I'll be pooped when I arrive home."

"No worries honey - how was the seminar?"

"Went like clockwork as always, dear. They've asked me to return several times in the next few months because they are on a major recruitment drive for Amazon. They'll be needing several hundred new staff and those people will all need to be inducted properly. So I'll see you tomorrow night and will text you when I touch down so you can call for the Chinese. I'll have the usual but can we have some noodles also, similar to the special fried rice because they do a special fried noodles too. Just thinking of the extra person and we don't want to be short of food now, do we?"

"Good point, will do. Bye now!"

"Bye darling!"

Raymond's New House

Raymond made the trip to Walmart and took several hours to go through the various departments. He purchased furniture to completely fit out the main bedroom and one other bedroom, including mattresses and bedding, bedside tables, a leather lounge room suite, a kitchen dining suite and all of the kitchen utensils he could think of – a refrigerator, the air fryer, kettle, frying pan, saucepans, crockery and cutlery – a television set, a laptop computer and printer, an office desk, a filing cabinet, cupboards and some portable lighting.

Though he may not have realized it himself, he was actually subliminally cleansing his mind of his life with his wife Natalie and starting a new beginning. It was dormant in the back of his mind that had he been certain of his Natalie being disloyal toward him and if he had known that the woman who introduced herself to him as Cassandra was indeed a single woman, he might have taken up her offer of some love and affection – and that might have become an ongoing relationship. Now that Raymond was aware that Phillipa is, in fact, not a single woman but a married woman with two daughters, he had resigned himself that he would never be with her and would not interfere with her marriage to Bradley.

Raymond's purchases from Walmart arrived that afternoon at four o'clock and Bradley was quick to arrive from next door to offer assistance which Raymond graciously accepted. The two Walmart truck drivers brought Raymond's furniture into the respective rooms and Raymond and Bradley arranged them how they thought was best. The job was all done by six o'clock.

"Well you're all set like a jelly! What's the big plan for dinner tonight Ray?"

"Dunno mate, haven't given that any thought yet, what would you suggest? Though I do need to unpack a few things for tonight and tomorrow morning – bedding, crockery, cutlery and the all-important kettle. Got to get up to a cup of tea in the morning – can't live without it."

"Tea eh? Not a morning coffee man then, Ray?"

"Nup! Can do a coffee after ten in the morning but until then it's got to be two cups of tea for me. Reminds me, have to set up the cappuccino machine too, eh!"

"Well I'm booked in at the golf club for dinner with four friends and it wouldn't be protocol to surprise them with an unexpected extra but there are plenty of options around here down the road there at the shopping precinct. You've got Maccas, KFC, Burger King and some great Indian and Chinese take outs there too."

"Yeah, thanks Brad, now that you mention it, I just might go the KFC for a change – haven't had that for a couple of years now. Make a nice change actually. Will buy some groceries while I am there too. Could go some honey wheat cereal then some bacon and eggs in the morning for sure. So bread, butter, sweeteners – all the usual! I'll get some beef and vege's because I like to knock up a flavored stew in the crock pot slow cooker, bit of a specialty of mine, throw in some garlic, cajun seasoning, paprika, cummin, black pepper, Worcestershire sauce and tomato paste. Usually make up enough for seven or eight meals that way."

"Sounds delicious Ray! Does your wife cook a lot too?"

"Nah! She's bloody useless when it comes to that. Natalie's idea of cooking is to buy some frozen meat patties in a packet and chuck them into a frying pan."

"Ha, ha, ha, ha, ha!"

"That's why I bought the air fryer Brad – we started doing seasoned fried chicken in the air fryer. She quite likes that! How about your Phillipa, Brad, is she a good cook?"

"Yeah she's very good actually – even makes up quite a lot of Thai and Vietnamese dishes, as well as the Chinese of course."

"You're a spoilt man Brad!"

"Yeah, well, she's probably better than I deserve – a really beautiful woman, physically speaking, is my Phillipa. In fact, guys go ga-ga over my Phillipa. She's been told she looks like a meld of Jaclyn Smith and Sarah Palin. Probably a blend of the two, actually, if that's possible."

"Well I hope she has rather more nous that our ex-Governor of Alaska, Brad."

"Ha, ha, ha! Yeah, right, pretty face but not a lot between the ears in most people's view."

"So when do expect your Natalie to make a visit?"

"Oh, I've told her that this trip is mainly about setting things up and leasing or even purchasing premises for the business and making some inroads to marketing with a mail campaign to local businesses before we make the big move. We'll bring some of our furniture from San Diego but we were due for an update and the removal costs were a factor, so we took it as an opportunity to update most of it. I didn't spare any dollars with what I bought today from Walmart. So she might be weeks or even a couple of months away. I'll make the odd trip back home before then to keep her in line. She likes to go to Las Vegas occasionally for the weekend with her work peers so don't want her to get too far out of control on that one."

"No! That can be the destroyer of marriages Ray – gambling - so be careful on that."

"Might even fly Natalie over to here for a few days, Brad, to check the place out."

"Yep, good idea, now I had better let you get on with your shopping spree and I had better prepare for my night out at the club. Oh and ... um ... the local sheriff is pretty hot around here on drink-driving so be careful about what you drink if you are going onto the roads. I'll be getting an Uber to the golf club for that very reason."

"Okay, thanks for the advice Brad. Hope to catch you tomorrow and thanks again for the invite to dinner tomorrow night."

Raymond locked his house and headed for the shopping precinct. He purchased all of the food he thought he would need for a week or so and before returning home indulged in a KFC dinner box, which he quite enjoyed. On his way home, he went through a hotel drive through and purchased a carton of beer, knowing that his new refrigerator would be quite cold by now. Raymond settled into his new house with his new television to watch the seven o'clock news then tuned in to Netflix to watch a favorite movie, Stargate, before hitting the hay. Prior to that he called his wife Natalie.

"Hello dear how is everything over there?"

"Going okay! I've had a bit of a look around and there are quite a few commercial properties that I could consider. Not in a hurry though so will take a few more days before deciding anything. A lot of good houses on the market here too. How's everything at home?"

"Had a call from an old college friend, Suzanne, so going out tonight to a bit of a re-union so might be home late but don't worry about me, you take your time over there."

"Yes, well I want to make an arrangement through U.S. Post for a pamphlet drop to local businesses to gauge the response before making final decisions, so could take some time."

"Okay Ray, stay safe, I had better get dressed, we'll catch up later."

Ray tuned in to Netflix and decided to watch one of his all-time favorite movies 'Stargate' starring Kurt Russell and James Spader, but fell asleep in his chair just as the team was going through the stargate for the first time. When he awoke, Ra the sun god was zapping Daniel Jackson's brain so Ray turned the television off and hit the hay.

The next morning Raymond slept in a lot later than he usually did. He would normally rise by about six o'clock every morning but when he did wake, he was surprised to see he had slept until eight thirty. He lay there in his bed for another thirty minutes – again something he never did – before rising to boil his kettle for a cuppa. He did not realize it but recent events were playing with his mind – the realization his wife had been having an affair, moving to his new area and into his new house, but perhaps above all, that he was about to see that woman again - Phillipa.

Raymond had no idea how she would react in the medium to long term but he was certain she would be absolutely shocked to see him initially. He was apprehensive about what she would do and say in her initial reaction. How would he explain himself? He knew he would have to wait until he was alone with her, away from her husband, to gauge her response. He knew she would be tight lipped for the first minutes up to an hour or more. So much was going through his mind.

Raymond treated himself to some honey wheat cereal then bacon and eggs, cleaned up his kitchen then spent an hour unpacking some more of the items he had purchased. The house was starting to feel like a home to him and he did realize he was starting to feel peaceful being alone and away from his wife, who had betrayed him. He then dressed to go into his garden at the rear of the house where he had noticed a few items had gone askew. He repositioned some portable drip-feed sprinkler outlets to the plants they should have been watering which seemed to be slightly parched. Raymond found a shovel in the shed and turned some soil over then did some pruning. Jennifer had left a garden bag behind with a phone number painted on the side, which he knew would be for the collection and exchange provider.

After just two hours working in the garden, Raymond sat on an outdoor seat and was feeling even more relaxed and peaceful now. Raymond had started his healing process and was starting to look forward to life as a single man, literally feeling rescued from his Natalie. At midday Raymond went back into his house to think about making a sandwich lunch but decided to have a beer. After consuming two beers, Raymond dozed off in a loungeroom chair. When he awoke he was surprised to see that the time was almost four o'clock. He really couldn't believe that he had slept such a long time in the previous twenty four hours. He recalled that it had occurred before after he was involved in a traffic crash several years ago, when he slept for fifteen hours the next day. He had put that down to shock.

Raymond sat in his lounge chair in contemplation, feeling some trepidation about his impending meeting with Phillipa but feeling some excitement also. He really did want to see her again. He kept thinking to himself that had he known of Natalie's disloyalty prior to meeting Phillipa he might have spent a night with her – but also realized that he only met Phillipa because of Natalie putting him to the test. He had decided to buy the house without knowing if Phillipa was a married woman and was surprised to find that out. Now it was up to her to explain what she was all about – providing a sex service to women when her husband seemingly knew nothing about that. Then a text arrived on Raymond's phone, from Brad. 'Ray Phillipa arriving at seven so feel free to come over just before that will order the Chinese for seven thirty Brad.' Ray responded 'thanks Brad will bring drinks'.

Raymond watched the six o'clock news then called Natalie but there was no answer. She was on the gaming floor in Vegas.

Raymond then showered and dressed and prepared the drinks he would take next door – a six pack of beer, an Italian Lambrusco, a Johnnie Walker scotch and a Southern Comfort with some lemonade and Coca Cola. He hadn't ascertained what Brad and Phillipa normally drank with dinner so he called Brad.

"Hello Raymond."

"Hello Brad, look I should have asked ... ah ... what drinks would yourself and Phillipa like me to bring over? I went overboard a little at the bottle shop today because I will probably entertain a lot of different people here in the next few weeks so, you name it I got it."

"Hey thanks Raymond, I'll have a beer and Phillipa a white sparkling like a Riesling or a Moselle would be good!"

"Okay, got that covered, thanks Brad, see you soon."

Raymond went next door and Brad welcomed him into the house. They sat awaiting Phillipa's arrival with Raymond growing increasingly anxious as the minutes ticked by.

Phillipa

The time finally arrived – a car pulled into the driveway and Raymond knew that Phillipa was just a minute away from gazing at him. His heart was trembling! Brad went to the front door and opened it to allow Phillipa inside.

"Hello darling, how are you feeling?"

"Hello dear, not too bad but won't be long out of bed I'd say."

"I have ordered the Chinese and Raymond is here from next door so come in. Let me take those for you and ... go and meet Raymond."

Brad took Phillipa's suitcase toward a spare room. Phillipa took several steps from the passageway near the front door toward the living room and noticed Raymond's shadow was just around the corner. She turned the corner, looked up and gazed at Raymond.

"Aaagh! What the fuck!"

Raymond opened his arms down by his side and tilted his head as if to say 'yes it's me and I'm here'. Phillipa whispered.

"What the fuck are you doing here?"

"Is everything okay, darling? I thought I heard you were quite startled. This is Raymond I told you about who is our new neighbor. Raymond Brookes, darling."

"Oh ... ah ... just a case of mistaken identity dear, I ... ah ... Raymond I'm sorry about that, for a moment there I thought you were an old friend from high school. You know you could just about be his twin brother actually ... ah ... Jeremy, Jeremy Corbett ... don't suppose you are though, he never mentioned a twin brother to me."

"No, Phillipa, I am Raymond Brookes and so very pleased to meet you. Yes, I bought the house next door and ... ah ... love it actually. The agent referred to it as a 'grand old lady' and I quite agree. Needs quite a bit of work though, but I've got time on my side so you'll see me around quite a bit I should imagine. Probably be out there in the garden for a few weeks to start with."

"Yes, it certainly is a stately old structure, that's for sure – and I don't mean that in a demeaning way – it's a beautiful house, Raymond."

"Yes it is and thank you for inviting me over for dinner. Now can I fix you a drink?"

"I'll do that Ray - you two take a seat in the living room and get to know each other a little. It could be a long friendship you know!"

"Well I hope so, but you did mention that you plan to move to Amelia within a couple of years Brad, so, we'll see what happens. Oh, Brad has invited me to join the Western Hills golf club where he plays so ... regardless of whether you do move we can always stay in touch."

"Great! Can't wait – and do you have a wife and children who are going to join you here, Raymond?"

Phillipa realized that for the immediate moment she would need to remain coy about having prior knowledge of Raymond Brookes, so as to not alert her husband, Brad, about where and how they had met – in a hotel in San Diego. She would reserve her true feelings for a later time when she and Raymond could be alone together.

"Yeah, I think I will bring my wife Natalie over in the next week or so to view the house but she will need a little time to tie up ends where she works and her network of coffee friends and so on. No kids though, I'm afraid to say, we missed out on that."

"Half your luck – just kidding! We have two lovely girls but they are with Brad's mother until tomorrow. I'll collect them in the morning."

"Here we are - a Riesling for Phillipa and a beer for you Ray."

"Ah, thanks Brad!"

"So Phillipa, Brad said you've been away in your work as an industrial psychologist!"

"Yes – I go away quite a lot actually, though I am thinking of slowing that down soon. Might take up a nine to five around here somewhere soon. That's a bit of a quandary for me though because Amazon have some heavy work on the way and it might be a little too much."

Phillipa had already started to wonder whether she could or should continue in the line of work she was engaged in – servicing women who want to separate from their husbands, considering that Raymond Brookes living next door is aware of her line of work.

"I must say darling, you had me just a little concerned there – thought you two might have been an item from way back."

"No such luck dear but, may not be too late, you just never know."

"Ha, ha – great sense of humor, my Phillipa!"

"Yes, I can see that!"

"So you play golf, Raymond! Well I hope you aren't too much of a hacker, my Brad plays of a six handicap you know."

Raymond wiggled his left thumb toward his chest then held up two fingers with his right hand.

"Two!"

"Two? My goodness – definitely not a hacker then, are we?"

"No, I do shoot sub-par occasionally at San Diego where I play – my best effort, a sixty six off the stick for forty four points in a Stableford comp. Also had a nett sixty seven in a Par comp once. And do you play golf Phillipa?"

"Uh, uh! Tried it once but I missed the ball!"

"Ha, ha, ha! I like that!"

"Tried surfing once too, but I fell off!"

"Ha, ha! You were right there Brad – your Phillipa does have a good sense of humor."

"Sure helps!"

"Actually Raymond, Phillipa does play golf, yes – and she's not too bad, plays off a twelve handicap."

"Twelve? I am impressed. I'm not so fortunate – my Natalie thinks golf is the best way to spoil a good walk. No, she's not into any sport actually, unless she plays indoor golf that I don't know about."

Phillipa gave a wry smile toward Raymond.

"So, what are your immediate plans Raymond after your first two weeks of gardening?"

"Long term – I am an accountant and have recently sold a large plot of land that was a farmlet so I did quite well out of that and now have an opportunity to expand, which is something I have always wanted to do. So I will take a look around Cincinnati to buy premises and do some advertising to bring in some clients, you know, develop a client base. Will be needing several staff from the get-go, with all of the tax changes our new President is touting."

"So you could offer me a 'nine-to-fiver', Raymond?"

"Ha, ha, ha – there's that wry sense of humor again. I completed a master's degree in corporate taxation legislation recently, Phillipa - and I do quite fervently believe in reigning in all of this tax minimization that Donald Trump and his cohorts have been flouting for such a long time."

"So politically, you are a Democrat, Raymond?"

“Yes, Phillipa – I think I’m too honest to be a Republican.”

Brad decided to chip in here.

“So you think of Republicans as being dishonest Ray?”

“Well not all of course but, their entire hegemony, Brad, is all about making more money for themselves and less for others. So that starts at the top and permeates its way down with various philosophies, such as the trickle-down effect to lift everybody up and ‘we create the jobs’ etcetera. The wealth divide in this country is just too great for me as a person who believes in the Almighty, me having been raised as a Catholic man and all.”

Phillipa looked at Raymond and gave just a subtle nod of concurrence, which Brad did not notice. Brad chipped in again.

“Well they certainly do employ a lot of people Ray. I recall that during Covid, Geoffrey Bezos had to take on an extra seventy thousand people at Amazon.”

“Yes, because people had to stay home and not go out to department stores spreading the disease and the technological changes that have occurred since the mid-eighties was always going to see a lot of people rise to the top. For the most part, those mega-rich people do seem to be okay people, at least superficially speaking.

“I suppose we will never know. Hey, let me get you two another drink.”

“Thanks Brad!”

“I mean, Bill Gates was heavily into philanthropy with his ex-wife as we know. But I do wonder if they retain too much for themselves Brad. I mean, why do multi-billionaires who have over a hundred billion dollars want to tweak the taxation system to give themselves even more? What can a person do with all that money and you have to wonder why so many really wealthy people at the top corporate level always seem to support the Republicans, don't you think?"

"Yes well there are quite a lot who do support the Democrats too, you know."

"Sure are Brad but, without being able to know, I'd say that split is about eighty to twenty the Republicans way. What would you estimate?"

"Don't know but, perhaps more like sixty forty! And as for what they might do with a lot of extra money should it come their way, they would surely invest that in ways that employ even more people and create more jobs and even develop vastly different ways of doing things. I mean, take Elon Musk, for example, even as the epitome of the Republican philosophy. Elon had hundreds of millions of dollars from his sale of Paypal before he launched Tesla electric vehicles, but he put his money on the line and took a chance – a huge chance with great risk – and succeeded. Now, who knows Raymond, that one individual who took a punt on that, just might have saved this whole fucking planet and humanity from extermination, considering what climate change is doing."

"Too true Brad, but you do realize that most of those who are in climate change denial want to continue exploiting fossil fuels and it seems their attitude is, to hell with the planet. That's where the excessive greed cuts in, I mean, I find it totally incomprehensible that they would jeopardize the future of planet Earth where their own grandchildren need to live."

"Yeah – point taken – unless Elon gets us to Mars!"

"Ha, ha, ha!"

They all laughed at Brad's humor and were certainly having fun already, but Phillipa was seeing a divide between Brad and Raymond on the belief front and she was not surprised at all.

That's when the doorbell rang and Brad accepted the Chinese from the Uber Eats driver.

"Hey, thank you so much, right on time so here's a fiver for you, young lady."

"Thank you sir – have a great night!"

"Okay, I have set the dining table and be careful, I put these plates in the oven to heat them so they are quite hot to touch. We'll place these dishes in the center and share them around, eh – ladies first."

"Looks like a great selection you've got there Brad."

"Too easy actually – Phillipa really likes the combination chow mein and the beef and black bean, I go the sweet and sour pork and the Peking duck and we always include the large special fried rice and noodles. So with four main dishes there should be quite sufficient here for us all. Sorry, should have asked you Ray what you might like."

"Oh I like ... ah ... combination chow mein, beef and black bean, sweet and sour pork, Peking duck and large special fried rice and noodles, Brad."

"Ha, ha, ha! Very diplomatic of you Raymond Brookes, but I do also like a chicken chow mein."

"Ah, yes, I like that too, Phillipa."

"So apart from the politics of the wealth divide Ray, you stated that it irks you as a Catholic man and you were raised as a Catholic. Do you think the church is as relevant now as it was when you were being raised by your parents?"

"Hmm ... very complex question there, Phillipa. Things have changed a lot, of course and when my father was a boy back in the nineteen fifties and sixties there was certainly a lot of sheer stupidity being inflicted upon the Catholic congregation."

"Such as?"

"Well, where do I start? Back in the day the church upheld that there were levels of sin that people committed – 'venial sin' and 'mortal sin' and – though more recently it now refers to 'serious sin' also. Venial sin was a minor offence such as stealing a small amount of money and mortal sin stealing a large amount of money. But mortal sin also included missing attendance at Mass on a Sunday, eating meat on a Friday - because Jesus seems to have been crucified on a Friday - and all forms of sexual activity outside of wedlock. So we were all supposed to be totally pure virgins with absolutely no sexual experience until our wedding night."

"Impossible!"

"Absolutely! So one has to ask how so many people who were supposedly intelligent, well-educated human beings could contrive so much bullshit – and why so many believed it and accepted it. So thankfully all of that has changed for the better."

"How so Ray?"

"Well Phillipa, it's perhaps still a moot point within the Catholic Church's doctrine but there is a growing movement at the top that now subscribes to what we refer to as 'anonymous Christian'."

"Meaning?"

"Basically meaning that all good people will be welcomed back into the kingdom of heaven – including atheists. So people who live their lives as good people but have no overt religious beliefs. It is based on the gospel of Matthew chapter twenty five versus thirty one to forty six."

"That seems like quite an open door there Raymond, that atheists would be welcomed into heaven considering they don't believe in it. My Baptist Church preaches that only people who have overt belief in Jesus will be saved."

"Yes Brad, a lot of American Protestant churches do believe the same, but it was way back in nineteen sixty five when the Catholic Church declared its document 'Nostra aetate' stating its new position in relation to non-Christian religions, particularly Islam and Judaism and focusing on ecumenism. So the concept of the anonymous Christian has emanated from there."

"So what does Matthew twenty five state Ray?"

"It's where the Lord separated the sheep from the goats. All the good people were welcomed into heaven – people who had fed the hungry and thirsty, sheltered the homeless, befriended strangers and visited the sick and imprisoned. At least, that's the basic gist of it. So much of the stupidity that beleaguered the church in the fifties has been expunged. I must state also that I, myself, do subscribe to the concept of 'anonymous Christian' totally."

"Well I have some born again friends who belong to the Assembly of God, Ray - and they cite the Gospel where Jesus said - 'you cannot go to heaven unless you are born again'."

"Yes, Brad and it's unfortunate that so many fundamentalist Christian churches interpret the Gospel so narrowly. That tag is something they bestowed upon themselves back in nineteen hundred and six here in the States, but we don't really have a right to do that now, do we? The question really is, what did Jesus mean when he said we must be born again. To me, it means we turn away from intrinsic human nature that is greedy and love other people as much as we love ourselves."

"Hmm ... that could be a moot point too Raymond!"

"Ha, ha, ha yes it certainly could be – the Christian bible is full of moot points, Phillipa!"

"You certainly have some quite complex views on politics and religion there Ray."

Phillipa had taken notice as a further insight into Raymond's character and was duly impressed. After dinner, the group retired to the living room, Brad brought out some more drinks then Raymond took a compact disc from his jacket and handed it to Brad.

"That was a really lovely dinner you provided Brad and Phillipa, so I would like you to have this music that I bought for you. It's one of my favorites. It looks like you still have a disc player."

"Yes we do and we enjoy listening to some quiet music don't we darling?"

"Oh absolutely - and what is that one Raymond?"

"Actually, it's a triple set of orchestral music by the Celtic Orchestra and it's pianist, Seamus Brett. The Celtic Orchestra recorded the albums 'Celtic Moods' and 'Celtic Inspiration' then Seamus Brett recorded 'Celtic Rhapsody' with his piano as the dominant instrument. My grandparents on my father's side came from County Tipperary so I suppose the melody is deeply ensconced within my blood."

"Hey thanks so much for this Ray, you didn't have to but which shall we play first?"

"Celtic Moods first Brad, okay!"

Brad removed the disc from its holder and popped it into the player. Phillipa was blown away with the soft gentle melody of the first track 'Easy and Slow'.

"Wow, Raymond, you have completely excelled with this, that is just so beautiful I can't believe that music. Wow! I'm definitely going to fall asleep to that one Raymond Brookes."

Phillipa had become even more impressed with Raymond's character and slumbered into her living room chair.

"Well I'm glad you like it and you have almost two hours of quality music there."

"Now don't go falling asleep there now, Phillipa - and you did say you would have an early night so we will share another drink with Raymond before he returns to his house shortly. Don't want to keep you up late either Raymond!"

"Don't worry I am ready to hit the hay now, so I'll be off soon. Must get a chance to visit the golf club with you Brad before too long."

"Absolutely Ray - we could get out there one morning next week when there is no competition so, probably Tuesday morning. Or you could even play in the comp on Wednesday afternoon as a visitor. The pro has hire sets of clubs but you might have to buy a pair of shoes."

"Sounds like a plan! Yeah Tuesday morning or Wednesday afternoon would be great."

"So what's the immediate plan for tomorrow Raymond?"

"I'll probably go back to Walmart, Phillipa, it was all a bit rushed yesterday and I will need to buy some decorative items to hang on the walls, you know. Might buy some painting prints or even a set of flying wood ducks."

"Ha, ha, ha – very funny, wood ducks!"

Raymond finished his beer.

"So I shall bid you good people farewell and head back home. Thank you so much again and when my Natalie arrives we shall return the compliment."

"Okay Raymond, thanks so much for coming over and catch up sometime soon."

"Thanks Brad, goodnight Phillipa."

"Goodnight Raymond! See you soon, huh!"

Phillipa was already planning to excoriate Raymond Brookes for turning up in her neighborhood and actually buying the house next door. He had better have a good explanation for this. Hopefully wouldn't be too long before she got the chance to talk though.

Nat's Surprise

The next day Raymond did some more work inside the house and in the yard. He had purchased a number of poster size prints from the photography section of Walmart to decorate his house. The following day he called his wife Natalie, whom he assumed, would have been away at Las Vegas for the previous two days.

"Hello dear, how is it all going over there in Cincinnati?"

"Well you may not believe it Nat, but I bought an old house and I have moved in, for now. Not sure how long I will stay here before I return, we'll just see. Been busy these last couple of days getting it looking better, still a long way to go though."

"You bought a house! Ray, what have you done? What a surprise, but so soon, Ray."

"Yes well, from the research I have done, I think this will be a good market to move into so, I bit the bullet."

"How much did that cost us?"

"It was eight hundred and twenty thousand but I do regard it as a good deal, despite the work it needs. So I would like you to come over here as soon as you can for a few days. I want you to meet the neighbors Brad and Phillipa and do some more interior decorating for me, okay?"

"And how long do you intend to stay there for this time around, I mean, do you think it might be a week or ... or ... a month or three months? You must have some idea – and are we going to move to there, Ray?"

"Points for discussion Nat, so we can talk about that when you arrive."

"Okay well not this next week but maybe the week after but, let's talk some more in the next few days."

"Okay well let me know when you think you can make the trip and I will book your fare, okay!"

"Okay Ray, thanks for letting me know."

Raymond was planning ahead and thinking that he would bring Natalie over to Cincinnati to meet the woman she had met in the hotel lobby in San Diego when she attempted to set him up with a prostitute. He was going to rely on the shock factor to bring Natalie to the realization that her marriage to him was over, before he would divulge all of the details about what he knew of her and her boss, Graham.

Raymond and Phillipa

It didn't take long for Phillipa to get her chance to talk to Raymond Brookes. Brad informed her that on Wednesday that week, he had to make a trip to Miami and would be away for one night, if not two, to inspect construction of a new bridge over a causeway. Phillipa took the chance and telephoned her mother.

"Phillipa, hello how are you?"

"Hi mom, I am really good thank you - and you?"

"Oh, just the usual dear, wondering what I will be doing today and tomorrow and the day after ..."

"Well I can help you on that if you wish because Brad is flying to Miami early tomorrow and after I take the girls to school I really want to spend the day shopping because I need to buy Brad a birthday gift for Sunday. So if you don't mind will you be able to collect the girls from school at three o'clock and bring them home."

"Oh happy to dear and do you have any idea what you will buy for Brad?"

"Probably some music because we still have a disc player but perhaps some DVD's of his favorite old films too. He likes Fleetwood Mac and Engelbert Humperdinck so I think that will be the go. So once I take the girls to school I will let you know and head off to Walmart."

"That's fine dear I will be too pleased to take the girls home and are you going to have a little function at home for Brad?"

"Yes, please come over for lunch about midday on Sunday, for Brad's birthday, okay!"

"Yes thank you, lunch time on Sunday and I will see you tomorrow afternoon, Phillipa."

"Thanks mom and we'll see you tomorrow."

The following day Phillipa saw Brad off in the early morning and prepared herself to shop early at Walmart as she wanted to be home from about ten o'clock. She purchased the CD's and two DVD's of Brad's favorite movies – "Aliens' and 'Predator'. Once back at home, Phillipa changed into some casual clothing. At ten thirty in the morning there was a knock on Raymond's front door, then his doorbell rang.

"Phillipa!"

"Yes, Raymond Brookes – time for us to have a long chat!"

"Ah ... yes ... okay ... ah ... please come in. Can I make you a cappuccino?"

"Yes, Raymond, you might have to make me a couple of cappuccino's today, I actually have several hours to chat to you if you don't mind."

"Well I suppose that is understandable because I do owe you an explanation, don't I?"

"Yes, of course, for what you have done but I must admit, I have some explaining to do myself, as you would know."

"Okay, please take a seat and I will crank up the coffee."

Raymond took the five minutes to make the coffee and placed some chocolate coated biscuits on a table in a bowl.

"Please, help yourself. Now where do we start?"

"Well I need to explain my role in this but, firstly, I really would like to know how on earth you found out where I live, I mean, you haven't arrived here as a pure coincidence, have you?"

"Ah no ... I will explain that, okay. As you know we met at the hotel in San Diego where I handed you the money from the repair job and you invited me in for a drink. That was a very wonderful experience for me because I had experienced very limited attention from Natalie in recent years. I felt that there was quite an extraordinary connection there with you, though obviously a lot of men would say the same thing because of your appearance. So I couldn't put you out of my mind for several days, Phillipa, but after two weeks that started to diminish, okay! Then, as fortune would have it, one morning, a few weeks later, I left home about half an hour earlier than usual to deliver some reports to a lawyer across the other side of the city and as I was returning to my business I observed you and a man exchanging details after what seemed to be a relatively minor traffic incident. That seemed quite extraordinary to me, so I had to ask myself if you had deliberately caused that incident."

"And?"

"I followed the guy to his place of work and had a chat to him. You should recall his name – Phillip Mason – right?"

Phillipa rather subtly nodded her head.

"Phillip had your card with the name Beverley Granger on it, so I suspected something rather surreptitious was happening, because you were unmistakably you. So, Phillipa, I staked out the hotel where we met and Phillip Mason arrived on que about five o'clock – and didn't leave until after nine o'clock. So I approached him again and I cautioned him by letting him know that a friend of mine had warned me that Natalie was trying to set me up for a divorce. Then he went his own way. Now, obviously, what transpired between you and anyone else is not my business and I don't expect you to divulge any details – that is all entirely your business."

"Yes it is Raymond Brookes! So what happened then?"

"What happened then? I went home and arranged for an investigator to ascertain your identity, okay? They caught the same flight as you out of San Diego the next morning and had you tracked to your house."

"Very interesting Raymond Brookes! What then?"

"I received a photograph of your house and saw that this house next door to you was up for sale, Phillipa. And I don't mind letting you know that, given what I was going through with my wife Natalie and the profound effect you had on my deepest psyche, I decided that if there was any chance of meeting you again and a possibility of a friendship, I would pursue that."

"So were they able to inform you that I am a married woman with children?"

"No! That was not the extent of their investigation – just 'this is where she lives', okay?"

"So then you bought the house and came over here to move yourself in and you met my Brad! So ... how did you feel about that Raymond, knowing that I am not single but married with children?"

"Disappointment, obviously, I had been hoping so much that you were a single woman Phillipa but, once I met Brad I started to give up on the prospect of there being any ongoing relationship between us. I just resigned myself to knowing that I would live here for a while, perhaps meet somebody else and maybe sell up and move on. Though I must admit, the glimmer of hope remained in wondering why you would be doing what you were doing while married with children."

"So you now want an explanation from me?"

"I don't expect you to divulge your home business to me, no! It's not my business what is going on within your home between you and your husband ..."

"But you must be wondering Raymond!"

"Well ... yes, of course it has had me totally perplexed, but, I just have to accept that it's not my business. So, entirely your prerogative, Phillipa."

"Okay, so let's have another coffee, okay!"

Raymond went to the kitchen and quite expectantly made the second coffee with some anticipation. He was hoping that Phillipa would open up to him and explain her circumstances.

"Oh, I forgot to compliment you on your coffee Raymond, thank you."

"Ah ... thank you I ... ah ... did work as a part-time barista at McDonalds when I was in college, so, pretty meticulous about the way I make coffee."

"I believe I do owe you an explanation Raymond, after all, I tried to play a part in the destruction of you marriage – though I had no idea that your Natalie might be the offending party. So what would you like to know, Raymond?"

"Brad told me you might sell up from here and move to Amelia. So if you don't actually mind me stating, I find it quite perplexing, of course, that your husband thinks you fly away once or twice each and every week delivering staff training and development packages to corporations and ... well ... what you are really up to is totally different, eh?"

Ray wasn't perturbed at the thought of them selling up and if Phillipa was intent on staying with her husband, he would resign himself to the fact that he would probably never see her again. He knew he could renovate and on sell his new house if Phillipa stayed with her Bradley. But he was hoping for an explanation from Phillipa.

"I don't expect you to be my moral compass Raymond Brookes. There are many things you are not aware of and I am not sure that I have an obligation to put you in the picture. It is very, very personal and very hurtful too, okay."

Raymond looked intently at Phillipa who seemed to be catching her breath as if preparing for something very significant. Then she slowly looked up at Raymond and took a deep breath before confiding in him.

"Raymond, my Brad is having an affair!"

Phillipa looked down despondently, took another deep breath then looked up again.

"As you know, Brad has a very, very successful engineering business and employs twenty seven people including engineers, drafting specialists, human relations staff and admin staff. A few years ago, that new estate down at Amelia kept him away for several nights at a time until late at night. That started almost three years ago. He would get home at nine o'clock, ten o'clock or later and sometimes for two or three nights in a week. So I took the trouble of driving down there to spy on him and it seemed every night that he was there, a woman was there with him – just the two cars parked in the carpark. Seemed a bit too suspicious for me so I took note of the car, of course - and made occasion to see who was driving it. That car is owned by his human relations manager, a very attractive woman named Roberta, who is just twenty nine years of age. I couldn't see inside the building but I had an inkling that my husband might be having an affair with her so I put my Brad to the loyalty test, Raymond - and he failed it."

"How did you do that?"

"One of his staff alluded that he was very close to a female employee, Roberta, so I had a person observe Brad and that woman exiting the building one night and they embraced and kissed quite passionately – and that was not an aberration Raymond, it was every night that they were there together."

"Hmm ... well you are probably right, but some might consider that to be anecdotal evidence, I mean, if it came down to lawyers fighting in court they would certainly argue that case."

"Yes – and that is why I engaged a woman to do exactly what I am doing now - and he fell for it. He fucked her, Raymond - and according to her, my Brad didn't take much convincing. I paid her ten thousand dollars which, I thought, was a very good investment. Now I am a woman of considerable fortitude, Raymond, so I thought, why don't I do the same."

"Meaning?"

"Meaning to go against my own religious upbringing and to derive a substantial income for myself - because some things in life are so significant as to take precedence over morality."

"Such as?"

"Such as the security of my children, Raymond! That is of the utmost importance to me, Raymond Brookes. I brought them into this world, this completely fucked up world and I want them to have a reasonable quality of life."

"That is entirely understandable, Phillipa. Any good mother would feel the same way so, I admire you immensely for that."

"Yes, well I have been living a lie in my marriage for almost three years but my husband is the cause of that, Raymond. For our marriage just five years ago, I was literally forced to signing a prenuptial agreement, okay, so I don't have any rights to any of Brad's vast estate. He is just thirty five years and has been a really successful engineer but is also an extremely self-centred person. The agreement was that, in the event of our marriage failing, I would be eligible for just five percent of the value of our assets."

"Just five percent?"

"Yes and he thinks that is fair because most of our income is derived by him, of course, but like most women who raise two children, I was not able to derive an income for many years while raising the girls. Not much has changed either, so if we ... when I do split ... I will be entitled to no more than about half a million dollars and he will undoubtedly, pay his top attorneys to reduce that as far as he can. So I just might need some concrete evidence and a good lawyer of my own."

"You seem quite positive about that, Phillipa – that you intend to split."

"Well I'll tell you two things Raymond Brookes. Call it female intuition if you will but I am positive that Brad is fucking that Roberta in his office when he is there with her into the night. He attributes his presence there to this huge estate he is working on, but why only the two of them there all the time? Nobody else works back with him and he's had a bed installed in one of the back rooms of the office – supposedly so staff can take a rest if they feel unwell."

"That does sound like anecdotal evidence to me, if you don't mind me saying so, Phillipa. Are you sure you are not simply surmising? But if you are right, you too may need to fund a top lawyer and have some more tangible evidence to go with."

"That's going to be very expensive – he'll try to run me short thinking that I do not have a lot of money. But unbeknown to my husband, Raymond, I make a lot more doing what I do than what I tell him about. He believes I charge four thousand dollars for the three days and he thinks that's really good money. But I charge ten thousand because sometimes I pay an accomplice to take the pics, depending on whether or not my client can provide someone of their own for that purpose. That is rarely the case, so I pay both our airfares and also the accommodation for my accomplice."

"If you don't mind me asking, who is your accomplice?"

"An elderly man named Arthur, who has a disability and cannot work again in his profession as a diesel mechanic.

When we were in the hotel lobby did you notice that man sitting not too far away gazing at his laptop?"

"Not really, no!"

"Well he was my associate – the one I pay to be there to take pictures Raymond. So he is very happy to receive what I pay him for flying around the country for a few days at a time. Arthur's wife died of alzheimer's disease a few years ago. He was there with his laptop when you were there Raymond."

"Yes, you said so before!"

"So I am in the process of accumulating a nice little nest egg of my own so that I can acquire evidence on Brad for my own lawyers, Raymond."

"And the evidence?"

"Well you do know what I do, Raymond Brookes!"

"Yes!"

"I have decided to set up my Brad in the same way – and, unlike the previous time, have that photographic evidence that I will need for my top attorney. You see, I was put onto this by a friend of mine from college who told me of a woman she knew of who was doing exactly the same – a very beautiful woman who would trap disloyal men. Which doesn't include you, of course – you were ah ... just one in ten, Raymond Brookes, if that surprises you."

"One in ten?"

"Yes, but what she was doing gave me the idea of doing the same myself, so I made contact with that woman and she spelt out the conditions upon which she would do the job, but, I didn't have the ten thousand dollars, so I decided I would raise that money the same way and pay her one day to test my Brad, which I was able to do after just three weeks of doing the same."

"So you set out on your course of action three weeks before testing Brad?"

"Yes, call it female intuition Raymond – a man doesn't passionately kiss an employee for several nights before saying goodnight without something quite serious going on. Problem is that hooker didn't procure photographic evidence, Raymond – I just had to accept her word for it."

"Have to hand it to you for your acumen and shrewdness Phillipa. That really is quite a master plan you have going there."

"Raymond, I decided that if my Brad was being disloyal to me I would not stay with him. I know it may sound like hypocrisy but I am only doing what I do to end the marriage and to look after my children. Now, once it is all over, yes, I can go on and establish a career in my profession but I want to start that from a high point for my girls – not dragging ourselves up from the gutter. With half a million dollars I will have to move, rent premises, pay school fees, buy a decent car, pay for health insurance, the list goes on."

"Yes, I know how it can be. We weren't so well off ourselves until relatively recently. Been through all that except for the school fees. Accounting has been competitive, even in San Diego – quite a few companies exiting Los Angeles for the peacefulness of San Diego."

"So you may not believe me Raymond Brookes and I fully understand if you don't, but if my husband had been loyal to me I would have remained loyal to him."

"Well, you seem very sincere about that, even though there is a speculative aspect of that, but ... yeah ... I believe that you would have been, for sure. I believe I can identify conviction when I see it, Phillipa."

"Which leads me to state, Raymond Brookes, that I have the utmost admiration for you and the way you responded to me when I put the hard word on you back then in the hotel lobby.

I must admit you didn't waste any time giving me short shrift for the sake of your own marriage now, did you?"

"Well, it was never going to be any different for me because of my deep religious conviction, Phillipa. You see, I was raised into the Catholic Church and I still hold my beliefs in eternal life, Almighty God, Jesus as Lord, heaven and all that, so ... never a contest, actually."

Raymond witnessed a very genuine smile come across Phillipa's face as she sat gazing at him.

"Now I realize you may not buy into that!"

"Hey, how judgemental are you mister? Quite the contrary, I was raised into the Anglican Church and, despite what I have been doing in recent times, yes, I too retain my spiritual beliefs and when this is all done, I will raise my daughters the same – and remain faithful to any man I am with in the future."

Raymond smiled and nodded subtly. He could discern Phillipa's genuine character. Then Raymond's front doorbell chimed. It was a delivery from Walmart – a rather substantial outdoor setting and Raymond signed the delivery docket.

"Hey thanks guys ... would you mind taking that around to the back patio area, the gate is unlocked, thank you."

"No worries cobber!"

Chemistry

Raymond returned to his discussion with Phillipa.

"So where do we go from here, I mean, have you raised the money you need or are you going to continue doing what you do for another six months, Phillipa? Oh, by the way, mom's the word from me, okay! You are doing what you have to do so, lots of admiration from me."

"I have heard that despite there being a prenup in place a good lawyer can procure a better settlement simply by threatening the other party with information that can cause embarrassment, Raymond, so I don't know but I might be reliant on that type of strategy. Brad is in good with various top end organizations, you know, at county level and within his professional and social groups, so my feeling is that he would not want his philandering to come out into the open, stultifying his name. So, have I raised enough money? How long is a piece of string? I might fall into quite a protracted legal wrangle in this Raymond, so my intention was to continue for another year, at least. Must say though, now that my new neighbor is aware of what I do, I have some mixed feelings about that, Raymond Brookes."

"Well that's understandable – not that I count for much though."

"Oh, you do, Raymond Brookes. You have no idea how much admiration I have for you with the way you responded to me when we met. I pushed you a little but there's no way you were going to accede, was there?"

"Ah ... no! There wasn't, Phillipa, as much as I would have liked to ... on the physical front, I mean. So now that I have interfered with your plans for the next year or so, if you decide you cannot continue, I can assist you financially in what you need to do. After all, I do feel responsible in that way."

"That's very good of you to offer Raymond but I don't expect you to do that. I might just have to go to my attorney with what I have got. You see, I didn't take the step of procuring photographs of Brad with Roberta or that hooker. So attaining a settlement will not be as arduous as it could have been – I'll just have to settle for the five percent."

"Hmm ... look, as you know my Natalie put you up to testing me. Do you want to know why?"

"Yes, why?"

"It's because Natalie is the one having an affair - with her boss, a man named Graham. When I go to golfing weekends, as I do quite often, being a good golfer, she goes to Las Vegas and stays with Graham in his room. So she is intent on splitting with me, Phillipa. She wanted evidence on me for the purpose of divorce. She possibly thought that she would have to fight against me with her attorney to procure half of my estate. That was never going to happen. So when she recently started making noises about what she might be entitled to, knowing that I was in the process of selling a parcel of land, I decided I would simply transfer her fifty percent without question – and I did. I transferred eight and a half million dollars to Natalie."

"So you sold the land?"

"Yes, it was a Godsend for me! My father encouraged me to buying a small decrepit farming property about twenty years ago knowing that eventually it would become residential at some point of time in the future. Phillipa, I sold the land for seventeen million dollars and transferred half of those funds to

Natalie the same day. That took her by surprise and she was ecstatic, of course, as she probably expected to drag that out of me but, I had already been alerted to her activities and I think, it's fair to say, of her intentions. So I thought I would negate all the crap that would emanate from going to court, paying attorneys and all that but, I have never been one to be greedy and have always been willing to give, not to take. Must say, I was pleased to see her go."

"Now, why am I not surprised by your attitude, Raymond Brookes?"

"Oh, there is another aspect to that also, I must admit."

"Prey tell!"

"You!"

"Me?"

"Yes, of course, as I have said, despite me turning you away for reasons that are of the utmost importance to me – I have my ticket to heaven and I am going to keep it - I definitely felt something quite substantial in your presence, Phillipa. You have heard the term 'chemistry' when people first meet, have you not?"

"Yes, of course!"

"Well a woman who assisted me to expose Natalie, a rather beautiful woman named Jessica, who is also a psychologist, explained that to me that it is real and pertains to eyes, facial expressions, lips, a person's smile, voice and other things too and that there can be a type of 'match' between two people even on first meeting. So that was there when I met you, Phillipa. There was just that something very special about your total being that clicked with me – and I am not referring simply to your extraordinary beauty, Phillipa. So when I made my profound decision to transfer more than eight million dollars to Natalie, I must admit I was already wondering how I could possibly find Cassandra Young. All I knew of you, Phillipa, at that time, was that you were not wearing a ring. So I had to wonder if there was even the remotest, possible chance. That is why I had the investigator find out where you live and why I bought this house."

"That seems like quite a few drastic steps there, Raymond Brookes, without knowing my status."

"I was working from the assumption you were probably single, Phillipa. So you don't have the evidence you need against Brad except perhaps an affidavit from that hooker. His lawyers will get him to deny that. They do that every day, you know. Money is their god!"

"Well I might have to work on that – get the evidence I need, you know, photograph Brad with Roberta and engage another hooker like that Lynette."

"So do you want me to spy on your Brad when he comes out of the office with that woman – for me to take the photographs you need?"

"Sounds like a plan, but with a camera with you that you can zoom in with, you know, get some close ups. You would park across the road within the carpark of a mechanical workshop. Always a few cars over there at night."

"I have a Nikon with a zoom lens, Phillipa. So, yes, I could do that and for that purpose, I will hire a car that Brad has not seen me in before. Then what happens, I mean, that Lynette probably can't set him up the same way again can she?"

"No, but she won't have to Raymond. She will just have to bump into my Brad again somewhere. He is always going to functions to do with his work so if she is there she can proposition him again. He'll go for her, don't worry!"

"How will she gain access to a function like that?"

“She won’t have to – she will only have to be entering the building as he is entering, then contrive some story that an invitee asked her to meet him there.”

“Hmm ... good plan, I like it! So, supposing he falls for it and you succeed, what then Phillipa? I mean, where would you like to live if you leave here and what about the girls, wouldn’t he want access to his daughters.”

“They are not Brad’s children, Raymond. We have been married for just five years. The girls are the daughters of my deceased husband Brian. Brian was a marine and was killed in a helicopter crash in Iraq. He was there with the United Nations as part of the peacekeeping mission. I met Brad about eight months after Brian died and he offered me security and a stable life but, after we had been married for two years his ex-wife attended a funeral for his grandmother and she whispered into my ear that he was an inveterate philanderer. Apparently he had at least three or four extra-marital affairs in the six years he was married to her. Which is not altogether surprising considering she informed me that in his early twenties as a college student he performed as a male stripper at hens’ parties. Apparently he handed out his phone number and website address quite randomly and is quite well endowed as a man - hence the bookings he procured - so he had numerous women maintain contact with him. So he may not have changed a lot since then.”

“Oh, I’m so sorry to hear that, Phillipa. You really have had quite a traumatic life, haven’t you?”

Phillipa’s eyes welled up with sadness and she gulped as she responded.

“Yes, Raymond, but not as traumatic as many people, as you would know. I mean, some people die as children, don’t they.”

Raymond was duly impressed with Phillipa's sense of perspective on life.

"So, where would you like to live, Phillipa?"

"Oh, plenty of wonderful places here in the States, of course, but I have always had a soft spot for San Francisco actually. Just love that song by Scott McKenzie – should have been a hippy you know."

"Ha, ha, ha – quite a sense of humor you have there, just born in the wrong decade, or two, eh? So you are thirty three years of age so born in nineteen ninety or ninety one!"

"Twenty first of December nineteen ninety!"

"So, do you have a plan for setting Brad up with this Lynette already?"

"Yes – I'm onto that! He's going to another conference next week in Philadelphia and I have all the details. He'll be staying at the Ritz-Carlton where the conference is, so I have already booked a room for Lynette so she can meet him there again and seduce him to her room. She won't be able to get there until the morning of day three but he'll be away for at least three or four days. He'll probably stay longer there with her if he can."

"Hmm ... so when he is away, just asking, would you like to make a sortie to the Bay area to check out some housing? I am willing to do that for you, to cover all expenses for the trip, but, you are still a married woman and I am still a married man, so we will have separate rooms if we have to stay out for a night or two, okay?"

"That's very good of you to offer Raymond – and yes, I would like to go and I would like separate rooms if you don't mind. I could tell Brad that I have a conference to attend - and I am sure my mom will take care of my girls."

“Great, so the day that Brad flies out we will fly out too, to San Francisco. Just let me know which day he flies out, I am sure I can book flights at short notice for the same day.”

“Now if you don’t mind me asking you Raymond Brookes, what are you hoping for in this? We have only known each other for a very short time and you know the circumstances in which we met, through your wife Natalie, so you don’t know me very well do you?”

“I have seen some very admirable qualities shining through already from you Phillipa McPherson - and if you are right about your Brad, you might be a single woman very soon. You will need to make a fresh start in another city and I can assist you with that. If our friendship comes to nothing then that will be my loss – and yours too by the way.”

“Ha, ha, yes, I think I can understand that already too, Raymond Brookes. I do like your values and your commitment already!”

Lynette

Now that the wheels had been set in motion for Phillipa to gain some concrete evidence about her husband's infidelity and for her to go to San Francisco with Raymond, Phillipa decided to make some final arrangements. Phillipa contacted Lynette to make a special request.

"Hello this is Lynette speaking."

"Lynette hello, it's Phillipa, great to speak once again."

"Phillipa hello, how are you and, yes, I am all set for next week at the Ritz-Carlton. Is everything still all go?"

"Oh yes, for sure, but I just wanted to make some additional requests if you don't mind."

"Okay what would you like?"

"Well on this occasion if you will be staying in Brad's room overnight, as long as he doesn't have someone else with him, I will be needing a photograph, let's say a selfie - of you and Brad in the hotel room together. Will that be possible?"

"Well yes, it should be but, I haven't informed you yet, I have purchased a portable pinhole camera that I will set up in my room and that will take a picture every few minutes if that's what you want. It's programmable you see, so every 5 minutes or every ten minutes, no problem. So I will endeavor to bring Brad into my room, okay!"

"Wow, that is such a great idea, you really are at the top of your game aren't you, I mean, I have never heard of something like that before."

"It comes in handy. As you know I do charge a rather high fee so my clients are greatly impressed if I do something above and beyond like that. And as you would understand it helps them in the divorce process quite a lot too."

"Well please do so with my Brad because he's a dishonest bastard and I just might need that to pin on him. Just censor the really explicit images okay. I just need to catch him in the room with you in compromising situations, so laying on the bed nude is fine but no sex scenes, okay! I don't need to see that!"

"Oh look, there will be hundreds of images I can choose from but thank you for letting me know and I will text you when I am all set up there and as we progress okay. I mean, if he is there with me he will need to take a toilet break at times, as you know. So I hope to keep you in the picture, Phillipa. Is there anything else I can assist with?"

"No, look, you've been wonderful Lynette, I am just so glad that someone can do this for me because I feel trapped in a really bad situation where I am, so thank you again and I hope to hear from you."

"Thank you Phillipa, goodbye for now."

Phillipa called her mother.

"Hello darling how are you?"

"Fine mom, but I need to ask another favor from you."

"Yes dear, what's that dear?"

"Well, Brad has been called to a conference of engineers in Philadelphia for Wednesday so he will be flying out in the early morning and, as my luck would have it, Amazon want me to be at their workshop in Seattle on Thursday so I need to fly out later on Wednesday. So asking if you can please look after the girls for two days?"

"Oh, would love to darling, they bring me so much joy I am always here for them and for you. Will you bring them to me on Wednesday morning?"

"I can take them to school but please collect them after three in the afternoon okay? And I should be back for Thursday afternoon but there's a chance it could be Friday sometime so I will keep you posted on that."

"Oh, thank you darling - I am looking forward to that so much, I do love your girls, they really are angels to me and you know that, Phillipa."

"Yes I know mom, as I do, they are just so special in our lives since Brian departed. So I will see you Thursday or Friday."

"Thank you darling, bye for now."

Now that Phillipa had put her plans in place, with Lynette ready to trap Brad and her mother willing to look after her girls for a few days, she decided to make one last confirmation with Brad that he was, indeed, flying to Philadelphia on Wednesday morning. Just to placate her own mind though, she asked Raymond to be outside Brad's office on Tuesday night with his Nikon zoom lens, hoping he could observe her husband kissing Roberta.

"Hello Brad it's me, look I've been asked to fly to Seattle on Wednesday for an Amazon workshop, so mom has agreed to look after the girls for a day or two, okay?"

"Yes, well I will be in Philadelphia for three or four nights so as long as your mom is okay with that!"

"Yes, she is ecstatic at being able to mind the girls and they have so much fun together – the girls really love their nanna."

"Yes, I know – probably a lot more than they love me!"

"No, it's just that they do see mom every week and she spoils them, so they really look forward to staying there. So, all systems go with you and Philadelphia, eh?"

"Yes, booked into the Ritz-Carlton – should be there by mid-morning so, will call you later on Wednesday and will keep in touch, of course, but see you soon - I'll be home later."

Phillipa called Raymond.

"Hello Phillipa."

"Hello Raymond, I have just spoken to Brad and it's all go for Wednesday, so would you please book our airfares for tomorrow morning and also, perhaps about five o'clock this afternoon, could you please park up in Mercers Pointe Drive which is off Newtown Rd. So to get there from the city you go south down Beechmont Avenue into Batavia Pike then Clough Pike, okay? Brad's building is on the right. Now Brad's car will be there, you can't miss it, but Roberta's car is a white Jeep. Also, the first time I observed their cars there together, which was about half past five, Brad's car was the only car there so everybody else had gone. So I left, but as I was driving north on Clough Pike, Roberta was driving the other way, so I am just wondering whether she does the same – leaves like everybody else does then goes back about half an hour later. Just saying if Brad's Cadillac is there alone, she might return within half an hour or so!"

"Okay, will do! I will book the two flights right now and accommodation too then set off for Turpin Hills."

"Thank you Raymond - you are my champion."

Raymond had procured his hire car and did what Phillipa had requested of him. He arrived at Mercers Pointe Drive at fifteen minutes to five o'clock as several vehicles were leaving the building across the road – Brad's building. Raymond observed Brad's Cadillac was parked closest to the building and the white Jeep was parked near the roadway. By five o'clock there were just five vehicles still parked up in the carpark, when a woman exited the building, accessed the white Jeep then drove away. About ten minutes later two other people exited the building then drove away in their vehicles. Now the stage was set for Raymond to observe whether Phillipa's suspicions of her Brad and Roberta were on the money. At approximately fifteen minutes to six o'clock and as darkness was falling, Raymond observed the headlights of a vehicle turning into Mercers Pointe Drive. It was Roberta's white Jeep. Roberta turned into the carpark and parked her Jeep alongside Brad's Cadillac, causing the security lights to brightly light up the entire area, then entered the building. Brad took several snaps of Roberta arriving. Then it was time to wait to see what transpired.

As Raymond's good fortune would have it, he didn't have to wait too long. Phillipa had cautioned him that he could be there until as late as ten o'clock, but on this occasion, Brad and Phillipa exited the building together at seven thirty. Once again the security lights lit up the entire area and Raymond was ready with his Nikon, programmed to the movie camera function. He observed Brad and Roberta standing behind her Jeep chatting for a minute, then Brad gave Roberta a hug and what seemed to be a grandmother kiss, before they parted to their respective vehicles. They both drove out of the carpark and Raymond called Phillipa.

"Hello Raymond!"

"Phillipa, hello, Brad and Roberta have just left a couple of minutes ago ..."

"And?"

Phillipa was eager to hear that her husband and that woman had exchanged a long passionate kiss in the carpark before leaving.

"Well I have recorded their parting gesture and all I can say really is, yes they embraced for a second only then exchanged a kiss that I would describe as one that a man would give his own mother. Okay. I mean, Phillipa, it was there but... ah ... to quote a line from a famous movie, it was just a wee pecker, okay. I'm sorry it wasn't what you expected but, who knows, they might have been in a hurry and they might have been up to hanky-panky inside the building."

The phone went silent for a few seconds as Phillipa seemed to be despondent before she replied in a rather subdued tone.

"Ah ... okay Raymond, thank you for doing that, it's so good of you to help me this way, I was hoping for more but I do have Lynette ready for two days after tomorrow in Philadelphia."

"Okay Phillipa, look I understand that you are hoping for another fail from Brad with Lynette and, as much as I like you as you know, I must state that what you are hoping for is something that I wouldn't actually wish upon anybody. I have recently experienced that trauma myself with my Natalie being unfaithful to me."

"Yes, I do understand that Raymond and we'll see each other in the morning. I will take the girls to school then meet you at the airport, okay."

"Okay Phillipa - goodnight darling."

Phillipa was a little chuffed that Raymond had referred to her for the first time as 'darling' but she was still a tad despondent that Brad had not given her more than a wee pecker of a kiss with Roberta. At the subliminal level, though she wasn't totally conscious of it yet, she was building hope for a new future with Raymond – in San Francisco.

Philadelphia

The next morning, Brad left home at six o'clock and took his eight o'clock flight to Philadelphia for the county engineering conference, arriving at nine thirty, then checked into the Ritz-Carlton hotel at ten o'clock. Meanwhile, Phillipa and Raymond had met at the airport at nine thirty for their ten thirty flights to San Francisco, where they would arrive at two thirty in the afternoon. They had checked in so they scanned their boarding passes and placed their suitcases onto the conveyor then waited to be called to enter.

"Hello Phillipa, how is everything, did you get the girls to school okay?"

"Yes, no issues there Raymond and thank you again for what you did for me last night observing Brad with that Roberta woman."

"Pleased to do that for you and I can show you the video while we are on the flight. Did I detect from your tone last night that you were hoping for something more incriminating?"

"Yes, well, as you know he has been caught out once with that Lynette and, like a lot of people, I was prepared to consider that to be an anomalous foible on his part, but if he is up to no good with that Roberta, then that makes it all quite different. No foibles there if that is happening, Raymond. That would be the end as I have told you. So in some way, I am actually hoping that my Brad does slip up with that same Lynette in these next few days."

They were called to enter the aircraft and displayed their boarding passes to the attendant.

"Good morning, you are seated to the right just the third row."

"Raymond! Business class! Well I have never, ever flown business class before - must have cost you a lot extra."

"Not really – just a couple of hundred extra, but we do have a four hour flight ahead of us Phillipa. I want you to feel relaxed rather than stressed."

Raymond, too, was contemplating what might transpire between Phillipa and himself if her Brad did fail the loyalty test with Lynette and wanted to impress her in every way possible, just in case there might be a future with her. While they were awaiting take off Raymond showed Phillipa the video.

"Hmm ... have to wonder what happens in that room with the bed though."

"Now we do have a long flight so we should try to get some relaxation along the way, Phillipa. Must admit, I was probably quite excited during the night so didn't sleep too well."

"Me neither, actually, but perhaps we had better get some nourishment before dozing off. I sure could use a fruit juice and maybe a croissant or a toasty."

"Yes, me too!"

"Now there is something that I need to tell you - something I have arranged without your knowledge, okay."

"What would that be Raymond?"

"I have explained to you how I found you – I had you tracked when you caught the plane leaving San Diego, by an investigator who sent me the photographs of your house."

"Yes, so?"

"Well I have engaged the same investigator to follow your Brad to Philadelphia and to stay in the same hotel, the Ritz-Carlton, to see what he gets up to before your Lynette arrives."

"Oh! Why would you do that, Raymond?"

"Let me put it this way. If your Brad is as devious as you believe he might be, there is an outside chance that he might actually go there to Philadelphia with that woman, Roberta, whom you asked me to take the photographs of. I mean, he doesn't know that you have arranged Lynette to be there and she won't get there until day three of the conference. So if your Brad wants to play up he might actually be taking that Roberta away with him on numerous occasions. You just never know. So I have provided the investigator with photographs of your Brad and that woman, Roberta, you could say as a backup strategy. Perhaps something will go awry at the conference and that Lynette may not come through for you the way you want her to."

"That's very thorough of you, Raymond, but honestly, if you had mentioned that plan to me before I am pretty sure I would have gone along with it. I do want to catch him out, you know. It will be very interesting to see if he comes up with something. You know, you are right - my Brad could have been going away with women on all of these trips that he makes. Why didn't I think of that before, it just didn't occur to me, Raymond."

"If he is there with another woman, possibly Roberta, it's going to be very interesting when your Lynette shows up."

"Ha, ha, ha, ha! Oh to be a fly on the wall then, Raymond."

"If that happens what do you think your Brad will do?"

"Good question – sheeze, that would pose quite a dilemma for him – Roberta or Lynette – a brunette or a blonde. Hmm ... just don't know."

"By the way, I phoned Brad's office this morning and asked to speak to Roberta and they said she has gone away for a couple of days, so I left a message for her to call me back – from my accounting firm. She won't know who I am."

"Very clever – so she probably has gone to Philadelphia with Brad."

"There's a good chance of that, yes. Let's wait and see."

"You know, sometimes when he goes away he doesn't call me at all – probably too busy with his lovers."

"Phillipa, the world is full of such wealthy men who take advantage of their wealth by indulging in a lot of sex with women. Your Brad is just one of them, so don't be surprised at what happens."

Phillipa and Raymond enjoyed their refreshment then both dozed off for almost three hours.

Back in Philadelphia, Brad had an hour or so before the conference re-commenced at eleven o'clock so he lay on his bed for fifteen minutes to relax, then went to the lobby to enjoy a beer. That was when Roberta arrived. She had gone into the office for an hour to do some urgent work so had caught a later flight.

"Darling, let me take your suitcase to the room, or would you like to enjoy a drink first?"

"Should be some in the bar fridge in the room, eh?"

"Yes, of course, so we will head upstairs and we do have about half an hour before I need to be back downstairs."

"Hmm ... just enough time to be quick, eh?"

"Take it slowly tonight, after dinner."

"Hope so, Brad!"

"So you've booked your return flight back to Cincinnati for the morning?"

Roberta was removing her clothing and pouring herself a drink.

"Yep, leaving at eight! Will go into the office mid-afternoon. Nobody suspects anything – they know I duck out for several hours every week even when you are there. You're quite a lucky man having such a beautiful wife and a girlfriend too."

"Yes, I know but, my Phillipa only gives me love and affection about once every week, sometimes twice, depending on her rigorous schedule. She's normally just too tired. Oh, by the way, I can deposit another five thousand for you today, okay."

"That's very good of you, Brad. You know, I will be able to buy my own condo soon, then you can visit me whenever you want to. Sharing with my younger sister Annabelle isn't exactly conducive to having an ongoing affair. We've been fortunate that she's had to go away occasionally but when I have my own condo she will invite her best friend to share the apartment with her."

"Meaning an open ticket for us to be together as we wish."

"Exactly, Brad! Now, come here my good man."

Fifteen minutes later, Brad dressed himself to go downstairs to the conference.

"I'll be back about five and we can have some drinks at the bar before we go to the restaurant."

"I'll see you to the conference room, then I'll come back upstairs for a sleep. Feeling a bit pooped now."

Brad and Roberta went downstairs in the lift and she accompanied him to the bar for a quick drink before she kissed him and he went to the conference room. Unbeknown to them, Sam Collins from Eagle Eye Investigations had recorded all of their interactions in the lobby area since Roberta arrived at the hotel. Raymond's plan had paid off, though he would wait to see what transpired from Lynette before he disclosed the information he now had, to Phillipa. Following the conference, Brad went upstairs and he and Roberta came down to the lobby bar at five thirty. Sam recorded them enjoying dinner then returning to the lift at eight o'clock together.

Sam Collins sent the details to his manager, Scott of Eagle Eye who forwarded the graphics to Raymond. He identified Roberta as the woman who was with Brad at the hotel. The next day, Roberta left the hotel to return to Cincinnati but on day three of the conference, Brad was sitting at the bar in the lobby at lunchtime again enjoying a beer. As he sat at the bar he glanced sideways and saw a woman he thought he recognized as Lynette. He jumped from his bar stool and rushed toward the lift but she had gone. Brad returned to his stool and finished his beer. He was almost positive that the celebrity blonde woman he had just seen was Lynette and wondered why she would be there. He was hoping to meet her again if, in fact, the woman was Lynette. Brad had a second beer before entering the conference room. The secretary of the Lawrenceburg County addressed the room for twenty minutes to welcome everybody, before the State Governor made a thirty minute speech, followed by the local Member of Congress also. Then it was Brad's turn to address the forum and he tried to gather his thoughts, which had been deflected into Lynette's direction.

"And now for his expert exposition pertaining to the main engineering aspects of this project, I introduce Mister Bradley McPherson who will augment the latest strategies for the bridge construction."

"Thank you mister chairman, I firstly want to state that I am involved in the design and construction of the new bridge at Lawrenceburg, about twenty miles or so west of Cincinnati, which has been in need of duplication for quite some time now. It is so commendable that our President Joe Biden has spent up really big on infrastructure recently, I mean let's face it, we just cannot have another incident like we had in Baltimore. The cost to the nation of that mishap has been so dramatic - the reverberation around the entire country is something like we have never seen before because of the movement of all that critical freight being impeded so greatly. So in view of that tragedy what we are recommending to the county is a design that we have drawn from the Chinese - that being a dual pylon suspension bridge where both pylons are several yards away from the river itself, so there can be no possible altercation between river traffic and the new bridge."

Lynette entered the conference room and took a seat in the back row. Brad was totally shocked to see Lynette enter the conference room and was very keen to talk to her, so ended his presentation rather abruptly and abandoned his front row seat.

"Now before I elucidate on this project I would actually like you to hear the drafting specialists expound upon the pylon design, because I need to take due cognizance of certain stress factors that will affect the height of the pylons and the clearance of the deck above the river. So I would like to hand over to senior draftsperson, Nicholas Brewer - and then I hope to address the meeting again later this afternoon."

Brad's initial cursory presentation took a lot people by surprise but he left the podium and, rather than resume his seat in the front row, headed toward the back of the room, exuding his usual confidence. Lynette was seated there where a vacant chair was alongside her.

"Lynette, hello, what are you doing here? I haven't seen you since we met two years ago."

"No, well I wouldn't expect to meet you either Brad, but I am here because my brother is in town as he has been awarded a contract and I haven't seen him for five years or more - so I am going to catch up with him while we are both here. What a coincidence, you being here! Is everything okay with you?"

"Oh, yeah, no issues with me except I reminisce about the first time we met. This meeting is going to break up in about five minutes for a one hour lunch break, so can I buy you a drink or lunch or ...?"

"Yeah, that would be great Brad, perhaps we can go to the restaurant across the road. They do a nice creamy garlic prawn dish that I had when I was here five years ago – doesn't do anything for one's breath though, so better get some mints – might get too close to somebody."

"Yeah ... fine ... we'll go to lunch then see what happens. Are you in town for a while or ...?

"Open ticket really! Probably stay three or four days. I might even stay for the John Fogerty concert here next week. My brother could have some plans for me too, just not sure yet."

"So ... ah ... where are you staying, Lynette, if you don't mind me asking?"

Lynette motioned with her right hand, indicating a room upstairs.

"I'm on the third floor Brad, room thirty four! Where are you?"

Brad took that as an invitation and was keen to fix a liaison.

"Hey great – I'm on the fourth floor so ... ah ... we could have dinner here tonight, too. Would you like to have dinner with me tonight?"

"Yeah ... great ... more creamy garlic prawns for me!"

"Ha, ha, ha ... you've not lost your sense of humor these last two years!"

"No and how did you get on with that woman you started dating, Brad, what was her name ... Penelope?"

"Ah ... got rid of her – took her to Vegas for a weekend and just could not drag her away from the gaming floor, I mean, after three or four hours I've had enough, but, she would sit there at that poker machine for eight or nine hours at a time. Bad news so I gave her the flick."

"You still single then?"

"Yes! Seems no-one will have me!"

"Hey, go easy on yourself Brad, you're quite a catch for any woman."

"And how about you Lynette, are you hitched?"

"Ah ... nope! Seems nobody wants me either!"

"Get away! You'd be fending off guys all day every day, so you are just playing hard to get, Lynette."

"Could be! Now I was just over the road there this morning for breakfast so I can order lunch using the app if you can tell me what you want. That will save a little time."

"Do they do a steak sandwich? If so, that will do me, something quick and easy, thank you."

Lynette placed the order for fifteen minutes time and they departed for the restaurant as soon as the conference ended for the morning. Upon arrival, they waited just five minutes for their lunch to be served.

"Hmm ... love these creamy garlic prawns."

"Yeah, a decent sized steak sandwich too. So what have you been up to for the last two years Lynette?"

"I have been really busy, actually, assisting a relative doing interior design, specializing in new homes and using auto-cad software. I find it gives me the opportunity to be creative and to use my imagination. It keeps me busy and the income is okay for now but I expect that to increase considerably in time. Apart from that I joined a golf club and get to play every Tuesday and Thursday in the ladies competition."

"Hey, that's fantastic, have you learned to hit the ball yet?"

"Very humorous, Brad – yes I have attained my handicap and I play off twenty four already. Lowered that by two shots already."

"Twenty four? That's a good start if you've only been playing a short time. You could be a champion in no time."

"What about you, Brad? What have you been up to?"

"Oh, I'm now involved in the development of a new residential estate just out of Cincinnati at Amelia. There's scope there for a couple of thousand houses so that will keep me occupied for years. Also in the new bridge over the Ohio River."

The couple kept on with general chat for several minutes until Lynette surprised Brad by deciding not to return to the meeting but to retire to her room instead.

"I suppose we had better go back now. I need to complete my delivery on the new bridge."

"Okay Brad please go ahead, but, I am not feeling the best so I think I will just head on up to my room. Feeling a little upset in the stomach, actually. I hope the prawns weren't off."

This was Lynette's way of avoiding having to point out who her fictitious brother was, as she suspected that Brad might want to talk to him.

"Oh, okay let me escort you to your room Lynette and if I can get you something from the drug store it is just down on the corner."

"Hey that will be great, just see me upstairs then perhaps some antacid powder please. That might do the trick."

Brad escorted Lynette to her room. She opened her door and slumped onto the bed.

"Look here is my key, so please get me something from the drug store and can you bring it back? Thank you Brad."

Brad went downstairs in the lift and entered the room to remove some documents from his briefcase, which he handed to another engineer he knew well.

"Hello Roger, look I have been caught up with a situation with a friend who has fallen violently ill after lunch so if I can't make it back in ten minutes can you just go through this and present my main points to the conference please?"

"See what I can do Brad – hope it's nothing too serious."

"They should be okay but if they need to go to the hospital I want to be there for them."

"Okay - I'll give it my best shot Brad."

"Thanks Roger, you're a champion."

Brad procured the antacid from the drug store and returned to Lynette's room. He wasn't about to give up a chance like this, with Lynette. He entered Lynette's room.

"Hey, how are you doing?"

"Oh, I have just relieved myself in the bathroom actually so I think that might have been the issue, so I am going to take a shower and be right back in ten, okay."

"Okay, well I might just duck back downstairs for a little while but I can return shortly to make sure you are okay. I'll lock the door as I go."

"Okay Brad, thank you."

Brad left and did lock the door but took the key with him. He delivered his address himself and returned to Lynette's room as she was coming out of the bathroom.

"Lynette, so how do you feel now?"

"Much better thanks Brad, but I think I might have a wee nap now."

Lynette lay on the bed.

"Reminds me of old times, Lynette. Must admit, I could use a wee nap too. Done a lot of traveling lately."

Lynette looked at Brad's eyes, then his chest, then his waistline, then his knees then his shoes, before returning her gaze back along the same path. Her manner of looking a man up and down was her way of extending an invitation. Brad didn't need much encouragement.

"So, I am sure they can do without me for the remainder of the conference if you don't mind me staying here with you, Lynette."

Lynette extended her arms to Brad, who quickly commenced removing his clothing. They took up their positions on the bed and stayed there for the rest of the day and into the night. After their first hour together and while Brad was in the bathroom, Lynette activated the minute pinhole camera which she had strategically placed near the television and recorder. She then had the evidence she needed for Phillipa.

The very next morning, Thursday, when Brad was in the bathroom again, she sent Phillipa a text to call her at eight o'clock, as she would feign that an urgent situation had arisen and she had to leave Philadelphia. She explained to Brad that she would need to leave as soon as possible that same morning and, using her cell phone, booked a flight to New York. When she left the hotel, she took the opportunity to call Phillipa.

San Francisco

Upon arrival at the San Francisco airport, Raymond hired a vehicle from Thrifty – a Toyota Lexus crossover, which also impressed Phillipa – then headed for the city.

"I have booked us into the Four Seasons Hotel in Market Street, Phillipa. It's nice and central to everything and as I said, separate rooms for you and me, okay."

"Oh, absolutely Raymond Brookes. I wouldn't have that any other way."

Within the back of her mind, Phillipa was experiencing a dilemma regarding how she would feel if her husband Brad did go with Lynette or, conversely, did not go with Lynette. She had ambivalent feelings about this, as a substantial change of life's direction was possibly confronting her. What would she do if her husband did, in fact, go with Lynette. She had been adamant that she would leave him but had no immediate contingency plans in place. With evidence from Lynette, she would confront him and ask him to leave the house and to sleep in that room at his office, before articulating her plans to move. She was also wondering what to do about moving to San Francisco if it did come to that. She might have to rent a very expensive place of abode until a portion of Brad's assets became available following a divorce. She was also developing a deep appreciation of the admirable character of this new man who had bobbed up into her life – Raymond Brookes. He was a good looking, quite sexy and sporting man too - and good golfer, was this Raymond Brookes. Phillipa pondered what her life would be like with Raymond. She had to admit to herself, that she was becoming particularly enamored with Raymond Brookes.

Raymond drove from the airport into San Francisco along route 101 to Van Nesse Avenue, turned into California Street then into Sansome Street to arrive at the Four Seasons Hotel. Raymond and Phillipa checked into their rooms then met downstairs to have a cappuccino and to plan their afternoon and possibly the next day also. Raymond had some maps at the ready.

"So the question is where do we start? Only have a few hours left today but all day tomorrow. Wherever it takes us we will stop somewhere tomorrow for a nice lunch, eh! What are you thinking about this afternoon Phillipa?"

"Oh, have to go across the Golden Gate Bridge Raymond, that's a must do, then head off up toward Santa Rosa and perhaps come back to the city via American Canyon and Richmond."

"Okay well I guess that is settled for now and this evening we can discuss what we do tomorrow."

Raymond and Phillipa set off from San Francisco across the Golden Gate bridge into Sausalito and took a drive through the small city for about twenty minutes before going on to San Rafael, stopping at Stinson Beach and Muir Beach along the way. Phillipa was impressed with numerous houses for sale in Sausalito but not either beach as a future place of abode. San Rafael was far more to her liking but they went on through Petaluma and Rohnert Park to Santa Rosa. Phillipa was not too impressed with Santa Rosa either, so they set sail back to San Francisco via highway 12 to Schellville, then south to American Valley and Richmond. They saw a lot of vineyards along the way, but really no place on the Santa Rosa Plain that they found too inspiring. Hopefully there would be some more inspiring areas to view the next day.

Upon arrival back at the Four Seasons Hotel, Phillipa and Raymond agreed to shower and meet downstairs in the restaurant for dinner, which they did. They ordered their dinner and sat talking about what they had seen during the day. For her entrée, Phillipa ordered a dozen oysters natural and Raymond ordered a dozen oysters Kilpatrick. For their main course Phillipa ordered creamy garlic prawns and Raymond ordered a fillet steak with roast vegetables. For dessert, Phillipa ordered a sherry trifle with ice cream and Raymond ordered a double banana split with ice cream. Then they ordered a cappuccino to finish off a lovely dinner. Whilst sitting there relaxing Phillipa started the discussion.

"I think that the areas to the south along the coast will be more to my liking. I am really keen to view the areas between Fairmont and Pedro Point. Last night I Googled homes for sale in the Pacifica area and there really are quite a lot for sale well below two million dollars so, I just might be in the market within that range before too long. Depends a lot on what Brad decides with his assets and pre-nuptial, I suppose."

"Hmm ... it might come down to that, yes – and maybe not. We should take a run down the Silicon Valley too, Phillipa – you know, the entire Santa Clara region - Sunnyvale, Palo Alto, Redwood down to San Jose."

"Do you think we will have time for all of that tomorrow, Raymond?"

"Oh, we certainly will if we make an early start."

Just then Phillipa's phone buzzed with a text message. It was from Lynette.

"Hello Phillipa, I hope you are doing well. I can send you the compromising photo of Brad that you need, whenever you wish.

Please let me know when. Also please call me at seven thirty in the morning as I want to feign an urgent situation has arisen to get away from Brad tomorrow, rather than Friday."

"So, an early start ... um ... what say eight o'clock?"

"Suits me! I am an early riser actually – can't sleep past six in the morning most days. You sure you'll be up by then?"

"I have two young girls, Raymond."

"Okay, enough said about that! Now, breakfast is available downstairs from six in the morning so perhaps we have an agreement that we just make our own way there depending on what time we arise. I have a saying you know, and that is 'never wake a sleeping person', so I will not disturb you, Phillipa, if I am up and about long before you. Though I might just wait there for you enjoying a cup of tea and reading the newspaper."

"Well I am looking forward to spending the day with you tomorrow very much, Raymond. But there is something I need to share with you right now. I have received a text from Lynette who can send me a photograph of herself with Brad. So I will ask her for that now if you don't mind ... as I urgently need to know, with certainty."

Phillipa sent her reply text.

"Thank you Lynette, please text me now, thank you."

The text with the image arrived about two minutes later. Phillipa opened the text and was shocked by what she saw. Her eyes lit up and her reaction was totally palpable to Raymond. She handed the cell phone to Raymond to view. There was a photograph of Lynette and Brad in the same bed, with Lynette dismounting Brad from what is generally known as the 'cowgirl' position, clearly displaying his face wearing a substantial smile. Upon viewing this, Phillipa knew that her marriage to Brad was over, as she had already pledged to herself. Raymond shook his head as if in disbelief – though he did not disbelieve. It was essentially what he had expected to see. Phillipa, too, was almost certain that her husband would succumb to the very beautiful Lynette – and he had. She had experienced some feelings of ambivalence over testing her husband again but now also felt quite some relief, knowing her suspicions had been vindicated and that she could now move on.

"Phillipa, what can I say? You did expect that this would probably happen again as it did before – you know that."

"Yes, I know Raymond – perhaps now knowing that it is true rather than being a suspicion has me in shock at the moment. If you don't mind, I need to retire to my room."

"Probably the best thing to do - we have a big day ahead of us tomorrow. Before we do, I can give you an update now on my line of enquiry through my investigator."

"You can?"

"Yes! You recall how I told you on the flight that I had Eagle Eye send a man to the Ritz-Carlton to see if your Brad was with a woman."

"Yes, of course but, I had forgotten that till now. So what type of update?"

"Their man, Sam, sent these photo's to his manager, of Brad in the lobby of the hotel."

Raymond opened his phone and showed Phillipa a photograph. She gasped!

"Oh, it's Roberta – so she did go to Philadelphia with Brad."

"Yes, but it seems she arrived there much later so probably took a different flight and she left the next morning."

"Oh my God, so that would have been so as to not arouse suspicion back at the business."

"Probably! I haven't shown you this till now because I wanted to see if your arrangement with Lynette came to anything but I also wanted to allay any compunction you might have had about what you had arranged with Lynette and to vindicate you testing your Brad this way."

"So in this one trip he has been with Roberta and Lynette. Fuck me!"

"Well I am actually pleased for you, Phillipa, that you now know the truth about your husband. He's a right cad, I'd say!"

"Yes and you know I do feel a sense of relief now, Raymond, knowing that my suspicions have been justified. It all makes sense now, so many trips away these last two years. He's financial enough to do that and being the boss, who's going to question him?"

"Exactly! That Lynette might have been his first slip up two years ago but he's probably been highly active with this Roberta for quite some time since then."

"Thank you for doing that for me Raymond, for covering that base. There was no absolute guarantee that Lynette would come through with the goods. Thank you!"

Phillipa and Raymond took the lift upstairs and arrived at Raymond's room first. He stopped at the door and looked at Phillipa to say goodnight.

"Raymond, can I talk to you for a minute please?"

"Sure! Come in."

They entered Raymond's room and Raymond offered to make Phillipa a drink of hot chocolate, then they sat together at the table provided.

"Now I want to make this clear, Raymond, that I am not suggesting that anything happen between us tonight, believe me, but I just feel that I need company, you know, just someone to hold me, if you don't mind. I haven't felt close to my husband, Brad, for two years now and what I have just seen makes me feel just so isolated. I hope you can understand."

“Well, Phillipa, you are quite welcome to sleep here in my room in the queen sized bed and I will sleep in the single bed there, okay?”

“No, look, I feel I do know you well enough as a man of morals and principle to believe that if we sleep together in the queen bed, you will not try to touch me up, but right now I would like to feel your arms around me. That is what I need right now, Raymond. Just to have a friend close to me to provide me with solace, but no hanky-panky, Raymond. I know you have that in you, am I right?”

Raymond couldn’t believe his good fortune, even though he was firmly intent on adhering to Phillipa’s stipulation of nothing to happen between them. But just to be so close to the beautiful Phillipa in that way was something he felt so totally honored about.

“Phillipa, I give you my utmost promise that if you seek solace with me tonight, I will respect that, okay. Might feel a little strange climbing into the same bed together though so ...”

“Well you go to bed first and I will go to the bathroom for a few minutes, okay – I need to undo my hair and remove some makeup.”

“Okay if you insist, I will be in the bed when you come out of the bathroom.”

“Thank you Raymond and please hug me if you don’t mind. It’s something I haven’t experienced for a long time. Now I will be just five minutes, okay.”

Phillipa went to the bathroom and Raymond dimmed the lights and climbed into bed wearing just a tee-shirt and his sports shorts. He was really excited to be able to share his bed with Phillipa even though he knew there would be love and affection between them. About five minutes later, Phillipa emerged from the bathroom wearing her nightgown and approached the bed. That was such a moment of magic for Raymond, that this beautiful woman he had met just months previously and who had blown him away with such deep emotion was wading toward him in his bed. Phillipa folded the blankets back and slumbered into bed, looked at Raymond who had extended his right arm to hold her. Phillipa sidled over to Raymond who gave her a gentle grandmother-type kiss atop of her head.

"Thank you Raymond – I do need to be close to you tonight and I do know I can trust you. Thank you, I will be asleep very soon now."

"Goodnight Phillipa."

They both fell asleep, to awaken at seven in the morning.

Pacifica

Raymond awoke before Phillipa, at seven o'clock, after experiencing some amazing dreams. He was quite surprised to realize Phillipa was lying next to him as he had no recollection of waking during the night. He gazed at the beautiful Phillipa's face for several minutes as she was sound asleep. Raymond couldn't help thinking to himself that to wake up next to this woman every morning for the rest of his life would be absolute bliss. But what chance of that? After almost ten minutes Raymond decided to arise and to boil the kettle for a cup of tea. He was totally fastidious about tea making and would pour boiling water into the cups for a minute to ensure the cups retained their heat – before pouring the tea. He was chuffed that, like himself, Phillipa drank tea in the mornings rather than coffee. Surely a good omen?

Raymond made himself a cup of tea, then a second cup, before Phillipa started to awaken. She opened her eyes and looked at Raymond.

"Who are you?"

"Ha, ha – very funny! Welcome to the world, hopefully a new world too! I'll start you off with a cup of tea or two."

"Oh thank you Raymond, my goodness I slept such a deep sleep I can't believe it. What is the time?"

"Just ticked over eight o'clock so, yes, you have slept for ten hours, Phillipa."

"Yes and thank you Raymond for comforting me last night. You can't understand how much that meant to me after seeing my husband in bed with that woman. I think that perhaps, psychologically, I must have substituted you, a good man, for that bad man – my own husband."

"Must admit I think we both fell asleep very quickly. I have no recollection of lying there awake, so, I suppose it just felt so natural to me. Now, here is your cup of tea, Phillipa."

"Thank you, Raymond! Hmm ... that is the very best cup of tea I have ever had, Raymond. How did you do that?"

"I brought my own packet of tea leaves, actually. I don't trust the crap these hotels provide – you know, those cheap shitty tea bags you normally get."

"So which brand of tea is this one, Raymond?"

"Lipton – it's Lipton red – and if I can't find Lipton red in a supermarket I will buy Dilmah."

"Hmm ... I've been drinking English Breakfast all this time. I'll have to swing in your direction when it comes to tea."

"Would you like a second cup?"

"Oh absolutely, Raymond, please."

"I thought you might! I always have two cups, sometimes a third if I get caught up doing something on the computer for an hour or more. So we'll head downstairs for breakfast after we shower then!"

"Sounds like a plan!"

"You can shower first, okay!"

"Uh huh!"

Phillipa and Raymond showered and dressed for their day out looking at areas around San Francisco, then went down to the restaurant for breakfast.

"Always start with an orange juice, then cereal, then ... hmmm ... bacon and eggs on toast for me. How about you, Phillipa?"

"I'll go the blackcurrant juice and cereal but poached eggs on toast for me. Then coffee!"

"Ah yes – the coffee for me too!"

They helped themselves to their juice and cereal and placed their main order with the kitchen.

"Should be on the road just after nine so lunch about one in the afternoon, eh?"

"Sounds good!"

Phillipa and Raymond finished their breakfast and set off at fifteen minutes past nine o'clock.

"Okay, so today we will head on down toward San Jose to check the Santa Clara region, but we will go via the coastal road as far as Half Moon Bay. Then we can take San Mateo Road toward San Francisco Bay. I assume you would want views of the Bay so we will look through San Mateo, Redwood, Palo Alto, Menlo Park and then go via the eastern side of the Bay through Fremont, Phillipa."

Raymond took 19th Avenue from the city center, turned into Sloat Boulevarde then turned southwards to take Skyline Boulevarde past the golf courses at Lakeshore and on to Westlake. Raymond then turned off the main road and took Skyline Drive through Westlake to Fairmont.

"Would be so nice to be living by the ocean like these people are, don't you think."

"Could do a lot worse, that's for sure!"

Phillipa then tinkered with her phone and the screen in the center console, connected Bluetooth and before Raymond could realize it, Scott McKenzie's 'San Francisco' was blaring over the audio system, which sent Raymond into raucous laughter. Now that really put them in the groove.

"Yay, San Francisco - what a great place to live!"

Phillipa played Scott Mckenzie's song repeatedly as they drove through Fairmont, Pacifica, Rockaway Beach to Shelter

Cove. There, both Phillipa and Raymond were enamored by the beautiful oceanic ambience to this entire area.

"What a beautiful area."

"Certainly is!"

"We should buy a Beetle, Raymond."

"A Beetle?"

"Yes – you know a Vee-dub - about a nineteen sixty eight model will do – and paint lots of flowers on it! Then we can drive around San Francisco listening to Scott McKenzie."

"Ha, ha, ha, ha, ha – that's quite a sense of humor you have there, Phillipa but, yes, a rather good idea that, actually ... ah ... might get kicked out of town though, in two thousand and twenty four. There's probably still quite a few old Vee-dubs lingering around here but they'd be somebody's nostalgia so you might have to pay a price. They could have lost all that love here by now. Makes you wonder what happened to all those people though, eh? Most of them would be well and truly retired by now. Somebody should do a documentary on that."

"Yes, but were they really sincere about the love aspect? I mean, it's one thing to grow long hair and place a colored band around one's head and stick some flowers in it and don a colored kaftan and oversized sunnies and cloth bangles, then lay in some long grass and think of ones-self as being hip, as they all seemed to do, but was it a genuine expression of their attitude towards other people, Raymond? I mean, when it comes down to the Golden Rule of life, were they essentially givers or takers?"

"Who knows ... shouldn't be too judgemental now, should we? That's quite an imaginative image you have portrayed of them, Phillipa. Obviously the sex was free and easy flowing with the advent of contraception but, as you say, were they genuinely good towards each other – and other people too?"

"I suppose that's right, Raymond - we shouldn't judge people without some knowledge of them. But I have to tell you, Raymond, that when we were in Santa Rosa, I checked Wikipedia and the Sonoma County has a population of about half a million people and that includes about five thousand homeless. So there could still be some old leftover hippies hanging around here. I wonder how many people got caught up in all that euphoria and came here to San Francisco from all over the States. There were probably tens of thousands of them, especially when Scott McKenzie's song was at the top of the charts. They would have come here from New York and Miami and Texas and Chicago ... and then found themselves parking cars and pumping gas, as the song goes - if they could find a job at all."

"Sounds like you might be just a little cynical about those hippies, Phillipa?"

"No, maybe not cynical - I might be a little envious, that's all. But, once all that hippie euphoria was over and people got older and returned to their normal life, maybe having gone back to where they came from and working in their usual job, did all that love expression have a lasting impact upon them?"

"Well, it may be inappropriate to generalize but, I suppose there's no doubt the long-term effect would have been quite diverse. Hopefully most of those people would have been far more loving and altruistic toward other people for the rest of their lives, but at the other end of the continuum, perhaps a minority would have simply reverted to being quite egotistical and mean, nasty and totally selfish toward other people, Phillipa."

"Yes – a positive effect on the majority, Raymond – and no effect on the small minority who went on to live their lives as the bastards they were, eh? They were just there because they got caught up in the hippie euphoria and to be hip and to have a good time. I like that summation of yours, Raymond!"

"Well you are the psychologist here. Perhaps some of your fellow psyches have conducted some research on the long-term outcomes of the hippie movement, Phillipa. You could look into that. Somebody might have completed their doctorate dissertation on the same?"

"Oh ... and then after the hippies had their day, there were those 'Jesus people' too – remember them?"

"That was a bit before our time Phillipa - early seventies I think. But yes, I do recall seeing a documentary about the 'Jesus Revolution'."

"And what's your take on that, Raymond?"

"Well, of course, Jesus added the love aspect to the Golden Rule – love your neighbor as you love yourself. So I hope all those hippies and 'Jesus people' remained as good people! To me, that's the litmus test of life."

"The litmus test of life?"

"Yep!"

"Elucidate for me, Raymond!"

"Goes back to my upbringing within the Catholic Church and being fed that stuff about Adam and Eve in the Garden of Eden – which, of course, is entirely metaphorical and means that we all did something to sever our relationship with Almighty God. Hence, I believe we are all here to prove our worth to be re-united again with Almighty God in the afterlife. To love other people and to give rather than take. So the Jesus people were probably more likely than the hippies to retain that all-important attitude to life. As for the hippies, a positive effect on most, probably! But I just don't know."

"I'd say they probably did – change for the better, I mean! We might bump into a couple of leftover hippies around here, Raymond, so we should ask them."

"Ha, ha, ha, ha! Very good idea that, Phillipa. But don't forget to enquire into any research your peers have completed."

Raymond looked at Phillipa with a sincere smile. She was starting to open up quite a bit and he was gaining some precious insights into her character – and she into his. They continued south from Shelter Cove through Moss Beach and El Granada to Half Moon Bay. As it was getting on toward midday, they stopped for a tea break at Granola's Coffee House.

"Looks like a cosy spot!"

It was a lot cosier when they got inside.

"Wow, yes, I could definitely make this my regular coffee house, Raymond. What a great little hideaway this will be."

Phillipa was even more impressed with the menu. A young table attendant approached the table.

"Good morning, may I take your order please."

"Hmm ... I'll have a turkey and avocado bagel with spinach please and a macchiato latte with soy milk! What about you, Raymond?"

"Was hoping to get a steak pie with chips and gravy. Was in Australia a few years back and it became my favourite lunch on the hop."

"Ah ... no, we don't have that on our menu I'm sorry."

"Might settle for a toasted ham, cheese, tomato and onion sandwich then, please - and a sixteen ounce tea."

"Sounds good!"

"What a quaint little spot this is – very comfortable! They would probably light that fire in winter."

"Sure is a nice, cosy spot all right!"

They stayed for about half an hour to enjoy their morning tea then decided to head for the bay area. When they got back into the car and before they hit the road, Phillipa played a Youtube video of Scott McKenzie's song on the center console showing people dancing and leaping about, riding trucks and buses adorned with colors and flowers and playing guitars.

"They look to be having so much fun don't they Raymond?"

"Sure do! They must have come from everywhere for the fun, the friendship, the singing and dancing - and the drugs and the free sex. Though they were protesting the Vietnam war also."

"Well it was a time of liberation from some very staid social norms wasn't it! I mean, just a few years earlier these people would have been under a very powerful influence from ultra-conservative religious persuasions."

"Yes, from hellfire and brimstone preachers to Lucy in the sky with diamonds - LSD. Quite a social transition, that! Okay, San Mateo here we come."

Raymond started the car then turned into the San Mateo Road and headed toward the Bay area. Phillipa used her iPad to check the house prices at a real estate website.

"Would probably need between two and three million to buy a decent house on the coastal strip – even more with ocean views. Saw two on San Benito Street and one on El Granada Boulevarde between two and three million – and one on Spyglass Lane."

"So once you separate from Brad, your share of the estate would max out at about half a million, you think."

"Yes - but doing what I have been doing I have more than that in a bank account that my Brad knows nothing about."

"Really?"

"Raymond, I have been able to derive an income close to half a million dollars in the last two years doing what I do, okay!"

"Sounds like quite a large number of liaisons you've notched up there, Phillipa."

"Yes, but I can revert to working as a psychologist again for about one hundred thousand a year. I have been making three times as much doing what I do – and that is tax-paid income I am talking about. So for the sake of my future and the future of my two girls, I have been taking the shortcut to grandma's house, Raymond. I am fortunate that I am now in a position where I could procure a mortgage to buy a home in this area."

"If you find that necessary!"

"What do you mean?"

"Well ... you just never know what the future holds."

Raymond started the vehicle and drove away from the café.

"There's a cemetery ahead on top of the hills, Raymond, only about four or five miles away and before we reach a reservoir."

"Well, could take a peek ... you might have to get to know this area quite a lot better, Phillipa. Could be some very good picnic spots around here."

"Do you like picnics, Raymond?"

"I find picnics to be very peaceful – a chance to get away from the grind of life, so it's a bit like ... time out!"

"Yes, I like to go for a picnic – especially to a place I have never been before - yes, peaceful, I like that! Spread out a blanket, open a picnic basket, enjoy some sandwiches and a coffee."

"Nup! Tea for me! Oh - and some raspberry cookies."

Phillipa glanced at Raymond and smiled.

"Certainly is a beautiful forest here, Raymond. In fact, there's a redwood forest just south of here on route thirty five."

After leaving Half Moon Bay and taking the San Mateo Road, they came upon an elderly couple by the roadside who seemed to be in a spot of bother with their vehicle.

"So, here is the entrance to the cemetery though ... ah ... I wonder if that couple there need some assistance."

"Hmm ... looks like it eh?"

"Hello there! Do you need some help?"

"You wouldn't believe it, ran over something that gave us two punctured tires. Got one spare which I've changed but need to take this one in to have it repaired. Would be most grateful for a lift to San Mateo. There's a tire shop there that we know of."

'Certainly, be pleased to help you out, we'll chuck the tires into the boot. Might as well get both repaired you never know what might happen. I am Raymond and this is my friend, Phillipa."

"Thank you Raymond, I am Keith and my wife Jenny."

"Hello!"

They put the tires into the boot and set off.

"So are you kind folks from around here?"

"No, I am from Cincinnati and Raymond from San Diego, but ... we are thinking of moving to this area so, scoping the joint, as they say. What about you?"

"Yeah, we are from San Carlos just a few miles south of San Mateo, been there for the last fifty years and probably die there too."

"Were you raised there, Keith?"

"No, neither of us were raised there. I was raised in Florida and Jenny in Texas but we both came here in nineteen sixty seven and we met by sitting on back of a truck to attend a music festival, in what was known back then as the 'Summer of Love'.

"Ah ... so a pair of retired hippies are we, then?"

"Very much so! About a hundred thousand young people converged on San Francisco that year from all over ..."

"A hundred thousand! That many?"

"Yes and it did have quite a profound impact on our lives, I must state. Jenny and I fell in love and decided to move to the bay area back then. I had finished college and Jen was in her honor's year and we were able to rent a house at Kensington just north of UCLA at Berkeley. We both had work so we were very fortunate that things fell into place for us, but what we experienced through the hippie movement at that time still has us feeling the love for each other and for humanity, I must say."

"And your honor's degree Jen, what field of study were you into then?"

"I completed a Bachelor of Arts degree majoring in sociology then my post-grad honor's degree with a thesis in religious fundamentalism, my master's was a content analysis of religious bigotry as espoused by fundamentalist Protestant televangelists and then I went on to complete my dissertation pertaining to an analysis of the so-called gift of tongues within Christian Pentecostalism."

"Hmm! That would have been interesting! I've heard about that phenomenon from some friends who got into that back in my college years about fifteen years ago."

"What did you study, Phillipa?"

"I am a psychologist Jen, though not working in my field at the moment but, it looks like I could be returning to my profession sometime soon, especially if I move from Cincinnati to San Francisco."

"And did you study a specialty area?"

"Yes, I completed an honor's degree and was involved in counselling foster children in my work for a few years before I had my two girls in my mid-twenties."

"Well, should be plenty of work for you in the bay area with so many families disintegrating because of the drug problem. Once the zombie drug gets hold of them there's no going back. They're virtually brain dead!"

"Xylazine! Yeah, a new level of destruction, that one!"

"What line of work are you doing now?"

"I'm a hooker!"

"Ha, ha, ha, ha ... go on, get away!"

"She's for real! Phillipa has been providing a very important service to other women to test the loyalty, or otherwise, of their male partners, Jen."

"Hey, interesting, way to go even, I like that idea, tell me more!"

"Well, it's a long, long story but, in short, I need to split from my very disloyal husband who has been fucking around and in the last two years I have made more money for the sake of my own security by being a hooker than I would have made in my profession. So I am now in a position whereby I can go my own way and provide my two girls with a worthy future."

"I like that approach Phillipa but, what does your man here have to say about that?"

"Oh, we are not together Keith as a couple, no, we are just friends who met recently and I am assisting Phillipa to move away from Cincinnati to the bay area. But we did meet because my wife Natalie got Phillipa to put me to the loyalty test."

"And?"

"He passed with flying colors, Jen – turned me down, he did! As much as I was disappointed, Raymond here is one in ten, I can tell you."

"Disappointed? You haven't mentioned that to me before."

"Oh, no, I ... ah ... haven't have I?"

“Hey you two guys are so very interesting and we will be at the tire shop soon so ... ah ... would you like to join us at our barbeque at our house tonight? We have some fellow ex-hippie friends coming over at six o’clock – a professional couple named Bill and Grace and Wayne and Sandra – who you would probably enjoy talking to very much, so just bring some drinks and we are providing all the food, okay?”

“Sounds great, yeah, just give Raymond your address and I do want to pick Jen’s brains about that dissertation you mentioned because I have some looney friends from way back who believe they pray to God in tongues.”

“Here, I have written our address on the reverse of my business card for you Raymond, now if you turn right here at South El Camino there’s a tire shop just down the road there on the left.”

They arrived at the tire shop and offloaded the tires to the workshop.

“Would you like us to stick around to take you back?”

“Thanks very much, but, you have been so good to us already and the workshop’s boy will take us back to our vehicle. It’s been great to meet you both and we hope to see you tonight.”

“Oh, don’t worry, I’ll make sure Raymond agrees to being there so, see you then. Bye Jenny!”

“Well, what an interesting couple they are, Raymond. I hope you don’t mind to me committing us to the barbeque but ...”

“Hey, no problem, looking forward to that enormously already! So from here we will back-peddle a little to San Mateo before we head on down to Palo Alto.”

The Bay Area

From the tire shop Raymond took route eighty two back to San Mateo then to Foster City before heading south on route one zero one toward Palo Alto, Santa Clara and into San Jose.

"So this is where it's all at – the high tech industries of the Silicon Valley, Phillipa."

"Yes, well, all of that area back there is rather too industrial for me to want to live there, don't you think?"

"Agreed! Not a patch on Half Moon Bay eh? I'd say the Pacific Ocean area is still looking pretty good for you."

"Love that coffee house, Raymond! Might make that my pad of respite, reflection and contemplation. Would be a great area to raise my girls and just look at that golf course."

"Okay so we head north and next stop could be Fremont."

"Says here the largest employer in Fremont is the Tesla factory with more than twenty two thousand workers. That's huge! Is also a 'tree city' Raymond."

"Yep, lots of trees that's for sure. Still very industrial, though eh? The housing looks to be very mid-market so you would probably get a decent house here for half a million but not our style."

"No and from what I can see on the iPad this entire east coast of the bay is very industrial. That's what you would expect from such a large city though, isn't it?"

"Yes, this next town of Oakland is a major port, one of the largest in California. A lot of similar housing too but more upmarket to the east there where the ranges are. Probably have a view of the bay from up there, Raymond. I did notice a beautiful house for sale in Spyglass Lane when we took the coastal route. Says here it is two point six million though."

"So we'll skip looking at the ranges to the east of Oakmont here and head towards Berkeley then Richmond before we head back to the hotel. We might need a catnap before we prepare for our outing tonight."

"Good idea, Raymond."

Raymond exited the Richmond Parkway at Tara Hills to head south again via the San Francisco-Oakland Bay Bridge to the big city. They arrived back at hotel at three o'clock and had a ninety minute nap to be refreshed for the barbeque. They had no idea of the impact the people they would meet would have on their lives.

The Barbeque

Once they had showered and changed their clothes, Phillipa and Raymond set off for San Carlos to be at Keith and Jenny's house for six o'clock. When they arrived for the barbeque, Jenny introduced Phillipa and Raymond to Bill and Grace and to Wayne and Sandra.

"Hey, so pleased to meet you guys! We've been told some of you were hippies back then also and that's how you met Keith and Jenny."

Grace spoke up.

"Yes we met, myself and Bill that is, at the Woodstock concert in August 1969 when we were both twenty two years of age and we've been together ever since. Strangely, we were on the same plane flying from San Francisco to New York but we didn't meet until day three of the concert. We were also both at the Monterey festival in June 1967 but we never met there either."

"What about you, Wayne and Sandra?"

"Strangely, same thing – we were both on the plane to new York in August 1969 but didn't meet until we were on the same flight back to San Francisco. Actually it was after we got off the plane and Sandra asked me which way I was headed. She was scoping for a free ride home to Rockridge and I had a lift from a mate back to Walnut Creek so Sandra's home was on the way. Had a bit of a chat on the way home, I asked for a date and here we are now, still married and loyal to each other fifty years later."

Bill took a bottle of beer from his cooler and handed Grace a can of Jack Daniels with cola. Raymond handed Phillipa a can of southern comfort and lemonade and helped himself to beer. Wayne fetched his beer and Sandra's can of Jacks. Keith and Jenny were placing steak, sausages and onions onto the barbeque which wouldn't be ready for a half hour and so gave them all time to chat. Phillipa and Raymond were keen to pick their brains about the hippie movement.

"So were you guys into the flower power culture in San Francisco at the time?"

Grace spoke up.

"Oh sure! We are your classical hippies from back then, it was magical, it was great, there were so many outdoor concerts and tens of thousands of people coming in to stay for a while. We were renting separate houses with others and we had a few people stay over for different concerts that were going and, you know, they are all still lifelong friends of ours and we still meet up occasionally. In fact, just three weeks ago we bumped into a couple at their local church when we were down in San Jose."

"Which church was that if you don't mind me asking?"

"That was the Anglican Church, Phillipa. We don't go to church very often but we knew that Brenda and Gavin quite often go to their local church and we were heading down that way for a picnic at a place called Twin Creeks so we popped in and there they were. We hadn't seen them for about eighteen months so it was great to catch up."

"You saw Brenda and Gavin, Grace! How are they?"

"Same as Jen! Always happy and pleased to catch up. Had a coffee with them in the church tearooms."

"So when did you complete high school, if that's not a rude question?"

“Oh, no there’s nothing rude about that. I was born in February of forty seven and Bill here in December of forty six, so we are just a few months older than Keith and Jenny. Wayne born in October forty six and Sandra in March forty seven. We were here in San Francisco just at the right time. It was a real buzz, I can tell you, something I wish every young person could experience in their life. Best years of our lives, for sure.”

Keith brought out some drinks for Jenny and himself and Jenny prepared some salads and rolls and the crockery and cutlery. Everything was set for a great evening.

“So tell us about your experiences at Monterey and Woodstock.”

“Oh Monterey featured The Doors who had just released their first album which included Light My Fire so ... ah ... was great to meet Jim Morrison in person as we did, just four years before his demise.”

“You met Jim Morrison?”

“Yeah, their album went to number one here in the States after it was released in the beginning of 1967 but they weren’t really a super group yet, so Jim and the boys mixed it a little with the crowd.”

“Yes they did really well with the girls, that’s for sure – hence the mixing, I suppose.”

“Can’t blame them though, eh?”

“Well there was adequate access to contraception so, yeah, it was a summer of love to be sure. Then at Woodstock we managed to see Creedence Clearwater Revival who had just released their third album ‘Green River’, so they were absolutely red hot at Woodstock.”

“Hey, I’m feeling envious already, you guys must do quite some reminiscing about those years.”

"Oh, absolutely and every few years somebody organizes a reunion somewhere in California and hundreds of people attend."

"They still making love?"

"Ha, ha, ha ... yeah hopefully, Phillipa, with their partners and nobody else, though a lot of them are single again so there'd be quite some loving going on there."

"Half their luck! So, Raymond and myself were discussing earlier today whether these overt expressions of love and peace, etcetera, were able to survive the test of time or whether people just, say, tripped out on a bit of a fad then allowed those worthy sentiments to attenuate somewhat in their lives. I mean, it stands to reason, doesn't it, that with so many hundreds of thousands of people involved in the hippie movement, after the euphoria wore off many of them would have returned to what we might refer to a 'normal life' and become real bastards! I mean, look at all the things that people do that are essentially, bad. People steal, they perpetrate acts of violence against others, they traffic illicit drugs, they scam others on the internet, they evade their due taxes, they rape, they murder. So I have to ask where does your bog stock hippie locate in all of that?"

"Now you're getting into Bill's area of expertise, Phillipa."

"Oh! How so?"

Attention turned to Bill so Grace put them in the loop.

"My Bill was so very good to me when I was undertaking my post-graduate studies that he worked on a full-time basis in a federal department to keep our heads above water, then after I completed my PhD in middle east studies, I was able to return the favor for Bill to return to study and he did. He completed his own dissertation in philosophy and ethics then assumed a role lecturing at UCLA in Berkeley where he worked for thirty years."

"Yes, life was very good to both of us I must admit, with Grace lecturing in middle east history and myself in philosophy and ethics."

"Wow, you good people were certainly up there in the academic world with Jenny's history in sociology so, ... ah ... what is your history Keith?"

"Oh, don't worry, my Keith was up there too – he completed his studies in international law and did a lot of work with the United Nations."

Wayne spoke up.

"I'm outdone! I am simply an auto body repairer and Sandra is my office manager."

"Now don't understate your own significance Wayne, you are a business proprietor and you have how many employees in your little business empire now?"

"Forty two!"

"That many – you only had thirty five last time we spoke."

"Yes but the EV's are here now so we have had to diversify quite a bit and put on a couple of top end sparkies to make sure nothing blows up."

"Ha, ha, ha, ha."

"There's some high voltage involved there you know."

"And what about you, Raymond?"

"Well I'm outdone too - I'm only an accountant!"

"Ha, ha, ha, ha ... don't denigrate yourself Raymond, we have all needed you many times, don't worry! We are absolutely no good with figures and I can speak on behalf of all my fellow lawyers on that."

"Yes, very glad for you to do my tax returns too, ha, ha!"

“Well I have to state, everybody, that after we have indulged in this very beautiful food that is now ready, we might have quite a bit to discuss before we call it a night.”

“Hear, hear!”

“I’ll drink to that!”

“You’ll drink to anything, Bill!”

“Nothing wrong with a drop, I always say!”

Phillipa was keen to return to the discussion about their hippie friends and whether the love was a fad or ongoing.

“So you mentioned that you do get together occasionally with a lot of friends from way back, so tell us about that and are they still together and in love?”

Sandra spoke up.

“We have a re-union about every two or three years somewhere in California. We mentioned Brenda and Gavin already and they became involved in the Jesus revolution sometime about nineteen seventy one when that was all happening and a lot of young people from different churches in the bay area took part in that too. So when we have a gathering there will be them and Richard and Leonie, John and Lynn, Tony and Amelia, Malcolm and Stehanie, Annette and Jacob, Peta and Ross ...”

“Wow, that many?”

“Not finished yet ... Patrick and Marie, Michael and Suzie, Phillip and Karen, Belinda and Brandon, Penny and Martin, Barbara and Andrew, Jimmy and Emily, Troy and Melanie, Colin and Mary, Nicole and Chris, Tamara and Dennis and many more too.”

“Yes, they are just the couples who always turn up and are still together but there are so many more who turn up occasionally and some others who are no longer together, but most are still together.”

Keith spoke up.

"And most of those you mentioned Sandra did take part in the Jesus Revolution through their church so I suppose it might be testimony to, not only the love we all experienced through the hippie movement, but the love that was reinforced through the Jesus movement."

"So it sounds as though you good people do believe that, for most people, the expressions of love you experienced through the hippie movement were genuine and had a lasting impact."

"Yes, I would agree with that Phillipa – it was a time when we questioned the fundamental values that were being touted at the time, society was extremely bent on consumerism, the war in Vietnam was grating on people ..."

"Oh, that was so shocking, the image of that poor naked girl screaming and running away from flames and surrounded by soldiers, oh I still shudder to think of that."

"Yes, me too Jenny."

"Dinner's ready!

Good or Bad?

They all helped themselves to a delicious barbeque dinner and sat at a long table together, where some of the chat continued.

"So Jenny's post-graduate studies pertain to religious beliefs, Bill's to philosophy and ethics and Grace's to history, Keith's to international law, Phillipa being a psychologist, I mean, wow, what an eclectic of knowledge we have here then. Makes me, the accountant, feel a bit ordinary I must admit!"

"Ha, ha, ha ... you might be the only sane person here, Raymond. The rest of us have got our heads all screwed up with reality. I mean, take this question for example, Raymond."

"Here we go – I warned you about Bill with his questions of ethics. He's been contemplating something for us for tonight. Now wait for it! What is it this time, Bill?"

They all laughed at this warning from Jenny. So Bill did not disappoint and he started.

"Are we good or are we bad?"

There were several seconds of silence before Phillipa asked for clarification.

"Ah ... what do you mean, Bill ... do you assume we are either good or bad and is there no in between? Some of us might be good most of the time and bad occasionally, so elucidate!"

"Well, Phillipa, consider this hypothetical situation that would have actually been manifest many times already in different places and at different times for different people – and I am going to give you two scenario. Scenario one, you are riding your pushbike along a road and you notice a wallet on the ground, so you pick up the wallet and find there is one thousand dollars in that wallet – along with identity of the owner. What would you do? Hand it back to the owner or keep the money? Now before you answer that in your own mind consider scenario two – you find a wallet that contains thirty thousand dollars with the owner's identity, rather than one thousand dollars. What would you do? Is this the litmus test of life? Are you a good person or are you a bad person?"

"Hmm ... good question there, Bill, I knew you wouldn't disappoint."

"Thank you, Jenny! Now do we all have our own answers within our minds?"

"Yes!"

"Yes!"

"Yes!"

"Yeah, me too!"

"So is anybody willing to share?"

"Well I know that I would return all of the money because I am a Catholic man and I have my ticket to heaven and I am not going to jeopardize that for all the money in the world!"

"Well stated, Raymond! I am really so pleased that you have said that and I hope that everybody felt the same way, that we would all return the money."

Everybody in attendance nodded in concurrence with Raymond's declaration that they would return the money in both situations. Phillipa spoke up.

"So is there no in between?"

"Yes, Phillipa, of course there is. I would postulate that every drug runner on this planet would keep all of the money and that every Catholic nun or priest, being people of rectitude, would be predisposed to renounce their human nature and to return all of the money. But different people, for their own different reasons, would return the lesser amount and keep the greater amount - or vice versa."

"Well, all of us are fairly well to do so it is understandable that a homeless person, for example, would keep all of that money, due to their extenuating circumstances?"

"It would be far easier for a homeless person to rationalize that, yes, Jenny. But some homeless people would return all of the money and some would keep the lesser and return the greater amount and vice versa for their own reasons."

"So, just to clarify, would that make the homeless person culpable and, therefore, a bad person in your view, Bill?"

"That is a matter for judgement, Jen, but I think ultimately, the Golden Rule cuts in here as it would everywhere and in all situations – do unto others as you would want to be done by! We are all conversant with that. It's the ethics of reciprocity! So let's not delude ourselves - there is nothing inadvertent about a decision to take from another person. To take something, anything, from another person is to incriminate ones-self in the eyes of the Almighty."

"That's one nasty question you came up with there, Bill and, speaking as a lawyer, I am aware of many exact situations that have been before the courts in this country."

"Well I must admit, it did make me think for a moment whether I would hand back either, because some people would think they might need the money more than the owner might – without even knowing the owner's circumstances. I mean, I'm going to split from my husband and still don't have the security I need to fend completely for myself and I need to provide security for my girls but, I did only take a second or two to make my decision that, yes, I would hand all of the money back."

"I can help you with your security, Phillipa."

Phillipa looked inquisitively at Raymond, who had a gentle smile on his face, but Bill wasn't quick on the uptake.

"Very pleased you mentioned that Phillipa, because that is the exact quandary that would face many people. But as my Grace has pointed out to me, life can become so very much more complex. Some people are placed into situations where their quandary is virtually incomprehensible. She put one to me just the other day."

Everybody looked at Grace.

"Well as you know I have lectured in middle east history so I did put the question to my Bill that Mr. Netanyahu would be facing a quandary every day while the war has been raging, about balancing the need to protect Israel and to bring the terrorists under control. The terrorists perpetrated horrific atrocities when they murdered more than twelve hundred people, but then fled and hid among women and children and in hospitals and schools and in residential areas, knowing that Israel would respond in the way that it has."

"So apart from considerations pertaining to who, exactly, is responsible for the demise of thousands of innocent Palestinian people, just how far should Mr. Netanyahu go in inflicting what the world's militaries refer to as 'collateral damage'? Most of the world's militaries have what they refer to as a 'CDI' - a 'collateral damage index', being an acceptable level of innocent lives that are expended for a greater cause. So I'm afraid that my question is one that I, myself, cannot contemplate an answer to. My reason being, that the terrorists have vowed to repeat the same atrocity in the future."

Bill responded.

"So that is what I mean when I say that I find such considerations to be incomprehensible. Does the Israeli Prime Minister destroy a house where he knows there is a terrorist with a child? But then what of a house with a terrorist with three children, or five children, or a house with three terrorists and fifteen children?"

"What do you think, Bill?"

"I have to be honest, Raymond. On that, I just do not know what to think."

Then Jenny spoke up.

"Well, what I can say from the sociological perspective is that it is such shame on humanity that we draw so many boundaries between us based on race or creed or ethnicity or religious persuasion, when we see Jewish and Arabian children and teachers within Israel living side by side at primary schools in total harmony. But that obviously requires people at the top being of a mindset that is prepared to nurture social cooperation and harmony. It's unfortunate that our political leaders cannot transpose that same philosophy across our entire society. I suppose at that young age, the children are too young to be socialized into all of the social prejudices that we adults know and understand. Reminds me of what Jesus said - 'unless you remain as little children you shall not enter the kingdom of heaven'. But what would he know, when, we have our political leaders to guide us?"

"So you know a thing or two about the Christian gospel Jenny? You did mention you conducted your post graduate studies in those religious areas of ... ah ... fundamentalism, bigotry, the so-called gift of tongues."

"Yes, Raymond, I am so dismayed at how so many of our fellow Americans here in the United States can be so credulous and gullible to follow the fundamentalist and bigoted Christian preachers who denounce all other religious belief systems and seemingly damn all non-Christians to hell for eternity. Some go even further and preach that even practising Christians who are not expressly 'born again' and do not pray in tongues will not be saved – many within the Assembly of God, for example."

"So they believe they pray in tongues, Jen?"

"Yes they do, but there is compelling evidence that what they are referring to - and what is known within linguistic science as glossolalia - is nothing but a contrivance and a product of the power of socialization. So my research and that of several others was able to educe the same phenomenon from study groups who had no religious persuasion, but given a suitable motive, were able to give us the same unintelligible gibberish that is entirely consistent with what the Pentecostals believe is the gift of tongues."

"So what inducement did you provide them with?"

"Money, of course! Our subjects were given instructions and paid a modest fee of one hundred dollars for just fifteen minutes of their time, to give us a rendition of unintelligible gibberish."

"What type of instruction?"

"Well many of them did balk at the requirement initially but we suggested they could imagine being stranded in the Amazon jungle and they had to communicate with the local native people, so then they got the idea. So they only had to givc us a thirty second sample as that was all we needed for the computer analysis. The resulting phonetics were virtually the same as what we have recorded at Pentecostal church services."

"So ... what motive do the Pentecostals provide to people to do this?"

"Well, receiving an overt gift from heaven, being a truly born again Christian, acceptance within their local community, the mystical aspect of praying the perfect prayer ... plenty of motives for people to follow."

"Yes, I've known people within my own Catholic parish who subscribed to that belief, as do some of the priests."

"So it is a fallacy then?"

"That's been the conclusion of all of the research into that peculiar phenomenon, but the people are indoctrinated into believing it – that it is the gift of tongues. Unfortunately, much of the spurious interpretation of the gospel comes with it. Some Christian churches denounce each other as heretics after reading the same bible – and they do that based on scriptural verse."

"Such as?"

"Oh, the obvious example is that of the Assembly of God and the Jehovah's Witnesses – two very extremist fundamentalist groups. They claim they believe in the Bible but completely denounce each other. The Assembly of God does not regard the Jehovah's as being born again and, therefore, cannot be saved. As for the Jehovah's Witnesses, they denounce all other religious belief systems including all other Christian churches. They are so notorious for their derogatory slandering and nurturing of enmity toward other churches in their magazines and exhorting their congregation to sever ties with their own family members, whom they depict as part of Satan's empire. They castigate any dissension within their congregation."

"Yes, they confound people with select scriptural verse and their predetermined interpretations of that, don't they?"

"Exactly Keith – and that despite their dubious origins with their founder, Charles Taze Russell, being a convicted fraudster and perjurer. Which is totally surprising considering he was under oath to Almighty God to tell the truth, the whole truth and nothing but. So the socialization process does tend to take hold of people because we are all credulous to some extent and we believe people we regard as having some degree of authority.

That is, essentially, the process of socialization and it affects all of us in our lives. Initially we believe our parents, then teachers and preachers but as we get older and wiser we might follow friends or work contacts more-so than the others."

"So Raymond, tell me, how do you think of Almighty God in heaven?"

"Me? Right! Well Jenny, being raised as a Catholic I have seriously contemplated such questions for many years so I have given that a lot of thought. When I completed my accounting degree we had to undertake an elective subject and I consciously avoided all of the rubbish I was fed in high school, you know, history, geography, politics, economics so I, too, decided on an elective unit in sociology. And having been raised as a Catholic person I was intrigued to learn about the sociology of religious beliefs. I suppose I was curious to learn more about all of that spurious dogmatism that is put forward by the fundamentalist Christian churches that I ... ah ... could virtually see through as an educated person - per se. You know ... all that rubbish that only 'born again' Christians would be saved or only Jehovah's Witnesses and that other religious persuasions were doomed to hell for eternity. I think all that bullshit should trouble any thinking, rational person."

"Yes, I do agree with that Raymond. Tell me more!"

"Well, last week when Phillipa and I were discussing this with Phillipa's ex-husband, Brad, I mentioned the Catholic declaration of 'Nostra aetate' from 1962, so essentially the Catholic Church finally acknowledged that all believers in God are part of one church on earth. That includes Muslim people, Hindu people, Buddhists and everyone else who believes in Almighty God but do not actually subscribe to any particular religious or spiritual denomination."

"Well with all that bullshit you mentioned one can hardly blame people for disbelieving, right?"

"Exactly, Wayne! You see, we humans do have an intrinsic sense of being able to differentiate between the genuine and the dubious to a great extent, particularly educated people - and when there are so many religious people peddling spurious theology, people of due discernment and prudence can see through that. Take those televangelists for example. They typically stand up there touting their stuff which condemns anyone who is not a born again Christian – including other Christians who are not in the so-called 'born again' fold."

Wayne spoke up.

"And what does that 'born again fold' mean, really?"

Jenny explained.

"Essentially people who profess to be born again are people who make a conscious decision to commit their lives to Jesus, usually after coming under the influence of a 'significant other'. That could be a section within one's own church or a friend or workmate or family member. They literally fall in love with Jesus, they fervently imbibe the Christian gospel and the words of Jesus that they consider to be the most precious. We all remember the miracles – the water into wine, the loaves and fishes, the ten lepers, raising Lazarus from the dead, the blind man who could see again, but the things Jesus said go over our heads somewhat. Through the Pentecostal movement, it is actually the things Jesus said that have so much of an impact on people."

Wayne chipped in again.

"Such as?"

"Well, where do I start ... such as ... 'I am the vine and you are the branches' or 'I am the way, the truth and the life' or 'no one goes to the father except through me' - so scriptural verse that can and does give people a deep-seated reason to be close to their Lord for the rest of their lives and a purpose for their lives also. It's unfortunate that such verse also give rise to frivolous fundamentalist dogmatism of the most bigoted kind."

"Such as?"

"Such as believing that only Christians will be saved."

"Yes, so many of them do, don't they!"

"So apart from all the things that Jesus did such as curing the sick and the blind and changing water into wine, the things that Jesus said become overwhelmingly significant."

"Hmm ...!"

"And not just those things but the incomprehensible concepts within some of Jesus' parables too."

"Such as?"

"The parable of the Prodigal Son. I think we have all heard it - about the son who took his share of his father's wealth and lived a life of debauchery then, after some introspection, which Christians would regard as repentance, returned to his father. Not only was he welcomed back by his father but upon seeing the boy in the distance, the father ran to the boy."

"Ah, yes, have heard that one, for sure, yes!"

"Then after the father threw a banquet for the returned son, his elder son became rather perturbed, but the father pointed out he had been granted eternal life and there was nothing more he could want. So, incomprehensible that people who genuinely turn to Almighty God, even at the last moments in their lives, can be welcomed into the kingdom of heaven."

"Hmm ...!"

"Which has a type of parallel parable, that being the vineyard workers. Some workers started work early in the morning and were offered a denarius and those who started late in the afternoon were rewarded the same – which gravely upset those who had worked all day. But, again, the Lord pointed out that they had been granted eternal life and what more could they want? So we are not to be perturbed when people do turn to God at the last."

"Hmm ...!"

"Also consider the parable of the Lost Sheep – the Lord left the other ninety nine to go off looking for the one who was lost."

"Left the others behind for the wolves?"

"No! The Lord knew they were already safe - in heaven. So I do reiterate that these parables have concepts that most reasoning people would regard as incomprehensible."

"Yeah, well, I suppose I could subscribe to that – and that explains why all the Pentecostal people get so carried away and carry on the way they do at their church service, does it? You know, the way they wave their arms around and sing out loud and all that."

"Well there's definitely been an infusion of the peculiar Afro-American sub-culture in the expressions of their joy in being close to the Lord, yes. But the reprehensible or blameworthy ones for the bigotry and the dogmatism are the preachers, who like to nurture ideas of exclusivity for the purpose of maintaining their flock - and cynics duly suggest that is to exact the tithings."

"Tithings?"

"Yes, the most prominent televangelists purport to be people of God and protrude themselves as such, then promulgate the requirement for their flock to give ten percent of their income to the church – and they require ten percent of a person's gross income, not net income. A lot of very susceptible people do so stringently for many years then, in retrospect, they realize they have virtually been defrauded."

“So with several hundred people giving ten percent of their income, the preachers can become very financial?”

“Try a few thousand, Wayne – and extremely wealthy not just financial. They can achieve multi-millionaire status, in fact, as most of them do. That’s when they buy their multi-million dollar private jet, ostensibly so they don’t waste time in preaching the gospel, then have the audacity to conceal their financial records from their congregation.”

“Yeah, I used to see some of them on television early in the morning years ago – that Hinn character and that Copeland couple and Creflo Dollar and others. Was all that really just a rapacious money racket?”

“That’ll be their problem Wayne. They elect to be oblivious to what Saint Paul wrote in Two Corinthians ‘Each one must give as he has decided in his heart, not reluctantly or under compulsion, for God loves a cheerful giver.’ Gloria Copeland expediently overlooked that and turned it into ‘you think the Lord wants to wrench your hand open to get your tithings?’. Her husband Kenneth stood on the stage twiddling his thumbs as he looked down with disdain and said ‘now you non-tithers’ – as if to infer that non-tithers might have a problem attaining salvation.”

"I recall seeing that other guy years ago - the guy in the white suit ... ah ..."

“Benny Hinn, Sandra!”

“Yes, that's him. He stood up there on the stage and said 'God wants you to be wealthy - and how can I preach that to you if I, myself, am poor'. So he expediently overlooked the fact that Jesus was born in a manger and rode into Jerusalem on a donkey. So Jesus literally epitomized humility and poverty and never acquired wealth – and that was his choice. He prayed each day for his 'daily bread' as in ‘The Lord's Prayer’ that he gave us - so enough to survive but never wealthy at the expense of others."

"Well said Sandra - and apart from that, it is just so totally untenable that Almighty God wants everybody to be wealthy, even just the eighty million believers within the worldwide Assembly of God - it's just never going to happen."

"A money racket, eh?"

"Could be Wayne - and that all started back in the nineteen fifties through pastors such as E.W. Kenyon and Kenneth E. Hagan. It has been an insidious disease within American Protestantism ever since. Many of those prosperity gospel preachers have been so absolutely notorious for their proclivity to inculcating blatant malice and spite toward all other religious belief systems – which is anathema to the Great Commandment of Jesus, to love other people. They incessantly debase and denigrate Islam, Hinduism, Buddhism, Baha'i and everybody else, which is an appalling affront to all other belief systems. I have such contempt for those shylocks and all of their ulterior motives – usurping so much money from their believers!"

"Yeah, I recall them getting stuck into that quite vehemently too!"

"Yes, there's no paucity of vitriol there! I'll tell you another verse from the Christian gospel, Wayne. 'No man can serve two masters – he will love one and despise the other. You cannot serve God and money'. They are the words of Jesus, Wayne! So those wealthy televangelists just might have quite a bit to worry about with the way they implore their flock to donate."

"To me, the exaction of tithings is blatant and flagrant theft, Wayne – and totally perverse when you consider Jesus led a life of such humility and poverty. And now it has become so pervasive – there are hundreds of thousands of Pentecostal churches here in the United States because a select coterie of people get smart, break away and crank up another church outlet, often in a factory unit somewhere to begin with. The smartest ones will then pool their assets and borrow funds to construct dedicated premises that can pass off as an authentic church. Then ten or more people can derive an income from the proceeds. They can also subscribe to a central agency to solicit their weekly sermon topics – basically what they are going to preach on Sunday. Years ago a lot of that came from the Trinity Broadcasting Network operated by Paul and Jan Crouch. Fortunately, the main scammers have come in for quite some rebuke from various sections of the media and the government too, having been required to open their financial records to scrutiny. A test of their level of rectitude but some not receptive to providing disclosure at all, though – deciding to refrain completely from disclosure."

Bill chipped in.

"Yes, Jenny has certainly got a handle on what motivates people into one form of religious belief or another – but that's her job as a sociologist – to provide the pertinent explanations for human social behavior, based on the assumption, too, that there is no Almighty God in heaven."

"Why would that be?"

"Well, because for all of the belief systems and the gospel and the holy Quran and the Jewish Old Testament and people's personal experience and all that, there is ultimately no scientific proof that there is an Almighty God in heaven. So the social sciences – particularly sociology and psychology – are literally compelled to provide explanations of such human behavior, based on that assumption."

"Hmm ... makes sense, I suppose!"

Raymond spoke up again.

"I have to admit that as a Catholic man I am the ultimate inclusivist. I believe that all good people will be welcomed into the kingdom of heaven, as per the gospel of Matthew chapter twenty five, verses thirty one to forty six, where the good people, the sheep, were welcomed into the kingdom and the bad people, the goats, were banished. So all good people of any faith or belief and including atheists too."

Wayne spoke up.

"Why atheists? I am an atheist! We don't believe in almighty God nor in heaven or life after death?"

"And many with good reason – some because of what they see as passed off in this world as religious belief, which makes them very cynical – and others because of their intelligence. I mean, conceptualizing existence can be a problem for many people, you know, the scientists tell us that our universe is expanding but, into what? Do we live in an infinite universe? And how can that be?"

"It's a head muddle that's for sure!"

"So, I believe that almighty God will not hold that against people – the critical aspect is whether we are good people or something different. So my church, the Catholic Church, now has many top theologians who subscribe to the concept of 'anonymous Christian', meaning people who are Christ-like by virtue of the way they live but have no overt spiritual or religious beliefs."

Bill spoke up.

"That sounds to me as if those theologians have risen up above all that crap your Catholic Church used to put out there and now have what we refer to within the discipline of ethics as the 'professional wisdom'. When I was in college I had Catholic friends there who believed they would be damned if they consumed meat on a Friday or missed going to Mass on

Sunday. I used to think 'what the fuck are they teaching their kids'?"

"That's a very good way of putting it Bill, that was all so contentious and my father has told me the same but I do believe my church has transcended that crap, which is now defunct. You've certainly got to wonder, though, how an institution comprised of so many well-educated and supposedly intelligent people can accept such spurious doctrine. Some of those ideas emanated from people during the middle ages and I'm talking about, in some cases, from one single person. So some errant-minded theologian came up with the idea that eating meat on a Friday should be a mortal sin deserving of spending eternity in hell – ostensibly out of deference to Jesus - and the Church went along with that. Surely, some of them should have been thinking, the Almighty God who created the universe cannot be so petty minded as to require such things of us."

"That's the power of religious socialization Raymond - the idea would have been to ensure high attendance at Mass every Sunday, but it's just so reprehensible to inflict that type of idea onto millions of people all over the world for, possibly, hundreds of years."

"So how do you think of Almighty God in heaven, Raymond?"

"Yes I have pondered that too and I think of God as being certain infinite qualities – obviously infinite intelligence, infinite power, infinite knowledge, infinite wisdom, infinite understanding and, dare I say it, certain human-like qualities that are also infinite – infinite compassion, infinite mercy and, above all, infinite love."

"Hmm ... must admit Raymond, as a philosopher you've got me thinking about that now along those lines. Infinite intelligence, infinite knowledge, infinite power I can understand, although as being infinitely discrete entities ... but infinite understanding and infinite wisdom ... hmmm? Quite perplexing those two!"

Wayne spoke up again.

"So, Raymond, just curious and don't get me wrong, even though I am an atheist and I do take some hope on what you have explained about the ... ah ... anonymous Christian, as you referred to it, meaning I might be given eternal life too ..."

"You are an exceptionally good man, Wayne, take it from me everybody, speaking as Wayne's wife, he donates a considerable amount of money to the Save The Children Fund and has already pledged that everything we leave behind us when we pass on will also go to the fund, so my Wayne is one of the best people I have ever known. As you know we don't have children because of my miscarriage, so we will be leaving a considerable sum to the fund and that was Wayne's idea, not mine. So if Raymond is right Wayne, you will definitely be granted eternal life, despite you being an atheist."

"So if you don't mind me asking, do you religious people still believe in hell?"

"Good question, Wayne and all I want say is that there is a Catholic saint, who was a nun – Sister Faustina Kowalska - who claimed to have been given visions of hell by an angel and she described it as a place where souls suffer from not being united with Almighty God, from knowing and feeling the wrong they have done, a spiritual fire that permeates their soul, being able to see devils and souls who are there with them, a terrible stench and cursing and blaspheming. So no physical fire as we were raised to believe but certainly a place of torture."

"Hmm ... better make a lot of money for the Save The Children Fund then."

"Ha, ha, ha, ha ... sounds like you will be okay, Wayne, don't worry too much."

"That's a wonderful thing you said about your husband, Sandra and my man Raymond is the best person I have ever met too."

"And you Phillipa? Where is your spiritual belief, if any?"

"Well as I told Keith and Jenny, I am presently working as a sex provider because a lot of women are being cheated on by their husbands and I need to split from my own philandering husband so I am busy generating as much of an income as I can. But, yeah, I was raised into the Anglican Church and do believe in life after death so I suppose I am hoping to turn the corner at some point and become a good person again as Raymond here refers to them. Just have to hope the good Lord will forgive all my sins."

"Yes, well, you might be able to change your lifestyle in the very near future, Phillipa, but we will talk about that later, in these next few days."

"So how did you two meet?"

"Phillipa tried one on me but I said no!"

"Ha, ha, ha, ha, ha, ha!"

"It was my wife, Natalie, who was being unfaithful, we know that now. We caught her out and she was plying for a larger part of our estate, which she didn't have to do. I handed her half and then some."

"Yes, Raymond made quite an impact on me I must admit. I don't mind letting you know that he is one in ten – the ones who said 'no' – and I don't mind telling you that all of the men who said 'no' cited their spiritual beliefs as the reason why they said no – just as Raymond did."

"That stands to reason – people devoid of spiritual beliefs have fewer reasons to be good! They'll get up to wrongdoing one way or another."

"That's probably true Bill. Then I was quite shocked when Raymond turned up in the house next door, but after he explained the situation to me I was quite blown away, actually - that he would go to that extreme, buying that house, just to find out more about me."

"I didn't know if Phillipa was single or married but, yeah, she made quite an impression on me."

"So are you two an item now, then?"

Phillipa and Raymond looked at each other and smiled.

"Ah ... no - not at this point of time but, who knows?"

"Well, you would certainly make a beautiful couple and, who knows, you might start a family of your own someday."

Phillipa and Raymond looked at each other and chuckled.

"We've not had any discussions along those lines to this point of time, Keith. So, might be time for us to make tracks back to the hotel and to thank all of you wonderful people for your hospitality and for the very interesting discussions these last couple of hours. It's been great to pick your brains on so many subjects, I feel like I've virtually been re-educated on some things."

"Thank you Phillipa and you Raymond for helping us out this morning with the car and ... ah ... let's all keep in touch if you do land here in the bay area."

"Certainly will, we'll get together again soon as - and lovely to meet you also Bill and Grace, Wayne and Sandra, it's been a wonderful evening.

They bade each other farewell and Phillipa and Raymond made their way to their car and left.

“So what did you think about our new coterie of friends Ray?”

“Great people - and I must say there was certainly no paucity of philosophies flying around in that circle, that’s for sure. Think I might have had Wayne worried for a while but from the testimony his wife has provided he hasn’t got a thing to worry about. I think that’s absolutely fantastic what they have committed to with the fortune they are amassing, to leave it all to needy children. Now you have two daughters, Phillipa, so we will take good care of them and secure their future, but I do need to let you know that, to some extent, I too would like to follow Wayne’s footsteps and leave a legacy of goodness behind me when I go. Okay?”

“And I will do the same, Raymond!”

Jess

Raymond and Phillipa arrived back at the hotel about ten o'clock and had a cup of tea before hitting the hay – in their separate beds. As she lay there on her side, Phillipa looked over at Raymond, who was falling asleep, for several minutes pondering what a good man he is. She recalled how she felt when she did meet him at her hotel in San Diego and how she was quite enamored by him. Now she was gaining insights into the character of this good-looking Raymond. She had thoughts running through her mind about whether her issue of financial security would be resolved if she and Raymond did become an item, after all, he had once mentioned that he could assist her somehow? Her ambivalent feelings emanated from knowing what her husband, Brad, was up to at the same time – being with that Lynette for two or three nights. It took Phillipa almost an hour to fall asleep, wondering if Raymond would want her. She was also thinking ahead – given the right circumstances, perhaps she could give Raymond the children that such a good man deserves. She was just thirty three years of age so to have to children was quite plausible. A son would be nice!

Phillipa eventually fell into a deep sleep and was awakened at seven thirty in the morning by the sound of the kettle boiling. Raymond was making himself a cup of tea. She looked over at Raymond and greeted him.

"Hello darling!"

Raymond turned and looked at Phillipa with a smile on his face.

"Darling, am I?"

“Ah ... sorry that was just rather spontaneous but, I won’t take it back. I feel so comforted waking up to see you, Raymond. Now, please make me a cup of tea.”

“Be three minutes – got to have the tea cure properly. No half measures on that one!”

Phillipa adorned her bedroom cape and strolled to look out of their window at San Francisco.

“Wow, what an absolutely beautiful city, Raymond.”

“Certainly is! Good view of the harbor from here too, eh?”

“Yes, oh yes! Amazing view from here. I can see that if I settle here in San Francisco, Raymond, I will be inclined to spend the odd weekend right her in this room. What do you think?”

“Sounds like a plan! Yep, I could certainly be in that. Here’s your cuppa, dear.”

Phillipa smiled.

“Dear, am I now?”

“Darling and dear, we are then - just now!”

“Ha, ha, ha! Yes, I can buy that! So after a cuppa we will head downstairs for some brekky?”

“Two cuppa’s – got to have two cups of tea every morning, okay?”

“I can buy that too, Raymond, thank you. And what do you think you will have for breakfast this morning?”

“Hmm ... I think maybe corn flakes followed by scramble eggs and sausages. How about you?”

“Me ... honey wheats then the same as you – then scrambled eggs and just one sausage.”

“Great, I’ll place our order now.”

Raymond was pulling on a sweater and was about to pick up his phone to order breakfast but just as he did his phone rang.

He didn't recognize the number so he swiped the phone to answer the call and pushed the speaker button.

"Raymond Brookes, good morning."

"Raymond, hello, this is Jessica, the psychologist who you met at the hotel in Las Vegas, how are you?"

"Oh, hello, Jessica, yes I'm fine, how are you?"

"Oh, no issues here but I have been concerned about you because of what happened so I thought I would give you a call. You must have been experiencing quite some mixed emotions these last few weeks, finding out about your wife's infidelity?"

"Well ... ah ... thank you for your concern, Jess, yes the first two weeks was quite an emotional roller-coaster for me but, I am being strong and quite looking forward to my new future actually - even bought a new house in Cincinnati and moved in. Left Natalie in our other house and ... ah ... I have decided I am going to sign that house over to her. Good riddance, I say!"

"That sounds like quite a substantial thing to do, Raymond, to part with an asset that way. Most people will fight for what they can get."

"Well, I am not most people, Jess. Besides, I have a far greater propensity to earn a substantial income in the future than Natalie does, so she can have that house. She doesn't realize it yet but I won't be returning to the house in San Diego and as soon as I get back to my new home in Cincinnati tomorrow, I will make arrangements to formalize our separation."

"Hmm ... well I hear what you are saying Raymond but I still have some concerns for you and you now have me wondering if you are adopting some type of a defense mechanism to subvert innermost feelings, so, I am willing to offer you some complimentary counselling sessions just to try to put you into touch with any underlying issues. Do you plan to return to San

Diego any time soon to formalize your separation? If so I could make some appointments for you."

Phillipa – herself a psychologist – was listening intently to this Jess.

"Ah ... no I don't have any plans to return to San Diego in the near future, I was just going to separate from Natalie via my attorney and hers."

"Now Raymond, you must remember that I was there in the same room where you stayed that night and I observed how traumatized you were when you realized that you wife had gone into the room across the hallway with her manager and, believe me, you may not recognize it yet but that experience can cut very deeply. So if you are not coming back to San Diego, I am willing to make a trip to Cincinnati to see you for a few days this week to provide you with counselling. How does that sound?"

"Oh I wouldn't put you out that way Jess, no, I think I am going to be fine but thank you all the same."

"No, I am not asking you to pay for my trip, Raymond, I am willing to cover that myself, although, I suppose if you do have a spare room in your new house I could possibly keep my costs down if you can put up with me staying there with you for a couple of days. I am very concerned about you, Raymond."

Phillipa was listening even more intently now. She whispered to Raymond and pointed to herself.

"I am your psychologist!"

Raymond got the message.

"Ah ... well, Jess right at the moment I am in San Francisco with a very close friend of mine as we are looking at properties for her to purchase and, believe it or not, Phillipa who is with me now is a qualified psychologist, herself, and ... ah ... Phillipa has had me on the couch picking at my brains many times already and she has been very helpful to me, so I can probably rely on my best friend here to assist me if I need any assistance. But look, thank you so much for being so concerned for me Jess and for the help you gave me in Las Vegas."

"Okay, Raymond, but let me know if anything changes, okay?"

"Okay, will do, thank you Jess. Bye for now."

"Goodbye, Raymond!"

"Sheeze! What a fucking nerve of that woman, coming onto you so strong that way, offering free counselling but would be great if she can stay in your house! Fuck me!"

"Ha, ha, ha ... no I think she was genuinely concerned for me, okay. She was in Vegas when Natalie and her boss, Graham, stayed in the same room and her room was opposite, so she allowed me to confirm what my other friend Roxanne had told me about their ongoing liaison. I had my own room around the corner but Jess allowed me to crash in her room that night. Must admit I was very badly hurt and she knew that."

"And is she the type of woman you might normally feel any attraction for?"

"Oh, she was an absolute bombshell in her own right, sure – late thirties, single, professionally qualified, yes quite a stunner actually. I took a couple of snaps while she didn't notice so, this is Jess."

"Wow! Bombshell ain't the word ... she's absolutely bloody gorgeous Raymond. Looks quite like Deborah Harry ... yep, a real blondie, that one."

"Deborah Harry eh? Yes I didn't actually draw the similarity at the time but, now that you've said it, she does look like Blondie, for sure. My father was a huge fan of Deborah Harry, still is I'd say. He showed me a video of Blondie singing ... ah ... what was that huge hit she had ..."

"Heart of Glass!"

"That's it, yes ... Heart of Glass."

"Well you don't have a heart of glass, Raymond. You have a heart of gold, in fact ... and that is just so benevolent of you to hand your existing house in San Diego over to your wife. I've never known anybody to do something like that."

"Quick way to get her out of my life, Phillipa. My new life!"

"Okay, well we are just going to have to keep that Jess at bay. I am your psychologist now, Raymond Brookes ... and I am looking forward immensely to picking your brains on the couch, as you say, okay? And I can refer you to the best attorney for separation - Baker and Hall. They have an office in San Diego and I have referred all of my clients to them with great satisfaction, so that can be taken care of quite expeditiously."

"Okay!"

Phillipa and Raymond enjoyed their breakfast during which time Phillipa really couldn't put that Jessica out of her mind. The nerve of that woman seeking to stay in Raymond's house while she provided him with so-called counselling. That Jessica would have this good man on the couch for sure, but not for counselling. 'Blondie', eh? While Raymond was preparing their coffee, Phillipa viewed the video of Blondie singing Heart of Glass on Youtube. She thought to herself ... 'shit, what a stunner of a woman'. Phillipa was now thinking less and less about what her Brad was up to and starting to appreciate what an amazing partner this Raymond Brookes would be. She was becoming so totally intent on sealing a permanent relationship with this very good man. Can't let that Jess get to him.

"Coffee, dear!"

"Thank you, Raymond. You make a great coffee too, I've noticed. How do you do that?"

"Too easy, really! I make it with half water and half milk then microwave it to get the heat back up. Just have to keep an eye on it to make sure it doesn't boil over in the microwave. Far better than having mostly water and just a little milk."

"I'll have to remember that one!"

They finished their coffee then went upstairs to the room to pack their belongings.

"So we should be heading for the airport by about eleven o'clock, Raymond."

"Yes should be home before five this evening – and your Brad will be home tomorrow sometime."

"He'll be on a morning flight so home early afternoon. My plan is to tell him that one of his staff sent me a text and a photo of him with that woman. If he persists in knowing who that was I will refuse to tell him, but if he pushes too hard I will just tell him that the woman he was with, Lynette, was sent in by me and that I know he has been with her before. I will ask him to move out of our house until I can find my new place of abode. And Raymond, once Brad does move out, do you think we could return to San Francisco because I want to make an offer on one of the houses I saw. I do have a sizeable deposit so I believe I can procure finance for the balance as soon as I secure employment in the bay area."

"You saw a house that you like already! Which house was that again?"

"The two story house in Spyglass Lane just south of the Half Moon Bay close to that Granola Coffee House. It had a couple of weeping willow trees in the front garden."

"Ah yes, I do remember that house and it is for sale through Pacifica Real Estate - for two point six million dollars though."

"Yes and it has views of the ocean and over the golf course. That is where I would like to live, Raymond."

“Phillipa, you might recall that at the barbeque last night I did say I could provide you with the security you need. You did smile when I said that, so do you want to know what I meant.”

“Yes ... I do recall you saying that Raymond so ... what did you mean?”

“Well I don’t want to come on too strongly Phillipa but, as you know, I will be ending my relationship with my Natalie and once I knew she was being unfaithful to me, I was so dismayed and dejected that I hadn’t got to know who you were. I couldn’t believe it when I saw you again and was able to trace you to your home. It just seems so fortuitous to me that the house next door to you was up for sale and that I have had this opportunity to get to know you a lot better and ... Phillipa ... I’m not making assumptions about how you feel but, I am prepared to buy that house for you and your girls.”

“What? Buy that beautiful house for me? What do you mean, Raymond. I have just told you that I can see a way of procuring that house myself off my own bat ... so ... you don’t have to do that for me Raymond Brookes.”

“Yes, well, as you say you have accumulated the deposit for that house but, Phillipa, it’s going to take you at least ten years to pay off that mortgage. I was blessed with the purchase of the rural property I bought many years ago so I am financial, Phillipa - and I do mean what I say, that I am not making any assumptions about how you might feel, but sometimes in life a person just has to trust fate.”

“So ... how do you think I feel about you, Raymond?”

“I have no idea – and I’m afraid to ask, actually.”

“Well, do you recall me saying to those people that you let me down – when you said no and turned me away?”

“Ah ... yes ... I do recall you saying that but I took that in jest, Phillipa.”

"Well I'm sorry that my outward expressions have been somewhat stunted these last few days, Raymond, but that is because I have had to ponder the fact that my Brad is with that woman and, as much as I am not perturbed to see him off, I have been dealing with this monumental change that is happening in my life right now. Raymond Brookes ... I did not make that comment in jest."

Phillipa approached Raymond and placed her hands upon his shoulders, looking intently into his eyes.

"I must admit I was actually disappointed that I did not spend those few hours that night with you, Raymond. You probably realize that I have been with a lot of men these last two years but I can honestly say that I never felt anything for any of them, Raymond. It was just a job for me and I was essentially an actor playing a role. But I must admit – you were different."

"Me ... ah ... how so?"

"Well, you are a good looking fit, intelligent, professional man, Raymond - and you came across as being a really personable character, you know, you interacted very amicably and you seemed very affable, friendly and you communicated really well too, so, I believe any woman would be attracted to you. As I certainly was at that time, Raymond."

"You were?"

"Yes and I have been ever since. I'm sorry that I have held myself back emotionally but, I hope you do understand this is a rather torrid time for me. You have been so good assisting me the way that you have and I should have been more loving toward you but, it's never too late, Raymond. I do love you Raymond Brookes!"

Phillipa planted a huge kiss onto Raymond's lips. Raymond put his arms around Phillipa and prolonged this first kiss as long as he could. He couldn't believe this moment had finally come and found his mind racing ahead contemplating his new life with this most beautiful woman. After a full two minutes Phillipa decided she should say something.

"I'm sorry I hadn't kissed you before now, Raymond, but I can assure you I have been wanting too. I have had an ongoing tickle of excitement occurring within, every moment I have been with you."

"Well ... ah ... I have been feeling the same way, in fact, ever since you told me that you were intending to leave Brad. I think I was overcome with hope but kept a rein on that because I wasn't going to get into false hope. That would not have been good for me."

"Now, Raymond, I can see what a really good man you are – one of the best, okay ... no, the best, Raymond. So I think it will only be fair if I put my savings into buying that house and rather than take out a mortgage, you can make the contribution for the balance and we buy that beautiful home in joint names and live there together. How would you feel about that?"

Raymond couldn't believe his ears and was overcome with emotion. He nodded his head in concurrence as he tried to speak.

"Well ... ah ... I think that is a wonderful plan, Phillipa, so yeah, let's work toward that direction. I can't believe I might have a chance of spending the rest of my life with you, Phillipa."

"I think we have both been blessed by the good Lord, Raymond. I hope he will forgive me of all my sins."

"Could be the reason we met, I reckon."

"Oh and, Raymond, I will never go with another man again I can promise you that. I meant what I said to you before, that I would always have been loyal to my husband had he not been disloyal to me, okay!"

"Don't worry I believe you!"

At that they gave each other a huge hug for more than three minutes.

"Now, we will need to be leaving here soon to return to Cincinnati and may I suggest that once we have put our separations from our spouses into effect, we would then be free to nurture our own relationship, okay? But not before."

"Yes, I was hoping we could put our separations into effect first, for sure. Now I haven't mentioned this to you yet but while you were in the shower this afternoon Brad called me and told me that he will be home tomorrow night but that he has to go away again for a couple of days leaving on Monday. This time to Houston. He said this will be the biggest contract he has ever had and he cannot miss the negotiations for anything."

"So home for just the two nights then off again."

"Yes, so I thought we could make an offer on that house with a holding deposit, which I am willing to provide, then make a quick visit back to Half Moon Bay to check it out and to seal the deal. We could leave the same day that Brad does. I'm sure my mother won't mind looking after the girls for a few extra days. They do love staying with their nanna. So how does that sound, Raymond?"

"Sounds great! I'll call the property agent handling that sale and send the holding deposit, myself, first thing in the morning – then book the flights. We can stay here again in this very hotel if you wish. I like it here!"

"That will be wonderful, Raymond – and I will inform my husband before he leaves for Houston that I will be leaving him and I will tell him that while he is away, I will be making my arrangements to live elsewhere."

"How do you think your Brad will take it?"

"There is nothing he can say that will change my mind. I am not going to be appeased, Raymond – in fact I am going to be entirely resolute in this giving him no chance to defy my stance. Brad will have to completely relinquish his relationship with me. So I envisage that my discussion with Brad will culminate in me being a single woman again and that the commencement of my new life is imminent, Raymond."

"Okay, that's good! It's best that I inform my Natalie at the same time, so I will give her a call as soon as we get back to Cincinnati and book a flight back to San Diego for a day or two. I'll call that attorney you mentioned and have the separation documents drawn up and serve those on her. She'll be happy enough to sail into the sunset with her Graham when she learns I am signing over the house to her."

"Seems like a lot of things are falling into place for us now, Raymond."

"Yes it does, doesn't it? Meant to be, I reckon! We had a saying at church a long time ago."

"And what was that?"

"The Lord works in strange ways. I think he has been pretty hard at work here with the way the dice are falling. You know, if I hadn't had to go to the other side of town that morning I saw you the second time, none of this would have happened for us."

"As you said, Raymond – it's meant to be. The good Lord sent you out there looking for this little lost sheep."

That educed a broad smile and a nod of concurrence from Raymond.

"Now I will take these suitcases down to the car and let's check out. Oh and I will book this same room again for next week, okay!"

"Excellent idea!"

Separation

Phillipa and Raymond left the hotel for the airport and arrived back in Cincinnati late afternoon and returned to their respective homes. Raymond booked a flight back to San Diego then called his wife, Natalie, to inform her that he would be arriving the next day.

"Hello dear."

"Hello Nat, just calling to let you know that I am coming home for a day or two arriving tomorrow. I have some business to take care of there but will need to return to Cincinnati on Sunday, okay?"

"Haven't heard from you for a couple of days, how's it going over there?"

"Actually I am in the process of securing a property right at the moment and hoping to finalize that early next week, so sorry I haven't been in touch, lot of things on my mind."

"Hmm ... well I am not really ready to make a big move yet but we can discuss that when you are here. My employer has asked me if we would be willing to move to Las Vegas but I told Graham I didn't think you would because you have purchased the house in Cincinnati."

"Ah ... yes I have and what he has suggested is a rather too precipitant for me at the moment. I am making plans here in Cincinnati. But I will be there tomorrow so we shall discuss, as you say. I need to fly by my attorney's office but should be home by mid-afternoon. So you will be home from work around five as usual?"

"Yes, I will see you then, dear."

Meanwhile, Phillipa collected her two young girls from her mother's house and was home cooking a roast dinner when Brad arrived.

"Hello darling, how has everything been with you? How was the trip?"

Brad gave Phillipa a small kiss on her cheek.

"Just cruising along as usual because I am able to present quite a lot of common material most of the time. I do have another appointment from Tuesday to Thursday next week so will be off again while you are in Houston."

"Hmm ... ships in the night we are, aren't we Phil? I could be away for three or four days, actually, maybe even longer! That Houston contract is huge – mainly for extensions to the freeway surrounding the airport so will keep us busy for a couple of years. There are some big cloverleaf bridges in that lot. Never seen anything like it."

"Should keep you out of trouble dear! Dinner is ready now if you are."

"Thank you, darling – I'll just scrub up!"

Phillipa sat there during dinner looking at her husband and thinking to herself just what a devious bastard he was – and probably always had been. She suspected that he was already scheming to be with another woman, possibly even Lynette, while he would be away during the next week. By contrast, she was also overcome with feeling at thinking what a beautiful man Raymond Brookes really is. She was starting to feel quite humbled that she had found Raymond Brookes – thanks to his wife, Natalie.

The next morning, Raymond called Pacifica Real Estate at eight o'clock to make arrangements for the purchase of the house in Spyglass Lane.

"Pacifica Real Estate, good morning Jill speaking, how may I help you?"

"Oh, good morning ... ah ... Raymond Brookes calling from Cincinnati. I want to make arrangements to purchase a property I saw near Half Moon Bay please."

"Good morning Mr Brookes I will direct your call to Johnathon who will assist you with that."

"Johnathon Cole, good morning."

"Hello Johnathon, Raymond Brookes calling about the house you have listed in Spyglass lane in Half Moon Bay."

"Raymond hello – yes, great location, beautiful house, how can I assist you?"

"Well if you send me the documents now to make an offer of settlement to purchase that house, I can forward the payment forthwith. I will just need to make that subject to a building inspection. Is that okay?"

"Yes, absolutely Raymond, we always recommend that an offer is subject to a building inspection but I am pleased to inform you that just such an inspection was conducted last week and we have purchased a copy of the report from the inspector for all prospective purchasers. So, we have that base covered if you wish to proceed Raymond. There is just a small fee for that copy, of course. Now if you do submit a holding deposit of just five thousand dollars which is refundable if you don't proceed, I can send you the report and if you are satisfied we can then close the sale. Will you need to apply for finance, Raymond?"

"No, I have cash and if I have the chance to peruse the report this morning, I can make the full remittance today, okay."

"Now that's what I like to hear!"

"Oh and ... ah ... myself and my wife will be coming over to San Francisco in a couple of days so would like to go through the house if you can meet us there. Best we do undertake an inspection before we finalize the transaction."

"Hey, done deal, just let me know when and I will be there. I will email you the documents now, the inspection report and the offer to purchase, okay?"

"Thank you Johnathon and look forward to seeing you later this week."

Raymond received the documents and spent half an hour perusing the building inspection report, submitted the offer to purchase and the holding deposit of five thousand dollars. Raymond called the attorney in San Diego to arrange for documents to be drawn up for his separation. He then booked two return flights to San Francisco for himself and Phillipa, leaving in four days, then headed for the airport for his four hour flight back to San Diego. For the next three days Phillipa feigned a case of thrush so that she did not have to have intimacy with her husband Brad before he left for Houston. She did not want to be intimate with her husband, Brad, ever again, knowing he had been with that woman.

Raymond arrived in San Diego after two o'clock and went to the offices of the attorney that Phillipa had recommended – Baker and Hall. He had provided the attorney with all the details they needed and they were able to provide Raymond with a document to serve on Natalie. Raymond arrived at his house before five o'clock, just forty five minutes before his wife arrived. Raymond made himself a cup of tea.

"Hello dear, how are you?"

"Hello Nat – not the best actually! You might like to have a cup of tea or a scotch, perhaps – and take a seat because we need to talk."

"Okay – I'll make myself a scotch and be right with you. You sound a tad serious, Raymond!"

"Yes, well, I have this for you – some documents from an attorney I have engaged. The time has come for us to go our separate ways, Natalie, as you might understand, yourself. We haven't really had a good relationship for a few years now and I have been informed that you go to Las Vegas with your company executives every time I am away playing golf for a weekend. As you know that is simply not a lifestyle that suits my character, so I cannot be a part of that nor have that in my life through you, I'm afraid. I have often wondered why you never seem to accumulate funds, considering that you do draw a good salary, so it seems to me it goes down the drain at the casino in Vegas. I must admit, that is the reason why I was so keen to provide you with your half share of the proceeds of the sale of the land - so that you wouldn't feel too dejected about your future without me. Oh ... and ah ... as you will see from what has been prepared by my attorney, Natalie, the arrangement includes you taking over full ownership of this house. I have my new home in Cincinnati now."

"So it's over?"

"Yes, I'm afraid so! I need to move on and to establish a new life for myself, in another city. There's quite a bit of hurt here for me, having been so assiduous in my business these last few years without you being there for me for emotional support, so, time's up, Nat."

"Well, sounds like there won't be any negotiation on that. I am surprised you are handing this house over to me though – normally people fight for assets don't they Ray?"

"Yes, I am aware of that but, even though you do have quite a good salary, I know that my propensity to derive an income is considerably greater than yours so, I am willing for you to have this house. My attorney has advised that you take these documents to your own attorney to effect the settlement through the district court."

"You have belongings here, Raymond. What do you propose to do with those?"

"I've taken a few things I need most of all – memorabilia, computer sticks, some trophies – they are in my car already. I won't be staying here tonight – my golfing partner, Reg, has invited me to sleep over at his apartment for the night. I'll be flying back to Cincinnati in the morning."

"Well, I'm sorry it has to end this way Raymond, but ... I must admit I have not exactly been a model wife for you these last few years ..."

Natalie started to tear up.

"I know you are a good man Raymond and I wish I could make things better but ..."

"Well it's all too late now, Natalie. I wish you the best. Now – I'll be off. Goodbye!"

"Goodbye Raymond."

As he headed to the door Natalie began to feel an enormous sense of loss as she had been with Raymond for many years, but at the same time had feelings of ambivalence, as she also felt a peculiar sense of freedom. She would be able to do whatever she wanted to do now, without having to account to Raymond. She had a lot of money in her bank account and he had given her the house. She almost couldn't believe that part of it.

Raymond drove away and Natalie decided to swing by Graham's house to inform him that she was now separated and a single woman again. It was just a twenty minute drive to Graham's house and as she rounded the corner heading towards his house she noticed a pink car had just pulled into his driveway and a woman had exited the vehicle and was heading toward the house. Natalie drove by Graham's house slowly, muttering to herself.

"Cheryl? Why would Cheryl Fagan be here at Graham's house at dusk?"

Natalie did a turn and went back passed Graham's house but Cheryl had gone inside. Cheryl was the personal assistant to the company's attorney and an extremely attractive woman, herself.

"Hmm ... could be about some urgent company business – I certainly hope so. Wonder how long she'll be."

Natalie parked up just a few hundred yards down the road at a Walmart car park where she knew she could wait without being bothered or moved on. She waited until darkness had set in then set off again back toward Graham's house. Cheryl's car was still there in the driveway. She once again did a turn and headed back to the Walmart carpark intending to do another drive-by about half an hour later. To her surprise, about ten minutes after she had parked up she noticed Cheryl's car also pulled into the Walmart carpark, stopped about a hundred yards away and Cheryl exited her vehicle. Natalie observed intensely and was surprised that Cheryl simply stood there by her vehicle. Then Graham's distinctive light-blue colored RAM truck entered the carpark, drove alongside Cheryl and she opened the passenger door and sat herself beside Graham. Natalie could see that they kissed and was duly overcome with dismay.

"What the fuck is going on here between these two? When did this start?"

Graham returned to his house with Cheryl and Natalie had followed, driving by as they pulled into his carport. Natalie then returned to the Walmart carpark and positioned her silver, inconspicuous Toyota Camry just a few rows from where

Cheryl's car was parked. She was determined to see how long they stayed at his house. There was much going through Natalie's mind. Her husband, Raymond, had walked out on her and her lover possibly had been two-timing her. What had she done with her life, she thought! Then again, Graham wasn't the only man she would be able to liaise with now that she was so very financial. She could open a profile at cougarlife.com and find herself a young stud, or two – or ten. Now that's a good idea, she thought. There's plenty of young men out there who would like to be with an attractive woman in her late thirties. Still, she wanted to keep an open eye on this Graham to see how long he spent with this Cheryl.

Natalie made herself comfortable with a rug she kept in her car, but fell asleep about eight o'clock. She awoke three hours later to see that Cheryl's car was still parked there at Walmart, then went back to sleep again. The next time Natalie awoke was almost four o'clock in the morning, Cheryl's car was still there so she headed down the road to the McDonalds drive through and ordered a muffin meal and pancakes. When she returned to the Walmart carpark, Cheryl's car was still there. Having had sufficient sleep she decided to just wait and observe.

She didn't have to wait long. No sooner had she finished her breakfast when Graham's RAM turned into the carpark and pulled up alongside Cheryl's car. There were still dozens of cars in the carpark so her vehicle, being as common as mud, did not raise any suspicion. Sure enough, Graham and Cheryl both exited his vehicle and he hugged and kissed her as she got into her car, then they both drove away.

Natalie didn't feel as bad as she might have. Graham had been a lot of fun at the casino and it was an outlet for her going there at his expenses every month, but she didn't actually feel love for him. He was older by fifteen years and she was now already contemplating finding some younger lovers. Natalie returned to her house and sent a text to Graham stating she was not well, would not be in for the day and was going to return to sleep. She drove home to her house.

At seven o'clock her doorbell rang and then there was a knock on her door. She viewed through her viewer that it was Graham standing at her front door. She was in her nightgown but opened her front door and peeped at Graham.

"Nat, I just saw your text and wanted to make sure you were okay ... ah ... how are you darling?"

"Oh, I have just been feeling some nausea and a bit faint also. I've only had a few hours of sleep but I'm sure it will clear after some more sleep so I might be in later but, thank you for your concern, Graham."

"Hmm ... well I don't have to be at the office for another hour or more, do you want me to come inside for a while ... ah ... been a week since we were last together you know."

Natalie took that as an offer to be intimate.

"No, Graham, I really just need to get another couple of hours of sleep so I should be in by midday, okay."

"Okay, well, will miss you Nat so get well, darl."

"Okay thanks Graham, I'll see you later."

Graham turned and walked rather disgruntled and muttered to himself.

"Buggar, missed out – never had two women in the one day!"

Also at seven o'clock that morning, Raymond headed back to the airport for his return flight to Cincinnati. Phillipa was at the airport to pick him up, as her Brad was at his office.

"Raymond, how did you go dear?'

"All good – served the documents, she shed a tear but I stood firm. I think my offer to her for her to have the house probably attenuated any regrets she might have felt. That house is worth almost a million dollars you know!"

"Yes, well, that would go quite some way to making a woman who was hoping to end her marriage feel not too bad about the occasion. Well done, Raymond! So, after I give my Brad the news, you will be mine Raymond Brookes."

"Still can't believe this is happening for me Phillipa. Oh and I have the tickets to fly to San Francisco the same day Brad leaves for Houston - and the sales agent Johnathon will show us through the house same day."

"Wow! I can't believe this is happening for me now, Raymond. You know, what I am looking forward to more than anything ... um ... what would you think?"

"The lifestyle and that café!"

"Ha, ha, ha, ha, ha ... shame on you Raymond Brookes, no, not even close, though it does have appeal, no, I will tell you if I just pull over off the road just here, okay."

Phillipa pulled into a truck bay then turned off the engine and looked intently into Raymond's eyes. She seemed to be gathering herself together and was quite hesitant.

"Ah ... what is it dear?"

Phillipa became quite solemn.

"Raymond, I have been living a lie doing what I have been doing for the last two years but, as you know, I have had my reasons. I have been working as a hooker to get away from Brad and you have come into my life as a total blessing to me. What I am looking forward to, more than anything, Raymond, is to once again be faithful to the man I love, just as I was with my Brian when he was with me. I am so humbled Raymond, that you have come into my life and, strangely, it is because of your Natalie that it has happened this way. Isn't it quite paradoxical,

Raymond, that Natalie's indiscretions have pointed me into a new direction of becoming a good person again, with you."

"That's the most beautiful thing I have ever heard, Phillipa – and you know that I will be loyal too don't you."

"Oh yes, yes, I do know that Raymond and ... I want to give you two children, Raymond. I am only thirty three years of age so I can do that for you. You are too good a man to not have children and you will be a magnificent father."

"Children? Hey, I have been thinking that will never happen for me, but, give me a hug, please."

Phillipa and Raymond hugged for several minutes with both feeling that a new life had just started for them. When they finally let go of each other there was a bit of a tear rolling down two faces. Raymond couldn't believe he would have children with this beautiful Phillipa. They arrived at Raymond's house and Phillipa went to her own house to call her mother.

"Hello mom, thank you for looking after the girls these last three day but, Brad is going away again in two days from now and I have another appointment also, so I am hoping the girls can stay with you again for a few days, say from two days after tomorrow."

"So soon again, well I am a little surprised but that's fine dear."

"Thank you mom, also when I do bring them over I want to talk to you about something that is quite serious and I think you need to know what is happening here."

"Oh dear, I hope it's not too serious and, yes, of course I will look after the girls."

Two days later, Phillipa took Brad to the airport for his flight to Houston. She accompanied him into the terminal and told him she needed to talk so offered to sit down for a coffee. She had decided this was her moment. Phillipa finished her coffee in a hurry as she wanted to walk away from Brad while he was still sitting there with his coffee.

"Brad, I want you to know that as you are going away for this next four days, I am making arrangements to move from our house while you are away. I have become aware of your philandering with other women, including that Roberta in your office - and I am no longer going to tolerate that. I have been making enquiries about a house in another city and I am going to make the move with my girls. There is no sense denying what you have been up to because one of your own staff has put me in the loop as to what has been happening between yourself and Roberta. Now I know you need to go to Houston and I acknowledge the pre-nuptial agreement so you don't have to worry about me taking legal action, in fact, I am going to resume working in my profession as a psychologist so I won't be needing the five percent that I am entitled to in the agreement. It's all yours, Brad - and good luck with all your other women."

Phillipa stood and turned to walk away knowing that she had spoken Brad's language – money – so was expecting that he might have nothing to say. He didn't disappoint, watching her walk out of his life and feeling the total fool for not being loyal to his wife, but true to form, was already thinking how fortunate he was that he would not need to hand any of his fortune over to her. Yes, his life had become all about the money – and women.

A Happy Ending

Two days later Phillipa took her two girls to her mother's house early in the morning then returned home. An hour later Raymond and Phillipa were in his house preparing for their trip to San Francisco when his doorbell rang. Phillipa was in an adjacent room as Raymond opened his front door. A yellow cab drove away.

"Natalie!"

"Hello Raymond, I hope you don't mind me coming here to see you but I really do want to talk and your new address was on the documents you served, so do you mind if I come in?"

"Ah ... I am just preparing to leave for the airport actually, so it's not a good time at all. My flight leaves in just two hours and I won't be back for three days, so ..."

"Well, perhaps I could stay here for that time until you come back?"

"Ah ... no, that is not a good idea you see ..."

"Who is it darling?"

Natalie heard the voice of a woman and looked quite startled at Raymond. Phillipa was approaching the door and Natalie asked the obvious question.

"Who was that?"

Phillipa appeared at the door alongside Raymond.

"Cassandra? What the fuck? Raymond? You never said ... How did ... you two ... what the fuck, Raymond."

"Hello Natalie ... we meet again and my name is Phillipa, actually. I have to thank you for arranging for me to meet your beautiful ex-husband, Raymond. Oh ... and by the way, we are aware of your liaisons in Las Vegas with your boss Graham so, there's no sense you trying to stay here, I'm sorry."

Natalie stared at Raymond.

"You didn't say anything to me about meeting Cassandra ... Phillipa ... again. How did this happen?"

"No, I didn't see any need to let you know anything once I found out about yourself and Graham so, I decided to move on and did not expect that you would ever meet Phillipa, actually. Now there's really nothing to talk about so you should call that cab to come back or an Uber and return to San Diego. You have everything you need, including your Graham."

"He is not my Graham – he has gone off with somebody else already."

"Huh! Well sorry to hear that Nat but, let's face it, you have been having a lot of fun at my expense and you will not have any problem attracting a far better man than your boss, Graham, so we wish you the best – really and truly! Phillipa and I will be together forever, Nat. What you arranged that led us to meet was fate for us both."

At that Natalie huffed, turned and walked away from the house holding her phone to call for a cab. She had received her comeuppance. Two minutes later her cab arrived and took her away. Within the hour Raymond and Phillipa had also taken a cab to the airport and caught their flight to San Francisco. Upon arrival they booked into the Four Seasons Hotel once again and into the same room. Phillipa spoke up.

"So, we should go to see the house tomorrow darling as this afternoon will be a bit late won't it – would be close to five o'clock in fact. You'll just have to call Johnathon to arrange the time for tomorrow, what's say ten o'clock? So for this afternoon we can have a rest and then go shopping and have a lovely dinner."

"Sounds like a plan – I agree. I'll call Johnathon now."

"Johnathon Cole speaking!"

"Johnathon, hello, Raymond Brookes calling, how are you?"

"Raymond, great to hear from you, are you in town now?"

"Yes, just arrived and hoping to view the house tomorrow morning if, say, ten o'clock would be okay with you."

"Perfect Raymond, I'll see you there, will your wife be with you?"

"Ah ... yes, Phillipa and I will both be there so, see you then."

"Oh and I can have the settlement papers ready for you to sign but I will need to insert names of both owners - so is it Raymond Brookes and Phillipa Brookes?"

Raymond looked at Phillipa, who nodded her endorsement with a smile.

"Ah ... yes, Johnathon, thank you for that and we will see you tomorrow."

"Okay, so long!"

Raymond disconnected the call.

"Wife, eh?"

"He said that, not me - and I was about to tell him Phillipa McPherson, but you seemed to be nodding your concurrence with you being Phillipa Brookes."

Phillipa looked at Raymond from head to toe and back again with a long, slow blink.

"I'll go with that – can't wait!"

Raymond smiled.

"Golly! Can't believe it, we'll view that beautiful house tomorrow morning and if all goes well, purchase that as our new home. As for now, I feel bushed – think I'll just lay down and rest a while.

Raymond slid off his shoes and flung himself onto the king-sized bed intending to rest for ten or fifteen minutes but was asleep within two minutes. He slept for three hours before Phillipa woke him to go downstairs for dinner.

"Golly! Sorry about that, I didn't mean to fall asleep, it just happened. Seven thirty ... time to get ready for dinner, eh."

"Obviously you needed that sleep, Raymond – I'd say a lot of things that have happened in your life recently have made you emotionally exhausted, so I thought it best to let you sleep."

"Sheeze! Better make myself a cup of tea before we head downstairs. So ... ah ... what have you been doing these last few hours?"

"Watching you!"

"Huh ... as if!"

Phillipa just smiled. She had, indeed, spent most of the last three hours gazing at Raymond Brookes with the deepest love she had ever experienced. Raymond made his cup of tea then they showered before proceeding to the restaurant. They returned to their room at nine-thirty.

"So a big day tomorrow for us, Raymond. We will see inside our new house for the first time. I can't wait! As long as there are no issues I can authorize a deduction from my bank account tomorrow ..."

"Phillipa – I am going to buy the house for both of us and if you want your name on the title deed as Phillipa McPherson that is not an issue with me. I can ask Johnathon Cole to redo the settlement documents."

Phillipa sidled up to Raymond and took hold of his collar with her hands.

"Don't worry, Raymond. I will be quite happy if we buy that house as a couple – mister and missus Brookes. I think our time has come, Raymond, to commence our own relationship now. I know you had previously convinced me to wait until we had informed our spouses that our marriages were over, before starting our own relationship and we have virtually achieved that by informing our spouses that we are now separated from them. But Raymond, hypocrisy abrogates belief – a person cannot profess to be a Christian person and steal money or be promiscuous within their marriage. Your Natalie had been unfaithful to you Raymond Brookes - and my Brad had been unfaithful to me."

"Yes, well, your Brad was raised in the Baptist church, wasn't he? With his philandering he certainly didn't act like a Christian man. When offered sex by such a beautiful woman as Lynette, a lot of men would succumb."

"You didn't, Raymond Brookes. Not with me, remember, I did put the hard word on you Raymond but you turned me down."

"Yes, but I do believe I have my ticket to heaven and I won't do anything to jeopardise my eternal fate, Phillipa."

"Then you generously handed your house over to your wife, Raymond. Few people would do something like that. Most people will fight for something like that, Raymond – through the courts in a protracted dispute with lawyers. You gave that to your estranged wife without a single thought Raymond Brookes. On that score Raymond Brookes, you are one in ten."

"If you say so, Phillipa."

Phillipa gave Raymond a protracted kiss on his lips. They then went down to the restaurant for dinner and enjoyed a special serving of Thai red curry.

"Wow that is just so delicious Raymond, don't you think? I've never had a lot of Thai food before. Now I am just going to have to buy a Thai food cookbook for our new house Raymond Brookes."

"Yes, I'll go along with that, for sure. Your Brad told me you are a good cook already, Phillipa."

"I like to be creative! Now I'm quite pooped actually after this very busy day so I won't be long out of bed, if you don't mind."

"Been a big day today and a very big day tomorrow too. I feel like I could crash also."

The couple returned to their room and made the short trip to Spyglass Lane in Pacifica the next morning. They were both blown away with the purchase of their new house.

"Raymond, this view from up here on the balcony overlooking the golf course to the beach is going to bring me immense joy every day for the rest of my life. Thank you Raymond for being such a good man."

"Well, I am sure I will be quite happy here, too, Phillipa."

The couple signed the documents to seal the purchase of their new home and returned to their hotel room. Once there, Phillipa again sidled up to Raymond, took hold of his collar with her hands and gave Raymond a long passionate kiss.

"So, despite our marriages being legally intact under law, don't you think a lot of people would regard both our marriages as being repealed on the spiritual level – and in heaven?"

"I suppose you could say that, yes."

"So you and I are a couple now, Raymond Brookes."

"Hmm ... well if you don't mind me saying so, Phillipa, I'll go along with that, yes."

"Well now, mister Raymond Brookes - take me to bed!"

Nine months later, Phillipa gave birth to twins – a girl first, then a boy.

Other books by author Michael Roses

“World of Words 500”
ISBN 9780975099896

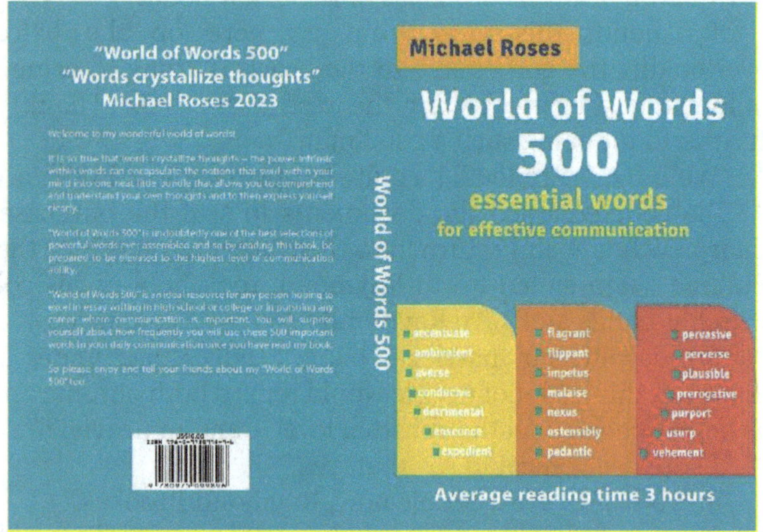

An advanced English vocabulary book comprised of 500 professional level words with definitions and three example sentences to demonstrate the usage of each word. A quick and easy 3 hour read.

“SAT 500 of the best words”

ISBN 9780646812748

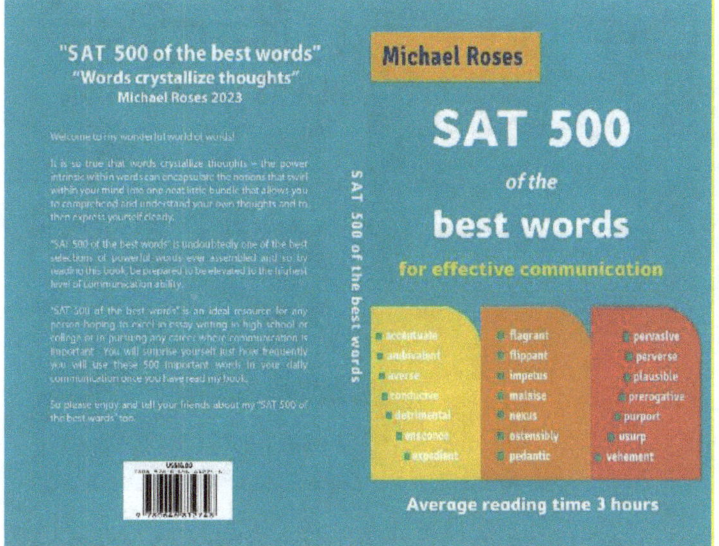

Same book as “World of Words 500” but with the different title, pitched toward high schoolers seeking college entry. Will elevate students to the top level in communication ability. Conducive to success in the SAT.

“UFO’s Aliens and Religion”

ISBN 9780645719000

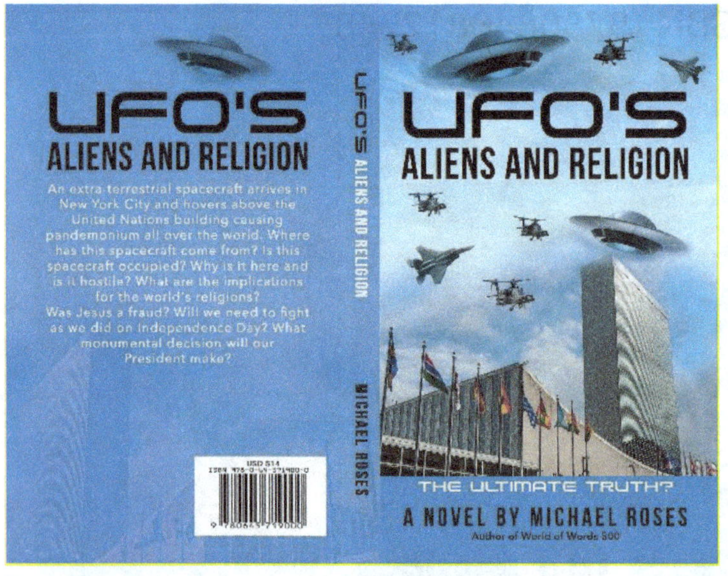

A plausible explanation of the existence of intelligent extra-terrestrial beings – who they are and where they come from, that provides hope for the future of humanity. Played out within an American family drama.

“Return of the Wagyl”

ISBN 9780975099841

An adventure in Australia and a very plausible concept to end drought periods in Australia and Africa, by flooding large salt lakes with sea water to increase evaporation into the Earth’s atmosphere.